Catalina

Markus Orths

Catalina

Translated by
Helen Atkins

The Toby Press

The Toby Press LLC

First English language edition, 2006

POB 8531, New Milford, CT. 06676-8531, USA
& POB 2455, London WIA 5WY, England
www.tobypress.com

ISBN 1 59264 165 2

A CIP catalogue record for this title is available
from the British Library Printed

Printed and bound in the United States
by Thomson-Shore Inc., Michigan

Prologue

The town of San Sebastián, on the Bay of Biscay, produced a number of individuals who almost made it into the history books. One such was Manuel Pessoa, a whaler, who was actually the true discoverer of America. In 1397, after the whaling and cod-fishing grounds off the Basque coast had been exhausted by overfishing, he sailed his boat to Iceland and from Iceland a further 1700 nautical miles south-westwards. There he became the first European to set foot on the shore of Newfoundland, and thus, in effect, of North America. But this was of far less interest to him than the Basque whales that abounded in those coastal waters; unsuspicious, placid creatures just waiting to be slaughtered. The wily Pessoa breathed not a word of his discovery to his fellow-fishermen, for what, after all, was the dubious, unprofitable fame of an explorer, compared to the secret knowledge of untapped whaling grounds? And so, year after year, he shipped mountains of whale-meat to San Sebastián, boiled down tons of blubber into highly lucrative train-oil, and hacked heaps of bones and teeth off the whales' skeletons, all of which brought him not fame but ever-increasing wealth. He was quite content to tell no one but his own children about his discovery of a land that had no business being where it was, since on all the charts available at the time that area was as white as the crests of the waves.

Or as white as the steam rising from boiling water, which grew to be such an obsession with the Basque engineer Blasco de Garay that in 1543 he set out for Valladolid, brimming with conviction, to lay before the ruling monarch the idea in which he so passionately believed. His concept was for a ship to be propelled by a wheel, and for that wheel to be driven entirely by the power of steam. However, the monarch that Blasco de Garay found himself dealing with was Charles I, son of Philip the Fair and Joan the Mad—the very same Emperor-King who had not scrupled to demolish a wing of the sublime Nasrid palace in the Alhambra and replace it with a clumsy stone monstrosity: the effect is like that of a cowpat dropped in the middle of a summer meadow. Although Charles was unreceptive to the engineer's idea, Blasco de Garay refused to be deterred and set about raising money from private sources in order to bring his plans to fruition. Unfortunately he achieved this only many years later, at an age when the brain is starting to decline. No doubt some errors crept into his final calculations, for the first steamship known to man, instead of advancing through the water, blew itself sky-high before plunging beneath the waves, where both it and Blasco's idea were lost from view for a very long time.

This happened within sight of the harbour from which in 1588 a man named Miguel de Oquendo y Dominguez de Segura set sail for England with the Spanish Armada. An amazing man, this, who rose from the position of simple shepherd to become a master shipwright and ultimately captain of the *Santa Ana*, one of the finest ships of his day. As well as being a shining example and a symbol of how far a man can go if he really sets his heart on something, Oquendo was also the originator of the expression 'from shepherd to ship's captain', which became a common saying, and was carried from the Basque country to the New Colonies, where it is still bandied about, in only slightly altered form, four centuries later. But history dealt Oquendo a poor hand, for he sailed with the Invincible Armada on the very campaign in which it forfeited that epithet, and when the battered remnants of the fleet eventually returned, humiliated and beaten by the English gunners, and the *Santa Ana* herself limped into the harbour of San Sebastián more or less a wreck, Oquendo died, a broken man, after only a few days on land.

Five streets away stood a certain house, a house that was called the Whale. (In those days every Basque house was given a name because, for the Basques, only something with a name existed.) And the Whale was where Catalina de Erauso was, if not born, at any rate conceived.

Part one

Chapter one

Losses

Catalina's mother, María Pérez de Galarraga y Arce, was a woman of considerable inner depth. One might have assumed that this showed itself in her extreme piety and the uncommon strength of her faith. On Sundays she stayed in church longer than necessary, and on Fridays she ate virtually nothing, at most lentils or dried cod. As a young woman, she attended the reciting of the rosary at the convent of San Sebastián el Antiguo and went to the Franciscans for the Stations of the Cross, to the Jesuit monastery for the adoration of the Sacred Heart of Jesus, and to the Carmelites for the annual celebrations in honour of the foster-father of Christ. She had twice made the pilgrimage to the tomb of St. James at Compostela, and had a great enthusiasm for saints in general: she had built up a whole collection of small pictures of them, and was the proud possessor of eighteen saints, all arranged in alphabetical order, starting with St. Agatha (against volcanic eruptions), St. Augustine (against losses of all kinds), St. Blaise (against throat infections) and St. Florian (against fires), plus twelve pictures of the principal saint, the Mother of God, whom María Pérez de Galarraga y Arce knew by all her names, so that when she had a request to make she could pray not only to the Virgen de la Esperanza but also to the Virgen de la Soledad, de los Dolores, de los Remedios, de la Misericordia, de los Desamparados and de las Maravillas, as well as to Nuestra Señora del Rosal. But a glance into her journal would have shown that those inner depths harboured something quite different, something waiting impatiently to be released, and when, on 14 February 1572, the twenty-year-old María Pérez de Galarraga y Arce forfeited that sonorous name by marrying the Basque merchant Miguel de Erauso, it seemed to her during the whole course of that day as though the feeling lodged deep within her were climbing up inside her body, through her belly and up to her throat.

After the wedding, María entered, for the first time, the house her husband had bought for her. Miguel had named it the Whale in memory of María Pérez's grandfather's grandfather's grandfather, for he had been none other than Manuel Pessoa, the discoverer of America, whose story María's grandmother would still recount to her. The Whale was a town house in the centre of San Sebastián, close to the church. It had a modest central patio, and the *alcobas*—the ground-floor bedrooms—were quite dark; Miguel led María straight to the upper floor, where a gallery looked down into the inner courtyard.

Inés, the maid, brought María a tray with a cup of chocolate and a plate piled high with *búcaros*—pieces of aromatic clay from the West Indies. María drank the chocolate and ate the clay biscuits. Then Miguel sent Inés back downstairs and showed María the two salons. The first of these had a tiled floor, tapestries on the walls, mirrors and some small pictures. The second was divided into two by a wooden screen. On one side, for the women, a quantity of cushions were arranged on a taffeta-covered dais, while on the other side chairs and stools were provided for the men. María Pérez stepped out onto the wrought-iron balcony, which had brass knobs at the corners. Leaning over it, she tried to catch the sound of the sea, but all she could hear was the splash of the neighbours' chamber-pots being emptied into the street. She went into the bedroom, where she found incense sticks burning and her pictures of saints hanging on the walls. She had asked Miguel to put the pictures up in the house—'in the house', she had said, not 'in the bedroom'. María Pérez took them down, carried them out of the bedroom and put them in the salon, then came back to Miguel, shut the door, let down the drapes over the small metal-grilled windows that had oiled parchment in place of glass, took off her wedding dress with its hoop petticoat—this was long before 1639, when a decree would ban the *guardainfante*, denouncing it as a 'whorish' fashion—knelt down before Miguel de Erauso, unbuttoned his breeches and shoved his member into her mouth. Though unsure how to set about putting on a lascivious look, she gave it her all, gazing up at her husband, squeezing her breasts together, sucking, turning her tongue into a whisk, trying out all the things she had often pictured in secret or discussed with other girls.

In this she perfectly reflected the mood of the times, for the Spaniards had fallen into an absolute mating frenzy, coupling frantically with each other as if they had all gone mad—or rather not as if they had gone mad, but as if, on the contrary, they suddenly had a clear vision of their future, a foreknowledge of the plagues that would ravage the land in the coming decades, and therefore felt the need to ensure a sufficient population to give Death enough material to work with. They were all shagging away for dear life; the *grandes*—princes, marquises and counts who were allowed to keep their heads covered in the Queen's presence; the *caballeros* of the chivalric orders of Alcántara, Montesa, Calatrava and Santiago; the impoverished *hidalgos* ennobled in recognition of their services during the *Reconquista;* the burghers of the towns, the craftsmen and shopkeepers, the soldiers, the countless poets and students, the peasants who had to pay most of the taxes, the shepherds and woodcutters, the ore processors and smiths, the vagrants and beggars, tinkers, town criers and muleteers, the grocers, peddlers and invalids, the porters and puppeteers, the innkeepers, eating-house cooks, coopers and executioners, the pimps, procurers and card-sharps, the Moors, gypsies and slaves. And no one shagged more insatiably than that reputed ascetic, King Philip the II. He might spend his days brooding over his state papers and putting off important decisions until tomorrow, but as soon as the sun went down he metamorphosed into a man obsessed with the succession. He brought his cousin Maria of Portugal to an early grave through child-bearing, and for four years mounted his second wife, Mary Tudor of England, to no avail; leapt with growing enthusiasm on Elizabeth of Valois, only fifteen at the start, who gave him two useless daughters and then died when the doctors failed to detect her third pregnancy; and finally mated successfully five times with Anne of Austria, begetting four infants who entered this world only to depart from it again, while the fifth, at long last, had both qualities required in a ruler: it stayed alive, and it was a boy.

They were all at it, whenever and wherever they could be, at customs posts and in taverns, at court and in the gutter, in the Alcázar in Madrid and in Seville's Triana quarter, on the Mediterranean and the Atlantic, in the Sierras and the Pyrenees, the boundless pastures of the Extremadura and the iron ore mines of Navarra, the olive groves of Andalusia and the forests of the eastern regions. And if they did not get results straight away they ate leek soup and red meat, which were considered 'hot' and supposedly heightened the sexual urge, they swallowed all manner of powders, ate crushed whalebone or drank the blood of slaughtered goats, to such good effect that in a single century the country's population doubled. Spain's very air seemed fecund with sperm, and the neighbours' rutting cries and shrieks of pleasure were ringing out from behind their parchment windows when María Pérez climbed onto her husband and rammed his stiff organ into herself like a knife, so that his testicles were immediately bathed in red. María did not cry out but concentrated hard as the two of them inexorably approached the end. Miguel too was at first wholly absorbed in what was happening, until he suddenly realized that he was engaged in a process of creation, of *pro*creation, and in a final surge, just before the dams burst, he cried, 'What shall we call him?'

María paid no heed; her ears were directed inwards. She dug her nails into her husband's back and shouted 'Miguel!' Then they sank down together in a pool of sweat, blood and seminal fluids. Miguel de Erauso stroked his wife's hair and said, 'Fine by me'.

Six months and many copulations later, María Pérez had still not become pregnant. There had to be some explanation for this. Her piety, which had been submerged under their marital orgies, now surfaced again with redoubled strength. Her diary shows her starting to recall all the 'obscenities' of which she had 'been guilty' in the bedroom. She suddenly believed that those 'sins', which for six months she had been describing as 'delights', were at the root of her failure to conceive. And so it came about that at night Miguel de Erauso found not a naked wife waiting for him but a white sheet with a hole cut in the middle and beneath it María Pérez, who informed her husband that from now on she intended to regard sexual intercourse in its true light, as an act that was indispensable for procreation but whose sinful side-effects, such as the immoderate expression of lust, she renounced from this day forth.

Despite this, another four months still produced no result, and with each day that passed María Pérez became more inclined to listen to the advice of her grandmother Isabel. The old lady's ancestral belief in the old Basque divinities had been channelled into a form of Christian superstition that now found fertile ground in María, who by this time was ready to clutch at any straw. Isabel impressed upon her granddaughter the information that the entry of the seed into the womb was a necessary but by no means sufficient precondition for conceiving a child. In addition to sexual intercourse, further rituals must be performed to win God's favour. She, Isabel, knew whereof she spoke: had she not herself conceived thirteen children? Admittedly eleven of them had got lost on the way or been stillborn, so she could not speak with authority about giving a child life, but about conception she certainly could. So María Pérez spent the next few weeks following her grandmother's outlandish precepts: she rubbed her abdomen against various old trees and statues of martyrs, prostrated herself on a saint's tomb, drank gallons of water from holy springs, brewed an infusion using scrapings from statues and water from a grotto, and, screwing up her eyes in a grimace, forced herself to swallow it; she prayed to St. Margaret of Antioch, St. Nicholas and St. Anne, and daily licked the dust from all the statues of the Madonna in the churches round about.

In her desperation she would even have undertaken the arduous pilgrimage to the shrine of Notre-Dame des Œufs at Gréoux-les-Bains, holding two eggs in her hand, one to be eaten on the spot, the other to be buried there and only dug up again on the following September 8th. Fortunately she was spared that journey, for at long last, well into October 1574, she achieved her goal—thanks to another of her grandmother's superstitious practices.

This practice was supposed to be carried out on the square in front of the church—at midnight, naturally. María was anxious to avoid any mistake and followed her grandmother's instructions to the letter. At the risk of being attacked, she walked through the dark streets of San Sebastián all alone—without her husband, who knew nothing of all this, without her grandmother, who was too old, without Inés, who was already asleep, and without having hired a man at the market to escort her. María Pérez placed her hand on the carvings on the great church door and touched the iron ring and the big keyhole that was on a level with her breast. At the first stroke of the bell she held out her right forefinger, while with her left she felt for the keyhole. Then she took a deep breath and looked up one last time to check that there was no moon, because that might spoil everything, but heavy clouds had gathered, and the town of San Sebastián was cloaked in unrelieved blackness when, with all the strength she could muster, María Pérez forced her right forefinger into the keyhole of the church door, ramming it in as far as it would go, not into the larger upper half, which would have been amply big enough, but into the part intended for the tail of the key, which was far too narrow. She was later to compare the pain to that of childbirth. In vain she tried to offset the pain by biting her tongue. She recited the prayer that Isabel had taught her, and it seemed to flow from her lips of its own accord; she spoke it aloud, with her finger thrust deep into the cold iron hole—your *right* finger, Isabel had said, to make sure it's a boy.

A trace of bile rose to María's mouth. The worst was yet to come: with her teeth clenched and her eyes and lips squeezed tight shut, she pulled her finger out of the hole with a jerk. It felt as if far more than just skin was left behind.

Wasting neither time nor tears, she started to run back to the Whale. All at once everything went black, and she fell, involuntarily plunging her injured hand into the filth of the street. Picking herself up, she tried to wipe the dirt off her finger, but it was almost unbearably painful to touch. She arrived home wet and dirty. Her finger, having lost not only the skin but also the outer layer of flesh, was reduced to a stringy mass of blood. But María Pérez did not mind this at all when she found, soon afterwards, that the pain and sacrifice had been worthwhile.

María comported herself perfectly during her pregnancy. She knew very well, having been told it many times, what a huge influence sensory impressions and the thoughts and imagination of a pregnant woman could have on the baby, and how something fleetingly heard or seen, an image or a harmless fantasy in the mind, could become a terrible reality in the womb. In the street she would avert her eyes at once if she encountered a misshapen individual, or a dwarf, a cripple, a beggar covered with festering sores, or a witch, for such monstrous sights would pass through her eyes into her mind and spirit, and thence directly to the infant inside her, leaving it disfigured. Instead she spent most of her pregnancy quietly and serenely at home, contemplating pictures of the Holy Family. She would spend hours staring fixedly at the infant Jesus. If she could absorb His perfection into herself, she thought, then her own child would follow the model upon which she gazed and become an exact reflection of the original, a true likeness of God.

After five months she no longer left the house except to go to mass, but even there she kept her eyes tightly closed while the priest placed the stole around his shoulders, for she knew that if she saw him do it the umbilical cord would wrap itself around the child's neck and strangle it. María Pérez would not allow herself even to think about the dangers of childbirth. Some expectant mothers died because they were malnourished or deformed by rickets. There were any number of miscarriages and stillbirths, or babies that tried to come out the wrong way, feet first, and suffocated in the birth canal. The dead babies were given a fast-track baptism, since otherwise they would be condemned to wander in limbo for all eternity. And it was not uncommon for the surgeons to announce in the middle of a delivery that the problems were too great, whereupon they would abandon the process and slash the woman open like a sack of flour—the only hope, according to them, of saving the mother and her child. This intervention would result in the death of both, and they would stuff the baby back into the place it had been so reluctant to leave, crudely stitch up the woman again, and give her a rudimentary burial in the graveyard.

When María Pérez gave birth to her first child, she lost only her right forefinger. For months, all efforts to make it heal had failed. Finally, it turned black. The doctor advised amputating the finger during the birth, for—so he informed them—birth pangs were the best anaesthetic. And so, when her time came, María's mother, her grandmother, a midwife and a whole crowd of other women stood on either side of her bulging abdomen, over which a Virgin's girdle had been laid; they gave María Pérez moral support, helped her, sat her up, held her hand, waited and finally set to and pulled the baby out, while at the same moment the doctor, using some dubious surgical instruments, removed María's right forefinger. And María's diary suggests that he had been right in his pronouncement, for when her hands held her baby she noticed for the first time that those hands now had only nine digits, and it was only when she passed the baby to someone else that she felt the stabbing pain of that loss.

The child was healthy, not a little monster; they examined its hands, eyes and face, it cried and kicked, and its father could not stop crossing himself with relief. Added to which it was a boy, and they called him Miguel. They did not cut the umbilical cord off close to his belly, as was usual in the case of a girl, but left a few inches to spare, and after washing the baby they did not pour the bloody water onto the symbolic ashes in the hearth, as they would have done for a girl—so that she would stay at home—but tipped it out of the door, into the street, because a boy must leave home and go out into the world.

In the years that followed, María Pérez was to bear six more children. What is more, she managed to conceive without performing any special acts of a religious or superstitious nature, which made her wonder if she had lost her finger for nothing. But she was unwilling to believe that anything happens without a reason; instead, her diary shows her pondering deeply on the nature of loss and concluding that for each child that was granted to her, something else was taken away.

While giving birth to Jacinta she lost the colour of her hair: as María Pérez screamed and screamed, it turned white as snow. For some reason the pain must have been far greater than during Miguel's birth. Even so, when daughter Jacinta herself was grown up, she refused to be daunted by her mother's recollections and during her twenty-three child-bearing years gave birth to seventeen living children. Twelve of them married and produced an average of six children each, who in their turn gave Jacinta twenty great-grandchildren during her lifetime. A simple calculation—subtracting those who died before Jacinta, and adding the spouses—yields a figure of a hundred and twenty relatives who attended her when she lay dying. Of course they could not all fit into the room at once, and for two days and two nights they took turns to keep watch by her bedside. Because it was a particularly cold winter and that room was the only place where it was really warm, the family members standing shivering outside were constantly pushing their way in, with the result that a continual stream of people flowed past Jacinta's deathbed, no one could sit down, and each stopped for only a matter of seconds to glance at her briefly before being pushed on from behind, so that after she had drawn her last breath no one knew precisely when she had died, or rather, who had been at her bedside at the moment of her death.

María's second son was named Sebastián. What María lost this time was the child himself. Held for a few moments by the midwife, he seemed oddly recalcitrant and ungainly, like a glove puppet; he stretched and drew precisely one breath, which seemed to be all he wanted. Then he looked straight ahead of him with veiled, unseeing eyes, before his little head, like that of a clown in a puppet-show, flopped resignedly down onto his chest, and a trickle of blood ran down his chin, as though while still inside his mother's womb he had popped a capsule of stage blood into his unborn mouth.

When she gave birth to Mari Juana, María lost three teeth. This second daughter grew to be a woman who far outdid her mother in piety. As a mere child—indeed, at an even earlier age than Catalina a few years later—she set her heart on entering a convent, and once there she rose ever higher, working her way up inexorably from the rank of an ordinary nun to that of prioress and later head of the whole order. This was not because she was driven by a pathological ambition, but because she took the figurative idea of 'striving upwards' too literally and thought that the higher she rose, the more she would *really* find herself 'up above', for 'above', to her, was synonymous with what was called heaven, and to be near heaven was her dearest wish. When she had ascended to the highest position in her order and realized that she could go no higher, she clambered, one day, to the top of the church tower and from its point climbed still further, into nothingness.

To the people watching from below it seemed for a moment as if Mari Juana were pulling herself up by a rope that dangled, invisible, from the clouds—while at the same time, some ten thousand miles away, a Zen master was telling his pupil that life was like climbing a pole, and that having reached the top one must simply go on climbing. But instead of trustfully pursuing her upward path, Mari Juana made the mistake of looking back towards Earth, which caused her arms to flail wildly as she regained her physical weight and lost her equilibrium, and those below could only look on helplessly as Mari Juana's mortal body plummeted to the ground and burst there, a red paint-bomb, while—and this they could not see, but they believed they saw it—the immortal part of her left her body and continued on its upward flight.

When Francisco was born, María Pérez lost her grandmother Isabel almost at the same time, and she had a fit of crying which so delayed the expulsion of the baby from her body that he was born congenitally slow-witted. The only livelihood open to him was the universally despised job of masturbation attendant at the casino. He had to hand the men, who often gambled right through the night, the tray-like receptacle into which they propelled their sperm: they would do this in a corner, without leaving the room and with a lack of inhibition worthy of the ancient Cynics. Francisco would then wipe off the whitish, sticky stuff that had often been sprayed right to the edge, and have the tray clean and ready for the next player. He did not mind this. The one thing he would have liked was to have someone to live with him, and, undemanding as he was, he would have been content with that, not presuming to think of such a thing as love. But in the whole course of his life no such person ever materialized, so that Francisco, who lived into extreme old age, died alone in the room that was all his meagre wage allowed, with no one to sit beside him and hold his hand as he breathed his last.

Of Mariana's life nothing is known. She was the sixth child to be born. So much can be gleaned from the baptismal registers of San Sebastián. But in her mother's diary we find only the enraged, teeth-baring scream of umpteen torn-out pages. We do not know what loss to María Pérez accompanied this birth. The diary is not resumed until 17 April 1585, the day Catalina was born, the day when María Pérez de Erauso, née Galarraga y Arce, lost the ability ever to give birth again.

Chapter two

The day of sun and rain

It would be so wonderfully appropriate, so luminously metaphorical, if María's last child—the legend-encrusted figure called Catalina de Erauso, later to be ridiculously and crudely dubbed the 'Lieutenant Nun'—if Catalina had been born in the Whale and if, after due determination of the child's sex, Inés had been instructed to pour the bloody water onto the ashes in the hearth but had stumbled as she carried the bowl through the hall, so that the water splashed onto the floor, ran along the cracks in the sloping hallway and flowed, unstoppably, symbolically, through the door and out into the world. That image, carved with craftsmanlike precision, might have formed the frontispiece to Catalina's further life. But the truth is that Catalina was not born in the house at all, but outside, already in the world. What is more, she was born on a day that still puzzles weather experts everywhere, one that the Basque meteorologist and chronicler Santiago de Etxeberria called the 'day of sun and rain'. The sudden downpour on that day will always remain a mystery, since it is a documented fact that the sky was a clear blue with not a trace of cloud when María Pérez, in the eighth month of her pregnancy, left the Whale accompanied by her son Miguel.

Miguel was then ten years old but, it is said, very advanced for his age. Although in addition to Inés the Erausos had hired another servant as a nursemaid, it was Miguel who, already at the age of six or seven, would be awakened in the night by the cries of a brother or sister who had had a nightmare, and would get out of bed, pick the child up and pace to and fro with it until it had calmed down. He also went shopping and did a great many things which were really the nursemaid's job, but she gladly took advantage of his precocious abilities to snatch the odd forty winks in the afternoon.

Miguel was a happy boy. This was because his father spent far more time with his son than other Basque fathers did. The reasons for this are debatable—perhaps love played some part in it, but the father seems to have been motivated chiefly by a sort of master plan which he pursued with single-minded determination. Miguel *père* had his life mapped out in a most satisfactory way. In his youth he had travelled to the West Indies with his own father and, being essentially lazy, had set a time limit on his working career: up to the age of thirty he would build up his business interests in the New World, and then he would return home, marry, reap the fruits of his endeavours and start a family. Up to now everything had gone according to plan: he had leased a silver mine in Potosí and, leaving his own father there as overseer, had returned to San Sebastián when he was only twenty-eight. The amount of money flowing in from the New Colonies would enable him to live with his family for a number of years enjoying, if not enormous wealth, at any rate tolerable prosperity.

The final and most inspired part of the plan was the firm expectation that his first-born, when he was old enough, would in his turn travel to the New World, take charge of the family's affairs there, and ensure that the flow of money continued unabated. Naturally, the son needed to be prepared for a task that was so vital to the continuing implementation of the plan. And since people are far more strongly motivated if they themselves want something than if they are acting on behalf of another person—even a father—Miguel senior made it his business to instil in his son an enthusiasm for that promised land. Night after night, while María Pérez sat beside them listening and knitting something more tangible, he was knitting in his son's mind an image of the West Indies as a kind of paradise. Avoiding all mention of any difficulty or unpleasantness that might await a colonist in the New World, he talked of 'endless beaches with pearly sands and turquoise seas', of 'breathtaking mountain landscapes and thick jungles', of 'uncharted regions' that could turn any colonist into an explorer and discoverer, of the 'deep respect' which a traveller in the West Indies encountered everywhere, of 'fabulous riches and treasures of all kinds' which made possible a life of 'the utmost luxury', of 'innumerable pleasures and pastimes' which the colonists could enjoy 'without restriction'; and later—with a sideways glance at María Pérez that was a plea for forbearance—he also talked of the 'beauty of the women there', who were 'available' to anyone. Miguel's eyes shone bright as he talked—bright with the silver of Potosí—and the son took all his father's stories for true coin, which of course for his father they literally were, or would be in his old age.

On 17 April 1585, several things chanced to coincide. Miguel senior was engaged on a week-long tour of San Sebastián's gambling dens. María Pérez was cross: her husband had not slept with her for three weeks. This was possibly because of her large belly, which was already unusually distended. All the same, she could not understand his avoidance of her, because during her previous pregnancies they had worked out an effective technique of suspended sitting which made the act possible almost up to the birth.

April 17th was an unusually warm day. María Pérez pulled the curtains away from the window and looked out. There was not a cloud in the sky. She could still not hear the sea. There was still an unpleasant smell outside. For two months she had not set foot outside the house and had, as usual, devoted herself to staring intently at pictures of the infant Jesus. Now she went into her son Miguel's room and told him to get dressed. The nursemaid was sitting with the other children, and Inés was out shopping. María felt like going on an excursion, something more than just a short ride: she wanted to escape from the stuffiness of the town and spend three or four hours breathing in the fresh April air by the sea.

The donkey trotted at a leisurely pace, with Miguel walking alongside. María had brought along a skin of water and two pieces of smoked cod wrapped in a maize tortilla. After half an hour the town was behind them, the smell was growing fainter and the air was starting to feel cooler. Near the shore there were a few fishermen's huts. They went a little further along, to where it was deserted and completely peaceful. María dismounted from the donkey and sat down on a rock. Her son ran the remaining hundred yards to the sea and took off his shoes. The water was cold, so Miguel did not paddle in the foam for long. When he turned back towards his mother he saw that something was wrong. A wind had come up from the sea, making her screams inaudible, but she *was* screaming—Miguel could see that because her mouth was wide open. She was waving frantically.

Miguel started running at once, his bare feet racing first over sand, then over hard shingle. María was sitting on the ground, panting. Miguel knew what that meant. 'I'll take you home,' he said. María shook her head and let out a roar. 'I'll fetch someone,' said Miguel. But María was already lying on her back, her legs drawn up and wide apart, her petticoat pulled back. Miguel was looking straight at the place, covered with black hair, from which he himself had once emerged. Or was that already the baby's head pushing its way out? Miguel grabbed hold of it and pulled, squeezing the new head; he did not know that a head like that was still very malleable while it was being born, and he pressed the nose down with one hand while with the other he bent the chin sideways so that Catalina could come out a little further. Two more contractions and Miguel was holding his sister in his arms, black-haired and covered with blood and mucus. María Pérez fainted. Miguel bent over his mother's chest. He could hear her heartbeat. And the baby? It was not breathing.

Miguel jumped up and tried to turn and run with the baby to one of the fishermen's huts, but there was something holding him back. He knelt down, took the umbilical cord between his teeth, had to chew on it a bit, and then the baby was free. Miguel ran towards the huts, and Catalina stirred for the first time. It was a hiccup. Then she parted her lips and gave a cry. A fisherman's wife came to meet Miguel, took the baby from him and dispatched her husband to assist the woman while she herself took care of the child. Running after the man, Miguel saw his mother being lifted from the ground, saw María Pérez slowly come to and nod weakly when the fisherman asked her a question, saw him hurry past, carrying her in his arms, towards the hut. Last of all Miguel saw his shoes. On his way to get them he thought how strange it was, after all that had happened, to go back to doing a thing like fetching his shoes. And then the rain started. In San Sebastián everyone who was out of doors at that moment stopped whatever they were doing and looked up. Miguel stopped and looked up. The listless donkey looked up. The fisherman's wife, holding the swaddled baby, looked up. The man carrying María looked up. And María Pérez, lying against his chest, looked up and thought: where are the clouds?

In the evening when all was quiet and his mother was asleep, Miguel stood alone in front of the mirror in the salon, trying to think, but the mirror snatched away this thinking time, sucked away his smooth young skin, his short hair, his childish features, his small stature: what Miguel saw was no longer a child, a guileless ten-year-old with hairless skin—no, Miguel saw a young man of eighteen or so with the beginnings of a moustache, with a sword, cloak, feathered hat and red and yellow breeches, ready to set off for the New World, and in the top corner of the mirror he saw his father enter the room and come up behind him; he put a hand on his shoulder and spoke a few last words to him before his departure. But Miguel was paying no attention, because he was thinking that before leaving he would have to say goodbye—to Catalina.

The first eight years of Catalina's life are inextricably linked with the ever-present name of her brother. Miguel fed her, giving her extra rations and trying to fatten her up, for following her premature birth Catalina was a puny child. Miguel put her to bed, said prayers with her and every evening added, 'Sun, sacred and blessed, return to your mother.' This had been a saying of his great-grandmother Isabel's, dating back to the time when the Basques believed in sun and moon gods; in Baxajaun, the shaggy lord of the forest, and the cave-dwelling god Mari, who could assume different forms. Miguel put Catalina's finger into her mouth for her to suck on until she fell asleep; he changed her nappies, washed her ears, nose, stomach, legs and the part he had no name for. When Catalina cried in the night it was Miguel who comforted her. Sometimes he took her into his own bed, where she seemed to sleep better. He helped her take her first steps and taught her to speak.

Catalina seemed to feel more at home with Spanish than with Basque, despite being told by her parents that Basque was the language of Paradise, since 'Eve' came from the Basque word *ezbai*, which means 'no-yes'. Ah yes, her parents: since one of the ships bringing back silver from America had been plundered by Portuguese corsairs and they could no longer afford the nursemaid, they were glad that Miguel saved them most of the work of bringing up Catalina, but on the other hand this led to a strange lack of closeness between them and her, and they had enormous problems with her, mainly because she was so strong-willed. If Catalina wanted something, she wanted it absolutely. And in order to get it she would sometimes have alarming tantrums and fits of profound, defiant obstinacy, screaming and stamping her feet until she got what she wanted, but at other times she would sink into an unchildlike, almost non-human state of apathy and unresponsiveness, and show such total submission and resignation that her parents were afraid that breaking the child's will might do her some permanent harm, and so to be on the safe side they would give in to her after all.

Catalina's own earliest memory was of movement. Of being carried, or rather of being dragged along. One day, when she was eighteen months old, she managed to crawl downstairs without anyone noticing, and reach the hall. She was attracted to the line of light around the door, which was slightly ajar, and felt her way along the wall towards it. Once outside she set off and took a few steps, but then, dazzled and confused, she lost her balance, fell over and ended up face down with her nose in the dirt. She did not cry out. No one noticed her. She put her hands in the stuff she was lying on. It was the family's excrement, which Inés had tipped out in the night, adding only a scattering of dirt on top. Catalina explored the heap of dung, poking her fingers into it, then rolled over on to her back and looked upwards. A blue cloth was spread up there, full of a hot brightness. She looked at it, her eyes open and unprotected, until they started to hurt. Just as she was narrowing her eyes, something moved between her and the sun—something that slavered, that licked her chin, slobbered over her lips, lapped at her face, that panted, nuzzled at her, snuffled and drooled. Making a bleating sound, Catalina groped around for anything that might protect her, found some thick, shaggy hair and pushed herself underneath it. Here it was warm and soft, and that tongue could not get at her. She held on tight and would not let go. Not even when the dog started to move. Clinging to the hair of its belly, she let herself be slowly dragged along. As her heels made furrows in the dirt and her head tipped backwards, she saw everything upside down: a light-blue sea, roofs like ships' hulls with upside-down houses as their cargo, people's feet and coach wheels on a sky made of mud. When she could not hold on any longer she simply let go. The dog went indifferently on its way. Catalina was left lying in the middle of the road. Someone picked her up and spoke to her, though holding her at arm's length to avoid getting soiled. Catalina saw a beard and a cap. Then she heard a different voice, a voice coming closer, a familiar voice and she knew whose it was. Miguel ran up to the man as fast as he could, took Catalina from him and carried his sister back to the Whale.

From then on he never let Catalina out of his sight. For the next few years he took her with him whenever he went to mass or down to the harbour. He read with her, wrote with her, played with her and told her about the West Indies. But he never gave her the slightest hint that he meant to go there himself in a few years; he simply repeated the things his father had told him, even reproducing his father's facial expressions, his father's gestures, and his father's embellishments. And just as Miguel had listened to his father, so Catalina listened to her brother, listened to the rehashed stories, even if at first she could not understand it all, and as time went on Miguel painted the West Indies in even brighter colours than his father had done, and that brightness became a brightness in his eyes which did not come from the silver of Potosí, as in his father's case, but from the sadness of the impending parting.

When Catalina was seven years old, a curious chain of events took place. It was the day of the Corpus Christi procession. The centrepiece of the procession was the monstrance, encircled by golden rays, in which the consecrated Host was carried through the streets under an enormous baldachin, surrounded by priests, monks and other dignitaries. All around were musicians playing strident music; groups of raucous young men wearing swords and performing dances; whalers and cod fishermen wearing the gold ring-and-chain earring which meant that they had spent a season hunting and fishing in the Davis Strait between Greenland and Baffin Island and off the Labrador and Newfoundland coasts; woodcutters shouldering their axes, shepherds with woollen smocks draped over their other clothes, peasants in traditional costume, with tall caps and crossbows, and miners from the iron ore mines; here and there among the throng, groups of merry-makers in brightly-coloured finery sang or shouted, already drunk even at this early hour of the day. When the roadside spectators saw the Blessed Sacrament they instantly fell silent for a moment, kneeling to cross themselves and murmur a few hasty prayers—but as soon as the monstrance had passed out of sight they promptly became as exuberant as before. Whistles from the crowd greeted the giant papier mâché figures, symbols of evil, that were carried through the town. These were the *gigantes* and *cabezudos*, giants and big-headed dwarfs, grotesquely brought to life by the slow, ponderous, lunging steps of the perspiring dancers concealed beneath them.

Last of all, but visible from afar, came the dragon, the famous *tarasca*, and as it brought up the rear the spectators fell in behind it. It was—in the words of Antoine de Brunel, who was travelling in Spain at the time—'a serpent on wheels, of vast dimensions, with a scaly body, a belly of horrendous size and a long tail, with terrible eyes and a gaping mouth with three tongues and rows of pointed teeth protruding from it', and the men inside the dragon worked the monster so skilfully, by means of long poles, that a good few of the onlookers had their caps knocked off. In short, there was such a crowd, so much pushing and shoving and such a din that you could not hear yourself speak, or tell who was in the procession and who was just looking on.

When the dragon was being carried past, Miguel bent down to Catalina, meaning to lift her onto his shoulders to give her a better view, but Catalina had vanished. Noticing that the undulating green scaly flank of the dragon did not quite reach the ground, she had run forward a few steps and slipped underneath the monster, joining the men beneath it in a dim twilight of trapped heat and suffocating air. She could hear puffing and panting and she could smell sweat, but before her eyes could adjust to the semi-darkness she felt herself being grabbed and forcibly ejected, pushed back out into the crowd, where she was at once caught up in a vortex, a swirling tide of flesh, legs and bellies, a maelstrom of revellers, until at last it spat her out and there were only a few more bodies to fight her way through. Exhausted and dripping wet, as if she had been washed ashore from a shipwreck, she came to a halt. She raised herself on tiptoe and called out for Miguel, but that was utterly pointless with all the hullabaloo going on around her.

She turned away from the crowd and saw an empty street ahead of her. With every step she took it grew quieter. All at once a man-sized billy-goat emerged from a side street. It was clad from head to foot in goatskin, walked on two legs like a man, and had arms that ended in claws, and horns on its head. It came up to her, bent down, thrust its horned head into her face, put its claws on her shoulders and emitted a repulsive noise. All this happened so quickly that Catalina gave a violent start and ran away in terror. Only after several minutes, when she was out of breath and had to put her hands to her aching sides, did she stop and look back. The goat had not followed her.

Catalina did not know this part of town. It was eerily quiet out here. Not a soul in sight. She had left everybody behind. It was as if the streets and houses had been emptied out and left hollow. Nothing. Except for those boys over there, six boys, and now she saw plainly that they were coming nearer. They were perhaps ten or twelve years old. Catalina was about to ask them the way back to the Whale when she realized that something was wrong. The boys gathered around her and began to push her about. One of them put out his leg to trip her up and she fell over, and the others pelted her with mud. When she got up they pulled her around in a circle by her hair, spat at her and knocked her down again. One after another they sat on her stomach, pressed her arms down into the dirt and boxed her ears. Up to this point she had not thought of putting up any resistance. But now, when one of the boys took his eyes off her for a moment to call something to the others, Catalina fought back, hitting the boy in the face as hard as she could. He gave a yelp of pain and Catalina thought she might manage to escape. But instead, like angry wasps, they all came at her at once and rained down blows on her, real punches, until, after one last blow struck her on the temple, Catalina passed out.

When she opened her eyes she was no longer lying in the street. She was looking up at a round, flat face very close to hers. The face belonged, as Catalina was to discover years later, to a woman named Beatriz de Aliri. Her nose was small, her eyes light-coloured, her mouth a long, straight slit. Now the woman sat back on her haunches and spoke. It was a peculiar, unpleasant rasping sound, barely above a whisper and yet full of fury. Beatriz was huge, in her mid-twenties, with angular shoulders and hair twisted into a shape like a tower, making her appear even taller than she already was. She spoke in a low but venomous tone, talking to Catalina in short bursts as if she were spewing out fire, with pauses in between. 'Covered in filth,' she said, 'the sofa, all this muck, think yourself lucky…' She paced to and fro in front of Catalina. She had a long skirt on and looked as if she were walking on stilts. Then suddenly she turned away and talked to herself. 'Whatever possessed me…filthy brat…nothing but trouble', she hissed, slapping herself on the forehead with the palm of her hand. She spoke disjointedly, spitting out odd phrases, while in the background a man, whom Catalina now noticed for the first time, scurried back and forth along the wall like a lizard that had lost its way. 'What are you scuttling about like that for?' asked the woman. 'Get some cloths to clean up with!' The man disappeared. Beatriz flapped her arms about like a bird with broken wings trying to fly, and now even her words sounded like a jay's chattering: 'Think yourself lucky, think yourself lucky!'

Catalina looked around. The room she was lying in was small, with windows that let in hardly any light; she could hear the sounds of revelry in the distance. The man brought the cloths and held them out to the woman. Quietly, as though she had no need to raise her voice, Beatriz hissed: 'What am *I* meant to do with them?' She flicked her eyes in Catalina's direction, and the man went over to her and handed her the cloths; his smile was crooked, almost apologetic, his look kind and soothing, as if to say don't worry, it'll soon be over. Catalina dried herself, though she did not know what there was to dry, since the dirt and blood had already formed a crust on her body. Bits of it flaked off and fell to the floor. Alarmed, Catalina knelt and scraped them up, but the more she picked up, the more bits fell off her. But Beatriz said nothing. Instead, she came closer, started circling around Catalina, viewing her from every angle. Suddenly with a different look in her eyes. All at once she had forgotten about the dirt and was talking about something quite different. Using an expression Catalina had never heard before, something to do with 'salt'. Obviously asking her something, but she didn't know what to reply. Then other words followed, frightening words that Catalina didn't know. Had something been pushed into her? Catalina shook her head. 'A thick rod, a sceptre, a chunk of meat, go on, show her your willy!' she said to her husband. But he had already vanished. 'Down there!' the woman said to Catalina. 'In there! Let's have a look!' And she knelt down in front of Catalina, lifted her skirt before Catalina could stop her, and reached between her legs, making her flinch. Then she withdrew her hand from under the skirt. 'Nothing!' she shouted, straightening up to her full height again. Catalina did not know if this was good or bad. 'Now let's have you out of here!' yelled Beatriz, and seizing hold of Catalina, dragged her out into the street.

'Where do you live?'

'In the Whale,' Catalina said.

'The Whale?' asked the woman. 'Where's that?'

Catalina told her the name of the street, and was grabbed and pulled along. The woman marched through San Sebastián with giant strides, grumbling when she had to make a detour to avoid the huge carts that were being rolled past for that evening's theatrical performances. Held by the hand and barely able to keep up, Catalina ran along beside her, and it was only now that the pain set in. Her head was pounding and something that did not feel like sweat was running down her back.

María Pérez was standing in front of the Whale. Beatriz de Aliri's voice suddenly took on a wheedling note. Her face seemed to spread as if it were melting; smiles, honeyed tones, she was talking about Catalina, fetched the girl in off the street, some food, and taking care of her, and as for the dirt in the house, well, obviously, the cost of cleaning up, no, that wasn't enough, after all, there was the loss of working time too, two hours at her house, she hadn't been able to do anything all that time, so if at all it would have to be, yes, that was certainly enough, no, really, glad to be of assistance, a child like that, you couldn't just, Christian duty, the way she was lying there, poor little mite. Beatriz took two coins, with a nod to María Pérez, and left Catalina standing there watching her strut away on her long legs, lifting the hem of her skirt, until she turned the corner and disappeared.

Miguel, arriving home soon afterwards, took the sponge from Inés's hand to attend to his sister, who told him what had happened. But Catalina did not mention Beatriz's strange words, which she thought about when she was alone in bed. She did not tell him how

Beatriz had touched her under her skirt—what that signified she had no idea—nor did she repeat the word which the boys had shouted at her a few times in between hitting her and which, as she lay awake that night, unable to sleep, preyed on her mind more and more: ugly. Next morning she secretly went up to the mirror and ran her fingers over her face. She seemed never to have noticed before that her nose and chin were a little out of true and that her eyes were washed-out, expressionless and brown.

❧

A year later her brother was standing in front of that same mirror, with his father behind him, talking to him; and when the father had said all there was to say, the son helped him dispel the awkward silence by asking for information that he already knew by heart so that his father was able to go over it all yet again.

'How long will the journey take?' asked Miguel.

'More than fifty days,' said his father.

'How many people will there be on board?'

'A hundred and twenty.'

'How many ships make up the fleet?'

'Thirty-three.'

'Who's the captain of my ship?'

'Francisco de Iñigo y Arturo.'

'When shall we leave Seville?'

'In May.'

'Where shall we land?'

'At Veracruz.'

'How shall I travel on to Potosí?'

His father told him.

'And my grandfather will be there?'

'He'll be waiting for you.'

'How will I recognize him?'

'You can't miss him.'

'Does he look like you?'

'He has our family name.'

'How much profit does the mine make in a year?'

'A reasonable amount.'

'Where's Catalina?'

'We've been looking for her for hours.'

She was not in the Whale. Nor in the street outside.

'She'll be at the harbour,' said Miguel.

And his father nodded.

The *San Marco* cast off and set a course for Seville. María Pérez pressed a handkerchief to her face. Miguel's father swallowed. Mari Juana crossed herself. Francisco, only half comprehending, slowly raised his arms. Jacinta shouted words of encouragement after her brother. Mariana stood dumbly beside her father and groped for his hand. Inés ran through the streets of San Sebastián, asking all and sundry if they had seen a little girl. Miguel, on board ship, craned his neck, scanning the shore. But there was nothing for him to see. Unbeknownst to anyone, Catalina was sitting in the church. She was waiting for the time to pass. She knew the ship would sail at about ten. She knew her brother would never go on board without having said goodbye to her. When the church clock struck twelve times and she could be sure that the *San Marco* was out of sight, she left her hiding-place and ran home.

'Oh, there you are!' cried her mother.

'Where's Miguel?' asked Catalina.

'He's gone,' María Pérez said. 'You know that.'

Chapter three

Blood on the wall

Like other convents, San Sebastián el Antiguo had among its inmates the three kinds of nun that have been so often described that they have become clichés. There were four of the so-called victim type, immured there against their will; there were two pathologically God-fearing nuns who took their fear of God to such extremes that they thought they experienced states of religious ecstasy because they heard the voices of saints, the Virgin Mary, even God himself, when in fact they were just completely debilitated by fasting and self-mortification; and there were two nuns drawn to the convent by their lesbian desires, who after their nights of homoerotic seclusion would appear at morning prayers limp and exhausted, with rings under their eyes. But besides these, the convent of San Sebastián el Antiguo had forty other nuns whose lives were wholly unexceptional, following a uniform routine of sleeping, rising, Hours, mass, confession, organ music, books to read or occasional quiet hours when they themselves could write books—saints' lives or biographies of women of exemplary virtue. Officially the nuns were strictly enclosed and were supposed to be kept apart from the world, *tamquam vere mortua*, as the phrase went—'just like a dead woman'—even before the Council of Trent. In reality, however, the regime was casual to the point of laxity: so long as the prioress was informed in advance, a nun could both go out and receive visitors, so that if her parents and relatives lived nearby she could see them at least once a week, and apart from praying, sleeping, eating and studying there was not really much for them to do.

Although the nuns had, in consequence, only relatively minor problems and worries, the prioress, Ursula Unzá y Sarasti, insisted on seeing each one individually once a month. Ursula wanted to be kept informed about everything and would not tolerate secrets. Each day a different nun would creep into the prioress's presence, cowering a little, for Ursula Unzá y Sarasti was a woman with two faces. On the one hand she was capable of truly superhuman goodness and understanding. She showed an exceptional gift for listening and sounding out the sisters who sat before her, training the full force of her eyes on their confessing lips as if she were trying not just to hear but actually to *see* their words: on such days she was able to analyse what she was told with great perspicacity and respond with sensitivity to each of the little problems laid before her. But at other times Ursula Unzá y Sarasti could be extremely nasty. On these occasions she would nod with an insincere smile while a nun confided her worries, and would then summarize what had been said in such a malicious manner that the nun was left looking utterly foolish. She would twist the nun's words in a way that made her feel that her problem was the silliest and least important there could possibly be, and that she must be the most pathetic creature in the whole convent to have dared to approach the prioress on a matter of such insulting triviality. After being dismissed she would then spend days agonizing over the problem of not really having a problem.

The prioress was a small, wiry woman. Everything about her was dark: she had black hair and eyes and brown skin that betrayed her southern origins. She also had hair growing on parts of her body where women generally prefer not to have any. But unlike others of her sex, Ursula Unzá y Sarasti wore her body hair with pride. It was as if she saw this luxuriant growth as compensation for her slight stature—indeed, she regarded this hair as a visible, God-given, natural endorsement of her leadership, lending her authority, dignity and, to put it bluntly, a touch of masculinity. In summer she often rolled up the sleeves of her habit so that the other nuns could see the bushy hair on her arms; it would never have occurred to her, as her moustache grew ever thicker, to pluck or rub away the hair as other women did. On the contrary, during a one-to-one interview she would often stroke the downy hollow between her nose and upper lip and try to twist an individual hair between her fingers, simply for the satisfaction of observing, with a fleeting glance, that the nun sitting before her was admiring her facial hair.

It was Catalina who now stood facing the prioress. She had made her way to the convent by herself, without her parents. She had insisted on it: the convent was no distance away, and she knew she would be able to see her parents whenever she liked. Inés had already brought her luggage the day before, and now Catalina had been led into the prioress's study. Ursula was sitting at her desk with her sleeves rolled up, writing something on a piece of parchment. There was not a word from the prioress, only the pen scratching away, and all that hair. After some minutes the prioress leaned forward, blew on what she had written as if to release the words into the air, then looked at Catalina and invited her to sit down.

Ursula was having one of her good days, and the room was filled with the amiability of her words. She even apologized for keeping Catalina waiting. And then the questions began. Catalina gave the answers that she thought a prioress would expect. She kept them short for fear of saying something amiss, and the prioress nodded, satisfied. The conversation was like hundreds of others before it: the prioress put her questions, the child responded, the prioress nodded and went on to the next question. But then something happened that caught Ursula's attention. Nothing special; just a tiny, almost imperceptible change of expression, the hint of a grimace, a slight contraction of the corners of Catalina's mouth. It was brief and fleeting, certainly unconscious and devoid of any ironic intent, but the prioress was always inclined to follow up any outward sign, however minuscule, and she decided to find out more about this little girl. So the benign expression was replaced by the searching gaze of the counsellor, the penetrating scrutiny of the examiner of souls, and Catalina was startled. In front of her were two eyes that instead of resting *upon* her seemed like a liquid flowing purposefully towards her, and Catalina was forced to lower her own gaze. Here was someone seriously trying to discover her true thoughts and intentions, someone determined to penetrate her innermost being. And that, thought Catalina, simply must not happen.

Only six weeks had passed since she had missed saying goodbye to Miguel. In those six weeks Catalina had fallen into a state in which, as María Pérez wrote in her diary, she seemed to be 'elsewhere'. She was not completely lost in her own thoughts—no, Catalina responded when she was asked a question, she did what was required of her, but all in a monosyllabic, introverted, mechanical way. Her life went on, but somehow without an inner spark. Sometimes she actually smiled, but the smile did not really come from within: she was merely doing the others a favour, acknowledging the fact of their presence. Often she would sit around somewhere staring straight ahead of her, spending whole days in solitude. The world had lost everything that she cared about, and she had been unable to prevent it. She had *willed* her brother to stay, but he had not stayed; she *willed* him to come back, but he would not be coming back. For the first time her will seemed powerless and useless, and Catalina abandoned herself to her disappointment. She would not allow herself to be angry, for there was nothing to reproach Miguel with. He had had to obey his father's wishes: Potosí, the mine, the job, the silver, the family's well-being. That much was clear to her, even then. Catalina tried to shake off the sense of having been deserted, which made her feel slightly soiled, and moved on to the next thought: if Miguel is not coming back, then there is only one way I can see him again. And so it is not hard to imagine how one night, lying sleepless in bed, she came to make that now celebrated childish vow to which she was to hold fast, through thick and thin, from the moment of making it. 'I'll follow him!' she vowed, and something new entered her life, something she could cling to from then on, forever, something she could passionately believe in, a goal, a purpose, a mission. She struggled to contain her excitement. It was not easy. It was too tempting to give herself over to dreams: images rose up of her brother at the edge of the world, and of herself sailing towards him. But how could she do that? She was a child, barely eight years old, a girl. Nobody would take her out there. At least not straight away, she thought, not right now. She would need to prepare the ground: she must study, think, and gain knowledge and understanding. And there was only one place in San Sebastián where a girl could do that.

On the morning after the night of her vow, Catalina went to her parents and told them she wanted to enter a convent. She wanted to take the veil and live the life of a nun. It was, Catalina lied, what she had always wished for. To her parents this came totally out of the blue. Her mother crossed herself; her father closed his eyes for a moment, pretending to think it over, but in fact it took him no time at all to calculate that it would be much cheaper to pay a small dowry to the convent now than a far higher marriage dowry in ten years' time. And so in less than two minutes her parents had given their consent.

Now the searching gaze of the prioress rested on Catalina, intent on discovering why she was really there. Unable to meet it, Catalina lowered her eyes.

The prioress said, 'Look at me!'

Catalina obeyed, and the next penetrating look from the prioress opened an even bigger breach in her defences. But, gritting her teeth, Catalina refused to surrender and fought to protect her secret. She kept telling herself, 'No one can get inside me against my will, not even the prioress.' Pouring all her resources of strength into her eyes, she gradually became more resistant to the prioress's gaze, until Ursula Unzá y Sarasti was forced to recognize that she was getting nowhere. Still, she knew that it always took several interviews to crack the kernel of a person—she had years of experience, great stamina and infinite patience—and she therefore gave up on Catalina just for that moment, certain that within a few weeks she would have found out what she wanted to know. So the conversation entered a phase of ceasefire, and Ursula recited the monologue which she had prepared for all new entrants to the convent. She talked of the duties to be fulfilled by a future nun, told Catalina the times at which she must attend prayers, handed her a loosely bound copy of the Rule of St. Augustine, explained about the daily classes and finally came to the most important thing of all, the first thing Catalina must learn if she was to stay in the convent and prove herself worthy, and that, said Ursula Unzá y Sarasti, was unconditional obedience.

Catalina's cell was not a cell in the true sense of the word, but a comfortable room in which her parents had hung tapestries on the walls in advance of her coming. There was a bed and bedding, a table with a tablecloth, some chairs, a basin and ewer, two candelabras, a picture of a saint on the wall, and a barred window. Everything was new to her; even the darkness was deeper and blacker than she was used to. Catalina was accustomed to the streets of San Sebastián, where oil lamps burned all night in front of the statues. There was nothing of the kind here. And it was absolutely quiet. No drunks shouting, no chamber-pots being emptied, no donkeys braying or cart wheels rattling through the mud, no footsteps, no curses, nothing but silence and darkness. She lay on her bed and hoped she would find herself yawning, for her grandmother had once said that yawning was a sign that you would soon fall asleep. But sleep was as far away as her brother.

Catalina stared up at the ceiling of the cell, but really she was below decks on a ship bound for Veracruz: lying in a dark, musty corner, she could hear the creak of the rigging and the breaking of the bow waves, she could smell fish oil, dirt and salt cod, feel the canvas covering her body and the hard boards beneath her. She sailed across the Atlantic until, exhausted but relieved, she reached the

New World, where, from on board ship, she could hear the Indians' drums—strange, three-beat signals coming from far away, always that same clear, incorruptible rhythm, the same three drum-beats over and over again—and Catalina could positively see before her the naked, red-painted Indians beating their hide drums. The drumming grew louder, came nearer, perilously near, as if they were planning some dreadful deed, as if they were hatching a plot, those savages, those creatures who might or might not be humans—as yet no one knew for certain. The sound was full of menace, so close to her now that Catalina heard it almost physically, and she jumped as her own door suddenly shook with the drum-beat, which was nothing but the knocking of the nun on wake-up duty, approaching relentlessly along the convent corridors. Passing from cell to cell, knocking, she had now reached Catalina's door, and knowing that there was a new girl here she opened her lips to call drowsily, 'Time for Lauds!'

Catalina sat up, took her new convent clothes from the chair and got dressed. Over in a corner she could see her leather trunk with its iron fittings. Opening it, she took out a knife that she had secretly tucked in among her clothes just before leaving home. She lifted the religious picture down from the wall and laid it on the bed. Then she pierced the skin of her forefinger with the knife, cut into the flesh, and raised her bleeding finger to draw a horizontal line on the wall, about a foot above her head. She returned the picture to its place, covering up the line, and licked her finger. 'When I'm as tall as that!' she said.

Catalina made herself as inconspicuous as possible. She avoided contact with both the nuns and the other girls her own age, and behaved like the kind of person who deliberately blends into the background so as not to attract attention. And she did not attract attention. Soon Catalina was part of the furniture, and no one took any notice of her.

Not to begin with, at any rate.

As far as religious observance was concerned—her comportment in chapel and church, in the choir and at prayer—she followed her companions' example and the rule of the convent. She simply did what everyone else did, with no thought for any underlying meaning. All her effort went into this imitation, these actions. However, she was often able to link the daily devotions to her real objective—the strengthening of mind and body. During prayers and masses she knelt for longer than required, so as to strengthen her thigh muscles; while singing the daily-repeated psalms, Catalina learned them by heart in order to train her memory; in the prescribed minutes of stillness after receiving the Host she tried to achieve a suspended state of absolute immobility without so much as the flicker of an eyelash.

As for the everyday life of the convent, here her conduct can only be described as exemplary. Catalina did whatever was demanded of her. Never grumbling, never objecting, docilely, without the least sign of resentment. She acquiesced in everything, and appeared quiet and contemplative. Unconditional obedience, the prioress had said. Moreover, when Catalina did a thing she did it properly. And so gradually everyone fell into the habit of burdening her with all the unpleasant tasks that no one else wanted. At first Catalina did not find this obedience easy: sometimes she had to lock her rebellious feelings inside herself as if she were stowing them away in a chest, and put the key somewhere out of reach. In fact she put it up so high that, when someone gave her a particularly repugnant task, even though she might mentally pull over a chair and climb onto it, feel around for the key and actually retrieve it, all this would take so long that she would find herself alone with the job, and then she would get on and do it and be able to congratulate herself on having managed, yet again, to subjugate her feelings.

She very soon found that what she was doing brought her great rewards. Whenever she overcame her reluctance to do something, she celebrated this as a victory. After each successful struggle against herself the victory was greater and more exhilarating. And this exhilaration was fed by two things—on the one hand a sense of possessing perfect self-control; the empowering certainty of being able to switch willingness and unwillingness on and off as she chose, and on the other a kind of superiority to the nuns, for they knew nothing of what really went on inside her and what her true intentions were.

As the years went by the nuns began to view Catalina with increasing admiration. They could not fail to notice the kind of person she was, or seemed to be. And so she gradually emerged from the shadows of inconspicuousness in which she had spent her first few years there. It started with the use of certain expressions: 'as good as Catalina' became a stock phrase. In all those years they had not had a word of complaint from her, they said; no arguing, no misbehaviour, none of the problems one usually had with novices—no, Catalina was an extraordinary person, a kind and selfless person, who had fought and conquered her own weakness. And at such a young age too! Even the prioress was amazed by Catalina's progress. In the first few months Ursula had trained her x-ray eyes on Catalina several more times, but the girl had managed to hide so successfully behind external actions, self-denial and the performance of duty that it became easier and easier for her to withstand the prioress's scrutiny. When Ursula realized that she could not do with Catalina what she had succeeded in doing with every one of her nuns—that is, turn her inside out and bring anything illicit or secret out into the open—it did not for a moment occur to her that her own powers might be at fault: instead, the longer the prioress observed Catalina's behaviour, the more certain she became that here was indeed an exceptional individual whose 'heart is truly white and pure, innocent and spotless', as she writes in the convent chronicle. And once she was convinced of this, she began to treat Catalina with great respect. She praised her conduct, at first only to the nuns but later even when Catalina was present. 'Look at Catalina,' she would say, 'and you will know how a nun should live.' Or 'She has not even taken the veil yet, but she already far surpasses you.' Or 'Unless you become like Catalina, you will never enter the Kingdom of Heaven.'

All this had some unfortunate consequences. The more Catalina was told that she was leading an almost saintly life, the more she believed it. The role she had adopted began to feel less like a role as her behaviour increasingly became an end in itself. The daily praise and reverential looks she received focused her attention on the outward appearance of her actions, and she fluttered her eyelashes at faster speeds, put on an even more pious expression in church and demonstrated ever greater stamina in her praying. Her performance as humble, kindly, ever-willing Catalina improved to the point where eventually even she forgot that it was only a performance. To the thrill of victory over herself was added the thrill of victory over others. For Catalina had become an example, a shining example. She caught the reverential, admiring glances of the others like butterflies that she could pin to the wall of her cell at night. For the first time she had achieved recognition, and over the next few years this recognition came to be what made her who she was, what held her together, what she strove for. She did everything in her power to make her light shine in the convent with an ever brighter, ever more unassailable radiance.

All went well until, in the summer of 1601—Catalina was then sixteen years old—the convent admitted that beanpole of a woman whom she had met once before in her life, Beatriz de Aliri. For some days before her arrival the nuns had done nothing but whisper about what 'poor Beatriz' had experienced, or rather, endured, in the past few weeks. The known facts of the case were that Beatriz had lost both her one-year-old daughter and her husband in quick succession, and that despair had driven her to the convent. But inventive rumour had it that the child had died by the hand of the husband, and that Beatriz had killed him. The truth, as always, was more complex.

Chapter four

Holding in and breaking out

As early as the year (of Our Lord) 1391, outbreaks of violence against the Jews in Spain had culminated in the massacre of untold numbers of those so-called false believers. To avoid being slaughtered, thousands of them had converted to Christianity. These converted Jews were known as *conversos*. But that did not spell the end of their persecution. In 1460 a Franciscan monk by the name of Alonso de Espina published a polemic against the *conversos* in which he lashed out at them with a logical deduction inspired, it would seem, not so much by a love of logic as by a delight in venting an intense hatred. His argument went like this: the *conversos* are not (true) Christians but (for the most part) still (clandestine) Jews; nonetheless, they are baptized; therefore, as baptized Christians who practise Christianity improperly they are heretics and ought at the very least to be killed. Further pogroms took place in the years 1467 and 1473, but whereas, at least according to some of the self-styled true believers of his day, Henry IV was weak and ineffectual—he was, they said, a vile, dirty man who was not averse to sexual congress with animals and even, it was claimed, with the false *conversos*, also known as *marranos* (pigs)—it was under the *real* 'Catholic Monarchs' that all those secret and sinister non-Christians living in Spain once again found themselves in acute peril.

The Catholic Monarchs were Isabella I of Castile and Ferdinand II of Aragon. Isabella was the First in more than name: *she* was the one who set the agenda. That was well known even at the time, and one sign of this is that her head—heavy with so much thinking and decision-making—presses down more deeply into the stone cushion on her tomb than her husband's does. For Ferdinand simply went along with whatever his wife proposed. It was Isabella who could no longer stomach all that tomfoolery with religion in her domains: her goal was unity of belief, the final, irreversible enthronement of the one true doctrine, the universal, natural, God-given Catholic faith. It was she who in 1478 had, to this end, invented the Inquisition, whose workings have so often been described and whose mission it was to track down, interrogate, torture and eradicate heterodox believers of whatever kind; it was Isabella who in 1492 sent Cristóbal Colón to China to instruct the pro-Christian Grand Khan of the Mongols in the Catholic faith and incite him to wage a holy war against the Muslims; she it was, too, who reconquered Granada, the Moors' last stronghold, in that same year. True, the history books accord the glory of the reconquest to Fernando; people called him 'the Bat' and 'the Hidden One', he was the saviour of Spain who completed the *Reconquista*, but once again it was Isabella who on 2 January 1492 insisted on personally driving the last Moors out of Granada, symbolically, so to speak, mounted on her horse and resplendent in her red and white armour. The Muslims were left with no choice but to head for the Strait of Gibraltar and sail back to where Isabella thought they belonged, or to embrace the Christian faith. Muslims who chose the latter course were known as *moriscos*.

But for all their zeal the Catholic Monarchs too failed to banish the Jewish and Muslim faiths completely from the country. Just as in earlier times the Christians had held their own against the Romans, so the Muslims and Jews who had undergone forced baptism devised ingenious stratagems which enabled them to go on practising their respective faiths in secret. The Muslims adopted the doctrine of *tagiyya*, which permitted an ostensible conversion to Christianity. Muslim prayer books were secretly handed down from one generation to the next. If the *moriscos* were forced to go to confession, they said that they had nothing to confess; if forced to observe holy days, they celebrated the Feast of St. John, which coincided with the Muslim feast of Ansara, so that they could start the day with their ritual ablutions. The *conversos* too had their subterfuges. They would say, 'In the name of the Father', but never 'and of the Son', they deliberately made the sign of the cross incorrectly, and they ate unleavened bread all year round so that no one would notice when their true, Jewish faith required them to do so during the feast of Passover.

Leo de Aliri, the man Beatriz had married—the shadowy figure Catalina had briefly glimpsed during the time she spent in the Aliris' house—was descended from one of those *conversos*. He was a master of dissimulation. No one could see how parts of the Torah which he knew by heart appeared before his mind's eye during the night, no one noticed that he would regularly cough or just mumble inaudibly when the congregation spoke the words accompanying the sign of the cross, and he had spent a long time honing his technique of crossing himself extremely fast and very convincingly, so that it would have taken a keen observer indeed to see that he omitted to touch his left shoulder.

Leo had come to northern Spain via Andalusia and Extremadura, and a convoluted set of circumstances had brought him together with the Catholic Beatriz. The two of them had immediately discovered a common interest of a kind conducive to an intimate relationship, and this interest found its expression in a secluded corner somewhere among the streets of San Sebastián. They had to get married: Beatriz was pregnant. This placed Leo in an exceedingly difficult position. The *conversos* generally chose like-minded co-religionists as spouses, since this made it far easier for them to observe their clandestine religion at home. Now Leo was forced to practise secrecy even in his own house. However, since Beatriz lost not only her first child but the next two as well, she was so preoccupied with begetting, conceiving, having her womb scraped out and mourning that she failed to pick up any signs of her husband's true religious orientation. At that time, incidentally, no one could understand why babies in the land of the Basques seemed so particularly disinclined to be born alive. Not until 1939 was the god identified who could be blamed for these botched acts of creation. He was given the name Rhesus. It turned out that this Rhesus—who was, perhaps, more of a monkey than a god—had endowed twenty-seven per cent of all Basques with a so-called negative factor. This meant that the babies ensconced in their mothers' wombs ran the risk, quite simply, of being poisoned by their mothers' negative blood if, as was quite often the case, the blood flowing through the child's own veins was positive.

Beatriz and Leo de Aliri did not let up on their procreative activities, and at last they succeeded in producing a living child. And now, like it or not, Leo had to attend the baptism of his own daughter. But the *conversos* had a solution for everything, so that night, when he thought his wife was asleep, Leo performed a special counter-ritual current among the Jews, which was intended to cleanse the infant's body, heart and blood of the Christian God who had been implanted there through baptism. Unfortunately for Leo, Beatriz was not asleep at all, but was standing in the doorway, covertly watching her husband and thinking, with a glow of maternal satisfaction, what a touchingly caring man the father of her child was—so besotted, so adoring that he could not bear to be parted from the baby even in the night. But as Beatriz stood there, invisible in the shadow of the door, and began to look more closely at what he was doing, the huge pile of stones in which her head had been buried all those years, blinding her to the truth, suddenly flew apart in a single, soundless explosion. She understood what was going on, saw her husband kneeling beside the child, saw not her husband now but a stranger engaged in exorcizing Christ, the Lord, from her own daughter's body as if He were a devil.

Leo was murmuring Jewish prayers, he had a little book open in front of him and was reciting verses which Beatriz had never heard before, he was singing, under his breath, religious melodies quite unlike those that were sung by decent Christian folk. She grasped the full extent of the catastrophe, its enormity, its irrevocability: she was living with a Jew, had for years been consorting with a Jew in the most wanton manner, had sullied her pure Christian soul forever with the stain of Jewish perversion.

Now, it is not altogether clear how the heavy vase that stood on the tall cupboard came into contact with Leo's skull: whether, as Beatriz testified to the investigating authorities, he lost his balance while performing the counter-rite, stumbled and crashed into the cupboard, thereby causing the vase to fall—a divine punishment, one might say, for what he was doing to the child; or whether Beatriz herself was guilty of reaching the vase down from the cupboard and hurling it at the back of her husband's head, her towering height adding extra force to the blow, before he had a chance to turn round. The baby was crying; Beatriz picked her up. She waited for her husband to regain consciousness. But he never did, because he was dead. Why the baptized investigators were so ready to believe the 'accident' version of the story, who can say, but the facts are that Beatriz was not found guilty and that the baby followed her father to the grave two weeks later, having suffered an attack of scarlet fever that proved fatal. Beatriz saw this partly as a consequence of the rite performed by the child's father, but also as a punishment of Job-like severity imposed on herself, not because she had killed someone—if she had—but because she had lived as the wife of a Jew without realizing it. No option remained for her now but to wash away her guilt, and this called for a washing facility commensurate with her great sin: a life in the seclusion of a convent.

Alongside the torments of guilt and self-pity, alongside her longing for repentance and her hope of forgiveness, a deep rage began to build up inside Beatriz de Aliri. If one could identify its successive stages, the sequence would go something like this: first there was only rage at herself, for not having noticed far sooner what was going on. Then came rage against her husband, for it was he, after all, who had so wickedly deceived her. Next, her rage was directed against what her husband had done to her, for which Beatriz used the word 'pretence'. Her rage against what her husband had done craved expansion, grandeur, universality; it developed into a rage against all pretence in the whole wide world, a rage against all hypocrisy and false witness, a hatred of the very spirit of the age in which she lived. But Beatriz came to realize that a rage against something general and abstract lacks an appropriate outlet, and so in the final stage of her fury she returned to the specific and concrete, once more focusing her rage on a tangible object. She vowed to herself that she would—'so help me God'—dedicate herself to the fight against 'hypocrites of every kind'. In an access of lofty Christian rhetoric she swore that she would become a 'tool of God' in the 'struggle for a life that is honest and transparent', the struggle to 'eradicate and unmask that most dreadful of all sins, the sin of pretence.' So, at any rate, she declared in one of her letters of confession, which was tucked into the convent chronicle and consequently never sent off.

Beatriz quickly picked up a trail that promised a worthy battle with which to open her campaign. Here was this convent brat, sixteen years old, Catalina—the fact that their paths had crossed before was, to Beatriz's mind, no mere coincidence but the work of Providence—and they all had her down as some kind of saint. That girl? Never! Beatriz watched Catalina closely. Whenever she was given an instruction she would acknowledge it with a silent, submissive nod before turning to go and carry it out, and for the merest fraction of a second there would be the twitch of a muscle in her face, one blink too many or a slight pursing of the lips which gave her away. This was anything but selflessness, Beatriz thought: on the contrary, it was arrogance, it was pride, it was self-infatuation taken to its extreme. Whenever Beatriz saw her kneel and pray, it seemed as if a light shone down upon Catalina's cheeks. This, Beatriz thought, was the most deep-dyed, nauseating hypocrisy. When Catalina's lips moved in silent prayer, she gave every appearance of true fervour, but in fact, Beatriz thought, she prayed only in order to be seen praying. Whatever Catalina did, Beatriz thought, she did to increase the awe in which she was held, to elicit some new, still more extravagant praise from the prioress. It was high time, thought Beatriz, that someone put a stop to her tricks. And after everything that had happened to her, Beatriz de Aliri considered herself ideally suited to the task.

With a certain sense of the dramatic, Beatriz now devised a plan. First she approached Catalina and talked to her—so far as this was possible, for point nine of the Rule of St. Augustine forbade 'idle conversation' and 'gossip'. Then, being much the older of the two, she gave the young girl all kinds of jobs to do—harmless, everyday things. Her manner was friendly, polite, appreciative. But as time went on her instructions became increasingly devious and malicious. She summoned Catalina to her cell and told her to clean it. Catalina obeyed without a murmur. While she was doing this, Beatriz confided to her that she had an irrational fear of dirt and could not possibly crawl into the corners herself. She needed Catalina's help, she said, and asked her to come by and clean the cell every day. From then on Catalina had to dress Beatriz, had to empty her chamber-pot for some trumped-up reason or other, had to help her wash herself. But all these humiliations failed to bring Catalina to the point where, as Beatriz secretly hoped, she would drop her pretence and, in a huge eruption of protest, finally show her true colours.

Sterner measures were called for. Beatriz tipped her chamber pot over and ordered Catalina to scrape up the faeces. When Beatriz was in bed with a bout of food poisoning from some fish she had eaten, Catalina had to catch the greenish vomit, wipe Beatriz's mouth and clean up the bed, which was wet and black from her diarrhoea. On top of all this, for some weeks now Beatriz had been constantly finding fault with Catalina and criticizing her for being clumsy. Systematically stepping up the torture, Beatriz subjected her to more and more accusations and complaints; soon she could do nothing right, and Beatriz continually found new words with which to berate her for her stupidity and ugliness.

When Catalina endured all this with apparent ease, when she performed every task, however disgusting, without the least hint of rebellion, when she seemed to regard each new torment as another golden opportunity to display her self-mastery and showed no sign of being about to concede defeat, it was Beatriz de Aliri whose patience finally ran out. On the night of 13th August, she crept along the corridors with a candle in her hand, opened the door of Catalina's cell, slipped inside and eyed the sleeping girl with undisguised hatred. She wished she could tear the deceitful skin from her face, plunge her hands into her breast and drag out what was hidden there. After observing Catalina for some minutes, Beatriz slowly bent over her.

Catalina opened her eyes and took fright, but she was unable to cry out. There, only inches away, she saw that face that had been thrust close to hers once before, and she was bewildered. 'You're so good,' Beatriz said suddenly. She said it calmly and sweetly. She set the candle down beside the bed and put her hands around Catalina's throat, very gently. 'You're so good,' she said, several times more, but the tone of her words changed from plaintive and half-admiring to vindictive and full of hatred. 'You're so good!' she shouted, and gradually her hands became throttling hands that made Catalina choke for breath. Then Beatriz sat up, drew back her long arm and rammed her fist with all her might into the face lying before her. Catalina spat, and her pillow turned red. The flame near the bed was smoking. Catalina looked at the blood. Then at Beatriz, who was waiting. Waiting for something to happen. For Catalina to defend herself, to hit back. And Catalina's fingers clenched into fists, her muscles tensed, her arm longed to rise, longed to strike—at last—a single retaliatory blow. Relief! But at that moment Catalina saw with vivid clarity her mother's raised index finger, her mother's right forefinger held up in admonition—but that finger was not there, it was missing, and the absence of the finger was like a cruel, stabbing pain. Catalina opened out her fist, kept her hand under the covers, gazed up at Beatriz and dispatched one last smile from her face —a gentle, excruciatingly forgiving smile—as if she were pushing it off a cliff. Beatriz turned pale; she stared wide-eyed at Catalina, rose heavily from the bed, turned, and left the cell without another word.

Catalina knew that this was her most spectacular victory. She wanted to celebrate it, silently, alone in the cell, with her unclenched fist still lying under the bedclothes. But she felt no exhilaration. The sense of triumph would not come. Catalina threw off the covers and stood up. She went over to the picture of the saint on the wall and laid it on the bed. It was weeks since she had last stood under the line she had drawn in blood. Pressing her nose to the wall, she placed one hand on the top of her head, touching the wall, then tilted her head back and looked up: she was very nearly there. And now her heels rose from the floor, her torso stretched and her neck strained upwards as far as it would go, until her hand covered the line.

Catalina got dressed. Mechanically, slowly, without reflecting on what she was doing. She stole through the corridors to the chapel, entered the sacristy, climbed onto a chair, opened the small, unbarred window and clambered through. She crossed the courtyard, to the chestnut tree that grew against the wall, climbed up and jumped down on the other side.

Chapter five

The cave of Ekain

Catalina walked into the darkness, guided by an obscure feeling within her that was no more than a faint twitching, a dying glimmer which she had to protect by cupping her hands round it. No one must come too close to her. When the moon appeared, it shone far too brightly for her liking, but it helped her to find her way. She walked without pause, heading east-south-eastwards and striking a straight course through the vegetation of the Atlantic Basque country. She took paths through fields, crossed almost impassable terrain, pushed undergrowth aside, waded through the small river Oria and covered almost twenty miles that night. Now and then she heard the rustling sounds of animals—voles, startled hares, deer, possibly sheep—and the wing-beats and cries of nocturnal birds. Stars rose and set again. It was a warm August night. Catalina's legs, wet from wading through the Oria, dried quickly. She crossed another river, and this time she was lucky, for there was a bridge right on her path. The first rays of sunlight appeared. Catalina did not stop. At this early hour there was no risk that there would be people about. It was not that she was afraid, she just did not want to meet anyone and have to talk: she wanted peace and solitude. This was only a dimly-felt impulse, not a conscious thought, for she was not really thinking at all as she walked along. She was simply walking—nothing else. A being devoid of thought, existing only in her muscles: moving, striding forward, fleeing.

At a certain point she stopped and scanned her surroundings, looking for a cave—dark, deep—looking for anything that would hide her from the eyes and words of other people. By now she had reached the hill known as Ekain, a limestone formation of the Cretaceous period, covered in trees and bushes—the last of the small hills stretching east-north-eastwards from the Agido, in the Deba region, less than a mile from the modern-day village of Zestoa. Catalina saw a sheep. She knew that when sheep spend the night in the open they seek out places that are dry, sheltered from the wind, warm. She followed the sheep as it scrambled up the hill and disappeared behind a clump of hazel and dogwood bushes and ash trees. Pushing her way through these, she found herself facing the entrance to a cave. It was a shallow arch, less tall than she was, but some seven feet wide. Inside, the passage grew slightly narrower. The floor was level. Just a few paces brought her to a dead end, where several sheep were huddled together. Startled by her presence, they bleated anxiously and, in an instinctive flight response, drummed their hooves on the earth floor. There was no sign of the shepherd. But he's sure to come, thought Catalina, to return these sheep to the flock. Also, the daylight was able to find its way even this far in: it was not dark enough for her. She turned round and went outside again.

Standing with her back to the cave entrance and looking eastwards, Catalina saw, directly below her, the confluence of two streams, the Goltzibar and the Beliosoerreka, whose waters combined to form the Sastarrain. She felt a draught on the back of her neck and, turning around, saw a small hole just to the right of the entrance. She moved closer and put her hand to it. The current of air was cool and an arm's width across. As she reached inside, bits of loose rock came away. Using both hands she pulled out further lumps until the opening was big enough for her. Then she wormed her way in, head and arms first, and found herself in a tunnel as low and narrow as a coffin. She would have to crawl on her stomach—so she did. A few yards further on her head still bumped against rock when she raised it. She briefly thought of retreating, but then she saw the darkness ahead of her, and the darkness was so profound, so dense, so stonily black and impenetrable that it beckoned to her, called to her, and Catalina suddenly knew that this was the very place she had been looking for; that all she wanted was to be swallowed up by this darkness, that she was crawling into a velvety, peaceful place far away from the piercing, all-revealing ugliness of the sun.

She propelled herself laboriously forward. Soon there was more headroom. She raised herself to her knees and continued, now crawling on all fours. Quite soon the passage became high enough for her to stand upright. When she turned to look back, she could only faintly make out the light from the entrance. She dusted herself down, then ran her hands over the cave walls. The rock was perfectly smooth, thanks to some tireless polishing-cloths—the pelts of bears passing in and out, bears whose bones had sunk deep down under the sediment of millennia. Catalina went on further, the layer of sinter crunching beneath her feet. The passageway broadened out. Now she was standing in the first main chamber of the cave, but could not see the paths branching off it. Instinctively she kept following the left-hand wall, and after a while she reached a dead end. The light from the entrance had vanished as if some thirsty maw had swallowed it.

When Catalina reached what she supposed was the end of the cave as a whole (though in fact she had only penetrated a short way into its stony entrails), she sat down. She thought that exhaustion would send her to sleep immediately, but she was wide awake. In vain her senses tried to resist. The silence and darkness were too strong. Her sense of smell put up a brief fight, but capitulated when she grew used to the musty, cold perspiration from the rock. Then there was nothing to stop the images hailing down on her: Miguel, a dog, the boys, shouts, the word 'ugly', a missing right forefinger raised in admonition, the empty harbour, Ursula's hair, and finally a face thrust close to hers, and once again Catalina felt Beatriz's hands on her throat, again she was being throttled and punched, again she clenched her hand into a fist, more tightly this time; and now, in her mind's eye, Catalina hit back, landed a punch on that flat face, and knew that in the long battle in the convent she had not been the winner at all, but quite the reverse.

Now, swept along by a landslide of violence such as she had never known, and with no means of holding it back, she mentally repaid with blows and kicks every humiliation she had suffered, revelling in the satisfaction of striking back and yet hating herself for finding pleasure in it. Sitting inside her, grinning, was that child, that sweet, pious caricature of herself that she had been for so many years—but *why*? Suddenly she no longer knew why she had done all that. She heard the prioress singing her praises in words that had become as much a part of her as if she had been branded with them, words that had been her light, her elixir of life. Now she ripped them out of her body. She saw herself from the outside, saw how she had behaved, saw that perpetual smile, that ever-compliant, sweet-natured, meek and modest smile which now metamorphosed into a grin, one that she wished she could cut out of her face.

A cold, wet cloth wrapped itself around her heart. Who *was* she? There was nothing left. Nothing inside, nothing outside. She could not even see herself any more. She wanted to take hold of herself, touch herself, wanted to place her hands on her body, but she sat there without moving, as if she were shackled. Wanted to cry out, prove to herself that there was actually still someone there, but she remained mute. Would it not be better if she never left the cave, if she never went outside again but stayed here forever, rotting away until the outermost covering, her skin which she could no longer see, no longer smell, was mouldy and riddled with worm-holes, until even her flesh was eaten away and liquefied, until even her skeleton, her teeth had crumbled to nothing? She uttered a scream. Her voice had found its freedom. Her hands too came to her aid, hands which touched her like hands that did not belong to her, hands which felt her, which confirmed that, yes, this was a human being of flesh and blood, a presence that was really present, a person, a living thing, this was she, she herself, even if she no longer knew who she was, what she was, what she should become, what she should do. She needed something to cling to. Now. At once. The hands that had taken hold of her body must become inner hands to drag something that was inside her out into the open. But there was nothing there. And so she reached into that emptiness and drew the void itself towards her, pulled the nothingness by its invisible hair, contemplated the absence, the extinction of all that she had been, and suddenly saw a glimmer. Saw a gleam. It grew strong, it gave her something to hold on to. She clutched the void to her breast and would not let it go. It was not just nothing. It was a physical sense of boundlessness, of openness, she looked at *nothing* and saw *everything*. Ways. Possibilities. She could see the back of the void, the far side of the nothingness; she felt as if she were standing on the highest point of the hill, and when she turned round to face in different directions there was always something different, something new to see. *She* could decide where to go, she could set off in a direction that was not prescribed by anything or anyone.

She stood up and, feeling the clothes on her body, took them off. Threw aside one garment after another. Wanted not to feel anything on her body any more. Wanted to revel in this new experience, to discard everything, to have the sensation of newness everywhere, all over her body, inside, outside. Naked she stood there in the cave, erect, with open eyes, her blindness turned into a source of strength, her lips parted, her ears intent, breathing and hearing and seeing nothingness. She wanted to draw it into herself, more and more, deeper and deeper. *Creatio ex nihilo*, she thought. God making the universe out of nothing. This is how He must have felt, how it must have been, standing like this in the blackness, experiencing the irruption of whiteness, the onslaught of emptiness, and transforming it into *something*.

Overwhelmed but suddenly lucid and sure of herself, Catalina knelt down on the floor. She felt elated. Before long she started to grope her way forward, and after a brief search found her clothes. As she touched them, she felt a piercing pain in the palm of her hand. It was not a snakebite, but the point of a needle which was in her pocket, together with a coil of thread. Only two days ago she had had to do some sewing for Beatriz, and now the needle and thread were the only things she had with her. To Catalina this was a clear sign, and what she now did took place in utter silence and darkness. Guided only by the invisible beam of her sense of touch, she fingered the various pieces of clothing and did what in those days only a woman could do: she started to sew. She sewed for what must have been several hours, and turned her blue woollen bodice into a pair of breeches and her petticoat into a shirt and stockings; she shortened and tore, sewed and patched, inserted and joined. She knew exactly what she was doing and what she wanted. To start completely afresh, a new person, stitched together by her own hands in the darkness.

At last she stood up and stretched. The clothes fitted. They were the right size. They hardly pinched at all. Once more she knelt down and felt around on the floor. She could not find what she was searching for. Her hands scrabbled about in the dirt. She crawled back the way she had come, with her right shoulder to the cave wall. Soon she was in the main passage again, could see, some distance away, the point of light that was the entrance. Catalina turned back again and entered the passage leading off to the right, which brought her, in only a few yards, to the vast main gallery. There she finally found what she wanted: a stone. It was a blade, and one of considerable archaeological significance. A flint blade with which, forty thousand years ago, a so-called Cro-Magnon man had not only kindled fire but also split open the skull of another Cro-Magnon man—for a thoroughly scientific reason, as it happens, namely to discover what went on inside a head like that, what there might be floating about in it, to discover the source of those vague stirrings, now brighter, now dimmer, that produced strange fancies inside his own skull too—a Cro-Magnon man who, finding nothing there to satisfy his thirst for knowledge, put the skull, since it was split anyway, to his lips like a goblet and quenched a thirst of a different kind.

Now Catalina pulled a handful of her hair as taut as she could and used the flint to saw away at it, close to her head, until the hair fell to the floor. She wielded the blade ferociously, off with it, one strand after another, and Catalina became a Samson in reverse, steadily gaining in strength as more of her hair was cropped. At last she ran an exploratory hand over her head and found that she was as bristly as a dog. Her hair lay all around her in a heap which over the next three and a half centuries would turn to dust, as would everything that had really happened in the cave. Layers of deposits would settle on top of the hair, so that there was no chance of Rafael Rezabal and Andoni Albizuri—the two researchers who on 8 June 1969 thought *they* had discovered Ekain—coming across it, though they did find the flint.

Catalina still had it in her hand. Before going back she gazed into the darkness one last time. She took a step away from the wall towards the centre of the cave and peered upwards. She wondered how high it actually was. Arching her body, she threw the flint up into the air as high as she could. She strained her ears in the darkness to hear what it would hit; whether it would reach the roof of the cave before falling down. But the stone did not fall down: it was as if it had stopped in mid-air, or were trapped by something, or as if someone had caught it. Catalina waited for a moment. Nothing happened. She recalled stories of the many-shaped god Mari, who lived in caves. But the stone had not been caught by the god Mari, it had landed on top of a fifteen-foot high pillar of rock in the middle of the gallery. Catalina, of course, could not see the pillar. The flint blade, which was found by Rafael and Andoni, is still there today, and is thought to provide strong evidence for the belief that Cro-Magnon man would ritually climb up such pillars, almost to the roof of a cave, to kindle a fire there in homage to the sun-god.

Outside, someone was approaching the Ekain hill. It was a man called Juan Bautista de Arteaga. He knew the cave, or at any rate the accessible smaller part of it. He felt drawn to its shelter now because the sun, hot as sizzling fat, was beating down from the sky. Juan's plan was to sleep in the shade for an hour or two, among the sheep if need be, until the worst of the heat was past. He hitched his donkey to a tree and took a few steps into the cave's dim interior. By now the sheep had gone. Juan spread out a blanket, lay down and closed his eyes. While he was doing all this, Catalina, in the inner tract of the Ekain cavern, was preparing to leave. She went down on her knees, blackened her face with dust, started crawling and finally lay down on her stomach to slither the last few yards back to the entrance.

Juan heard a sound. He opened his eyes just as Catalina closed hers against the dagger-thrust of the sun. He stepped out of the cave entrance just as Catalina poked her hands and her dazzled head out through the other opening. And Juan Bautista de Arteaga saw something emerge from the rock beside him, a spiky-headed monster, a stone man rolling towards his feet, so that Juan, in his fright, could think of nothing better to do than to draw his sword and let out a loud and terrible yell.

Chapter six

Juan Bautista de Arteaga

I rode out into the gloom of a sunless morning, slumped on the [donkey of myself?], unable to clear my mind of what had happened, unable to engender a single new thought, reduced to a mere [cape?], the world a ghostly presence, the clouds like [bleached ashes of the sky?]' So runs—more or less—the not wholly decipherable opening sentence of Juan Bautista de Arteaga's memoirs. The rather erratic raw text consists of 3,422 closely written pages of manuscript, never published but, as of a few months ago, available for inspection in the archive of the Centre des recherches sur le siècle d'or en Espagne.

We learn from these memoirs that Juan was born in Vitoria. He was both the first and the last-born of the Arteaga family. At his birth, however, it was not—as so often in the Basque country—his mother who forfeited her life, but his father. For on that same evening he celebrated his child's birth with some friends and got blind drunk. Singing as he lurched across the stone steps of the church, he lost his balance, fell over backwards and, unable to put out a hand to break his fall, hit his head on one of the steps. He broke the base of his skull and did not get up again. This mishap does not seem to have cast too much of a shadow over the future of the truncated family, for mother and son lived on, relatively unaffected, in the unmortgaged house that their husband and father had left them.

Even as a boy Juan Bautista had a passion for collecting, which he was to indulge in different ways throughout his life. He was forever bringing home all sorts of things, regardless of what they were: odd pieces of brass, bits of wood, stones, broken tools or scraps of clothing. Whatever he found, whatever people threw away, he brought home and crammed into his room until it was full to bursting. He would rearrange all these corpses of objects each time he added something new to the collection; perhaps he was trying to make the house he lived in a little less empty. Juan's mother, Anna Bianca Arteaga, worked hard to support them both, toiling day and night fluting the fashionable ruffs that were then so much in demand. Another reason why she worked so hard was that she shared the passion for ennoblement that was rampant in Spain at the time, and dreamed of giving her son the chance to go to university, for the title of Doctor would mean that he, at least, would be raised to the ranks of the nobility. For the sake of a 'de' between his first name and surname, for the status that this conferred and the well-paid positions open to a Doctor, Juan's mother scrimped and saved, pinched and scraped and hoarded every last crumb of money.

And at eighteen Juan did indeed go to the university of Alcalá de Henares, to study medicine. Anna Bianca had bought him the short black soutane-like student's gown called a *loba* and, rather than the square academic cap, the cheaper peaked cap. Like every other freshman, Juan was greeted by the established students with unpleasantly crude rituals: they 'made him white as snow', in other words they covered him with their spittle, mocked him for the resplendent newness of his gown and the prim and proper way he wore his cap, jeered and whistled at him, pretended to feel the material of his gown and pulled at it until it tore, and squashed his brand-new cap. However, these trials and tribulations did not go on for days, as they did for most freshers, because Juan quickly realized what was expected of him and stood his tormentors a meal, which immediately won them over so that they accepted him as one of themselves from the very first evening. Of course these were not students of noble birth, who could be recognized by the costly silk of their gowns and above all by the veritable army of servants following in their train: preceptors, tutors, cooks, pages, valets, footmen and grooms; rich students leading a life of luxury in a house bought, or at least rented for them by their parents; students who would ride to lectures on horseback, attended by their retinue of servants, who then waited outside the university, ready to escort their noble lords home again; students who for the most part had been admitted to one of the *Colegios Mayores*, whose alumni obtained the best appointments in church and state.

Juan was one of those students who managed as best they could outside the colleges, many of them living in boarding-houses. Under the regulations issued in 1534, the boarding-house landlord was required not only to satisfy the students' proverbially large appetites but also to protect them from the 'temptations' and opportunities for 'moral transgression' that lurked everywhere. To obey the letter of the law, he would have had to give his charges a pound of meat each day, as well as soup, a dessert and an 'appropriate amount of bread'; in addition it would have been his duty to lock the main door at half past seven every evening and check each morning and evening that all the students were present; to make sure that they were attending lectures as they were supposed to; to prohibit idle and unnecessary conversation among them, instead imposing set hours of study; and see to it that they did not under any circumstances spend their time playing at dice or cards. But the landlords and students together managed to sidestep the legal requirements by reaching a compromise that was agreeable to both parties: the landlord cut down on the daily rations, filling his own pockets with the money he saved, and in return he allowed the students complete freedom to do as they liked, letting it be no concern of his whether they were sitting dutifully in their rooms and studying, or staggering drunkenly from one brothel to another.

So the students were able to lend substance to the myth that theirs was a life of untrammelled liberty, dedicated to the pursuit of pleasure, though at the price, as Quevedo writes, of being gripped by 'the claws of Hunger incarnate' and being served 'a soup so clear that Narcissus, had he tried to drink it, would have been in even greater danger than when he saw his reflection in the water of the pool'. The *capigorristas*, the poor students, based their hopes of financial solvency mainly on subsidies from home. Whenever a letter arrived from their parents, they would tear it open at once, their eyes greedy for money. But instead of the material support they had hoped for they would generally find only a litany of parental advice. That evening there would be a ceremonial burning of these letters and those received by friends, accompanied by the chanting of the *Paulina*, a savage parody of the Lord's Prayer. To get his hands on any money, therefore, a student had either to work as a servant, enter into a liaison with some barely respectable barmaid, apply for a licence to beg, or simply steal. If students chose the latter course and were caught, then, under the terms of the 1492 Pragmatic of Santa Fé, they were subject not to local jurisdiction but to that of the *Scholasticus* of the university.

As well as being exempt from military service and excused from paying taxes, students also had an enormous influence on the appointment of the university's Rector and of the professors. Candidates for a professorial chair had to demonstrate their erudition in a competitive debate held in front of the students, who would then vote on them. But although the authorities did their best to prevent any attempts at bribery by the candidates, there was no limit to the students' venality, and they would happily give their vote to anyone who promised them a mule, a parcel of land, jewellery, slaves, or anything else that could be converted into cash.

Juan Bautista was a model student—that is to say a student who followed, with the utmost dedication, the models he saw before him. He went out on the town with his friends, squandered what little money his mother sent him, got drunk, gambled, won, lost, got entangled with women and would not have dreamt of doing any studying. He was living like any young man who has left home for the first time and is breathing in his new freedom like a drug—a young man pulled this way and that by different moods, and experiencing everything with great intensity. It was that phase of experimentation, of discovering who you really are, how you appear to others and what you can achieve; a phase when everything is permissible because you have no definitive picture of yourself but are still, as it were, painting that picture, trying out every conceivable style; it was a time of life when feelings are powerful, when thoughts are new and fresh and every experience is a wind of change, throwing into confusion all that has gone before; a time not yet dulled by the mustiness of repetition and the treadmill of resignation, but filled with hope, strength and a thirst for action.

Juan was uncommonly good-looking. He was nearly six feet tall, with thick, dark hair and black eyes, and at eighteen he already sported a proper pointed beard and was extremely popular. He had assembled a whole horde of friends around him. It was almost as if, since the crowded student boarding-house in Alcalá, unlike his mother's more spacious house, could not accommodate his mania for collecting objects, he was left with no choice but to collect people. Juan was the focus, the fixed point that held his friends together. And so he was always one of the party when they set forth to—as they say—paint the town red.

On one of Juan's visits to Vitoria, after he had been a student for about two years, he found his mother in such a poor physical state that she was completely unable to work. Anna Bianca Arteaga sat motionless in the house, emaciated, gaunt and frail. For weeks the gout in her fingers had prevented her from making any ruffs. Now her money was almost completely gone, and she was considering selling the house so that she could continue to support her son. Horrified, Juan dissuaded her from doing any such thing. Then he watched the doctor treat his mother, prescribing sweat cures and bleeding her copiously three times, but all to no avail. After two weeks of fruitless treatment the doctor told them to wait and see what happened, left the patient a diet sheet to follow, and departed without indicating when he might return. Juan waited for three days while his mother followed the diet, but when there was no improvement he told her that from now on *he* would take charge of her treatment, that they could forget about the doctor's instructions, that he, Juan Bautista, had already learned more in his first two years of study than that incompetent quack had in his whole life. But when Juan tried to apply to his mother's case the medical knowledge he had acquired so far, he realized that it was actually very limited—indeed, that really he had no systematic medical knowledge at all, only a few names and anecdotes that he had picked up here and there and happened to remember.

All the same, he gave Anna Bianca regular treatments: three times a day she had to bathe her hands in heated sheep's milk into which he had stirred some herbs or other. While she did so, he talked encouragingly to her, assuring her that warm milk was the latest medical discovery. Only a few weeks earlier a lecturer had mentioned that the Divine Vallés had used milk baths to cure the King himself of podagra. And in dealing with gouty complaints, the efficacy of milk treatments was *sui generis*. While treating his mother Juan used as many words as possible that were bound to be unfamiliar to her and would therefore impress her all the more. He quoted statements by eminent Spanish doctors, and enumerated all the newest medicinal herbs from the West Indies, which the famous Nicolas Monardes had brought together and named in his *Historia Medicinal*, and which, if they were ground very finely and stirred into milk—so Juan said, making it up as he went along—were a reliable cure for gout.

His mother believed every word her son said. She did not know what 'podagra' or '*sui generis*' meant, and she had never heard of the Divine Vallés, but she nodded in response to everything Juan said, not without pride. After only a few treatments her symptoms gradually abated, until finally they disappeared altogether. This was due not so much to the placebo effect—to her faith in the medical authorities and remedies—as to her motherly wish that her son should be proved right and become an outstanding doctor. For this to happen, it was of supreme importance that Juan's first attempt at healing should be a complete success, and so she and her body instinctively did their utmost to make it so.

After his mother had regained her strength, Juan began to take his medical studies far more seriously. He tried to catch up as quickly as possible on what he had missed in the first two years. He took a part-time job in order to lighten his mother's load. But the examination for the Licentiate was so expensive that he had to slave for six months to pay off his debts. Not only were there the honorariums for the professor, the bedells and the examiners, he also had to pay the masters of ceremonies and the workmen who had decorated the façade of the university with tapestries in honour of the occasion, as well as the drummers, trumpeters and bell-ringers. Everything was precisely laid down in the so-called *Ceremonial*, even the banquet which Juan had to give and which, with his mania for meticulous record-keeping, he describes down to the last detail. There was a salad consisting of fruit, vegetables, lemons, jams, sugared almonds, preserved cherries and pickled eggs, followed by partridges, pigeons *à la neige*, chopped poultry garnished with slices of bacon, sausage, pieces of rabbit and veal, and a fish platter with salmon, eel and dorados, while for dessert a white blancmange made of milk, almonds and sugar would not do, no, it had to be eggs *à la royale*, and to finish with there were cheese and Seville olives, aniseed bonbons and wrapped sweets, wafers, and of course the toothpicks which could be employed to bridge the belching silence of repleteness. But all this was as nothing compared to what his doctorate cost him.

Juan had to organize a huge procession with refreshments, hire a richly caparisoned horse, buy a new suit of clothes made of velvet, and after the examination lay on a *corrida* in which five bulls were killed. He had to make a whole series of 'gifts' as prescribed by the university statutes: fifty florins each for the *Scholasticus* and for Juan's sponsor, who placed the doctor's cap on his head in the church, two gold pieces for each of the Doctors who took part in the ceremony, and a hundred silver *reales* apiece for the bedell and the university notary, as well as gloves, bags of sugar and three brace of chickens for each of the above, and sweets and delicacies for half the town at the bullfight.

When at last his debts were paid off, Juan returned to his mother's house in Vitoria, and began to practise as a doctor. All the things he had collected as a child he now threw away to make room for a new collection: whatever money was not needed for day-to-day living he invested in books and medical equipment. Among other things he bought the works of Amusco, Aguero, Monserrate, Calvo and Alcazar, and of course the chief writings of the royal physicians, Diaz's *Compendio de cirugía* and Vallés's *Methodus medendi*; he purchased pirated handwritten copies of Pereira, Cristóbal de Vega and Villalobos, and besides the essential surgical instruments he also owned a multitude of jars containing human extremities, entrails and other body parts preserved in alcohol, some of which came from the collection of the Valencian anatomist Pedro Ximeno. He would not allow his mother to work.

Now and again Juan visited friends from university who had dispersed from Alcalá to places all over Spain. In August 1601 he spent a few days in a village on the Atlantic coast. 'On the way back,' Juan writes in his barely decipherable record for 14th August, the day on which he was to encounter Catalina, 'the sun was hard and hot and [swarming?] so high up in the sky that it was starting to lick up my blood right through my skin, my donkey was creaking beneath me like the [sails of a weary windmill?], I was longing to have a rest and recover some strength, so as to [...]. Flies, they had to be seen to be believed, were buzzing around so impudently [...] that there was no catching them, and my donkey's ears too would give a backward [twitch?] every now and then. Then I remembered the Ekain hill, which [towers?] above the Goltzibar and Beliosoerreka streams, I remembered that small, shady cave whose refreshing coolness is also sought out by all manner of sheep around the middle of the day. I made my way there [...] Before sleep could [blindfold?] my eyes I heard something, and stood up and went to investigate the source of the sound. Some stones had come [stumbling] out of a gap in the rock to the right of the entrance and turned into flesh, into living skin: there was a hand, black with dirt, then a head, a body, by now the [creature?] was half out of the rock and, unable to stop itself, slid down the small stony slope, landing right at my feet; I drew my sword and shouted to drive the apparition away. The—as I now saw—young man, who was no less alarmed by what *he* saw, jumped up and stretched out his hands defensively. For a while we stood there, and spent silent seconds looking at one another, each assessing whether the other posed a threat or whether one might prepare, in a spirit of trust and human reciprocity, to strike up a conversation.'

Chapter seven

A second baptism

'Who are you?' asked Juan.

Catalina was still shaky on her legs, wet and messy, an unlicked calf. In the cave she had taken a decision, but she had not yet given a thought to what her life would be like now, how she would behave towards other people, what exactly she would do or say, what kind of manner she would adopt. She parted her dry lips to reply, without thinking at all of disguising her voice, without reflecting that now, as a man, she would have to give it a darker timbre: she completely forgot that her light, girlish voice, accustomed to praying, trained through singing and seldom raised above a sharp whisper, would betray her the moment she spoke to anyone. Awkwardly she managed to get her tongue moving, said 'I…' and then stopped short, taken aback by the sound of her voice, which had dropped of its own accord to a lower pitch. 'I…,' said Catalina, and gave a start, because her silent cross-country march, the time spent in the cave, the long hours without speaking, the thirst, the lack of sleep, all of those things had lent her voice such a dark tone that for a moment she herself thought someone else was speaking from inside her.

'Who are you?' asked Juan.

Now Catalina took her time. She needed to clear her head a little, to collect herself and put her thoughts in order so that she could see her way more clearly. She was glad that her own voice was helping her, reminding her who she was, or rather who she wanted to be.

'I'm…,' she said, and broke off.

Had she any chance at all? Wasn't it ludicrous even to try? What good were the altered clothes she was wearing? What good was any new name she might adopt? Wouldn't it be easier to put an end to all this before it had even begun? Wouldn't it be simpler to say, 'Catalina', and tell him the whole story? But when she thought the name 'Catalina', she felt, for the first time, that she was thinking of someone else.

'…Francisco,' Catalina said.

She was giving it a try. She put all her strength and conviction into that name. Nonetheless, she fully expected that the tall, black-haired man facing her would, with a single word, bring the fragile, new, unconvincing self that she had created crashing down. 'Francisco,' Catalina said—her voice hard, dry, deep—and she could already hear the stranger laughing and saying, Francisco?—no, a girl can't be called that. 'Francisco,' Catalina said, and waited for his annihilating response.

'Francisco?' asked Juan. 'Francisco who?'

There was no disbelief in his voice, no doubt. The man repeated the name she had given herself, accepting it at face value. When Catalina heard the name spoken by another, it began to seem strangely real, solid and tangible. If *he* believes it, Catalina thought, then everyone else will too. And if they believe it, so can I.

'Francisco Loyola,' she said.

This came from somewhere deep inside her. She could not think what had suggested that particular name. She had been standing stooped and cowed before the stranger, but now she straightened up, a plant stretching towards the sun.

'What are you doing here?' asked Juan.

Catalina's first impulse was to describe her flight from monastic life. Where were you, the man would ask. At San Sebastián el Antiguo, she would have to reply. But surely that's a nunnery, he would say—no, that was no good, the truth would not serve here either. She would have to re-invent her history: having sewn herself a set of clothes, she must now stitch together a new life-story. She could not do it on the spur of the moment. But she must think of *something* to say right now, the man was waiting for an answer.

'I was attacked,' her gruff new voice replied, already a little louder, a little more confident, and Catalina lowered herself into that deep tone, bathed in it, began to explore the new voice, to play with it.

'Attacked?' asked Juan.

'Attacked,' said Catalina.

Anything was possible. Now that he had accepted her new name, now that she herself had begun, for the first time, to believe in the person she wanted to be, anything was possible. And anything might have happened before their meeting.

'How? When?' asked Juan.

But 'anything' was rather a lot to cope with just now. Too much. And besides, one question would only lead to another. Catalina wanted to gain time, recover her strength, have something to eat and drink, think carefully and produce a well-crafted story that would arouse pity without straining credulity, so that this man would believe it and be willing to help her. 'It's a long story,' said Catalina, determined not to become embroiled in details. And to discourage him from asking further questions she pretended to be exhausted, putting a hand to her forehead as if she were giddy and about to collapse, and just at that moment she really was overcome by giddiness, a black veil of faintness really did descend over her eyes, and she swayed and sat down, putting her hands out behind her. Juan went to fetch a skin of water. Catalina drank from it, and it did her good. It strengthened her. It mended the cracks in her lips and flushed the dust from her throat. Then Juan gave her bread and sheep's cheese.

After that Catalina would have liked nothing better than to lie down on the ground somewhere and be covered over with darkness and peace, but she could not afford to show weakness, and so she pushed her exhaustion aside.

'Where are you heading for?' she asked.

'Vitoria,' Juan replied.

'So am I,' said Catalina without thinking. She was about to add that she had an uncle living there, but she bit her lip just in time, for she was no longer Catalina de Erauso, and if she was not Catalina de Erauso then her family also did not exist, and if her family did not exist there was no uncle in Vitoria. The thought filled her, all at once, with exhilaration. It gave her an undreamed-of, all-consuming sense of freedom, a feeling of independence so overpowering that it left no room for doubt, fear or uncertainty. She was no longer herself. She was a different person, a person who could do things Catalina could never have done, say things Catalina could never have said. From this moment there was no going back. Everything was before her.

'Will you take me with you?' she asked, and for an instant she was horrified by her own question, for coming from a girl it was an outrageous question, an immoral, whorish question. But that momentary shock was succeeded by a sense of power. She was no longer a girl, she was a man, a stranger even to herself, someone who would surprise her in everything he did because all possible deeds still lay before him.

'Yes,' Juan said at once. 'It's always better for two people to travel together. This region isn't safe.' The true reason for his quick assent was different. 'That young man,' Juan later wrote, 'sitting before me at the entrance to the Ekain cave, there was something that seemed to [connect] him with me, I felt that something—what it was, I could not say—drew me to him.'

'Where are your shoes?' asked Juan, pointing to Catalina's feet in their dark blue stockings.

'They stole them,' Catalina said, glad that she had left her flat nun's sandals behind in the cave. Juan took a spare pair of shoes from his bag and handed them to Catalina. While he was packing up his things, Catalina slipped the big shoes on and took a few steps to see whether she would be able to walk in them. She caught sight of the body-sized opening she had made in order to get into the cave. She bent down, picked up the stones that she had pulled out and closed the hole up again. It is hard to say why she did this. Out of respect for what had happened in the cave? In veneration of the god Mari, whom she thought she had encountered? Out of fear that what she had left behind in there might take on a life of its own and emerge from the darkness to come after her? Perhaps there were elements of all three; what is certain is that Catalina left the entrance exactly as she had found it and exactly as it was when Andoni Albizuri and Rafael Rezabal 'discovered' the cave almost four centuries later. Rafael felt the same draught that Catalina had felt. He called to his companion, '*Andoni, emen zulo bat zeok*', which means, 'Andoni, there's a hole here'. They then removed the lumps of rock that Catalina had removed once before and looked at each other, and Rafael asked: '*Ze egingo diau?*' ('What shall we do?'). '*Aurrea!*' said Andoni without hesitation, a word that has become the battle-cry of the region's archaeologists: 'Come on!'

On the way to Vitoria, Catalina's overtiredness, like that of a child that has stayed up too long, turned into over-excitement. She was thrilled by the nakedness of the world around her. She saw everything as if she were seeing it for the first time, looking at it with new eyes that she herself had set in her face. Nothing clouded her enthusiasm. She drew deep breaths of air into her flat chest, which suddenly struck her as masculine. Juan sat on the donkey, and Catalina walked alongside him. She had said, 'I'd rather ride on St. Francis's mules'—in other words, walk—because she was afraid of giving herself away. She could not remember exactly how a man set about mounting a donkey. It was too long since she had seen it done. She only knew that it was quite different from the way a woman did it. She let Juan ride first and memorized his sequence of movements so that she would know what to do when her turn came. Altogether, she never took her eyes off Juan. As unobtrusively as possible, out of the corner of her eye and under cover of the cap which Juan had made for her from a piece of cloth, she observed every movement, however small, and stored it all in her memory: how Juan spat, making a sort of purring noise as he brought a lump of mucus from his throat up onto his tongue before pursing his lips and spitting it out onto the ground; how every now and then Juan scratched his stomach with four scrabbling fingers; how he patted the donkey's neck just below the ear and soothed it with a few words; his gestures when he talked, the sudden jerk of his arm, the way he plucked at his nose, his whole repertoire of finger movements.

During those hours they spent on the road, Catalina was like an empty vessel eager to be filled. As well as observing, she asked endless questions. And Juan answered them. About his home town, his studies, his mother's house and his work as a doctor.

'You wouldn't believe how many sick people there are,' Juan said.

'Tell me more about what you do,' said Catalina.

'Well, it depends.'

'What on?'

'On the illness.'

'What was the last illness you treated?'

'Marsh fever,' said Juan.

Catalina was practising. She was pleased that she was managing to ask all these short questions in the same deep voice. This was her real reason for questioning Juan so closely. She wanted to see how her voice would develop, now that she had had some food and rest. Although she noticed that it kept trying to creep upwards, back to its natural pitch, she successfully forced it back down, and with each new question it became easier to hold it at the lower pitch.

'Marsh fever?'

'That's right.'

'What is that?'

'No one really knows where it comes from,' said Juan, rubbing his chin. 'But the patient often loses a lot of hair, is deathly pale and has swellings like those you get with gout. The man I was treating was already old. The point came when he couldn't walk any more. The gouty swellings on his feet burst open. Some nasty stuff came out. You can't imagine how it stank. And it was so noxious that the wounds just wouldn't close up again. Then he developed dropsy and abscesses.'

'What does that mean?'

Juan explained.

'And what happened then?'

'He couldn't move any more. He even lost all movement in his hands. Incidentally, our king has the same illness. His valet has made him a chair on wheels, with a horsehair mattress. Unfortunately the man I was treating had nothing like that. He spent all day lying in the rotting bed of his body.'

'And what did you do?'

'I put him on diets and ordered milk baths.'

'Did it do any good?'

'He got diarrhoea and grew more and more thirsty. He wanted to drink all the time. I wouldn't let him.'

'Did you manage to cure him?'

'No, he died. In the end he summoned his family to him. His body was festering, riddled with open sores and covered in lice. The smell he gave off was so bad that you could only go near him with a cloth tied round your face. He showed his children his body and said a few words about the transience of life. Then he closed his eyes, for the last time.' Juan was astonished. Normally an account like this would set people yawning, and their attention would wander. But with every sentence that Juan uttered, this young man called Francisco Loyola showed more interest and asked more searching questions. This, Juan thought, was someone who wanted to know all about the subject, a man who was not satisfied with just a general explanation.

Under Francisco's insistent questioning, Juan described his work at length, explained aspects of human anatomy and indicated the difference between the male and the female skeleton. He found himself giving a detailed and exact account of how he had removed a stone from a patient's bladder, and not only what method he had used—the Spanish or the Italian—but why he favoured the Spanish method when even the King's own physician, Francisco Diaz, used the Italian method. And all the time, Juan was talking to his companion with the greatest of ease, as if he had known him for years. But because in fact he knew nothing about this youth—where he came from, where he was really going, what he was doing at present or had done in the past—Juan decided after some time to swing the conversation round to him, and so he asked Francisco about the attack that had been made on him.

Catalina still needed a little more time to invent her story. So first she rubbed her nose and scratched her stomach and also, in order to do something that would appear natural in a man, scratched her chest, which she found oddly exciting; after this she collected saliva together in her mouth—not quite managing the purring noise, but making a weak, halting sound—and spat it out onto the ground beside her. This cleared her head, and she started to speak.

'I was on my way to Vitoria,' said Catalina, 'when suddenly there were six men standing in front of me. They stole my donkey. My sword. My dagger. My money. My shoes. Then they dragged me into the cave, right into the depths of it. They left me in there alone, without a light. It took me a long time to get out.'

'Is the cave big?'

'It's vast.'

'I only know the small front chamber.'

'There's no comparison between that and the part behind the stones.'

'And you live in Vitoria?' asked Juan.

'No.'

'But you said that was where you were going.'

'I'm looking for work.'

'What kind of work?'

'Any kind.'

'What about your family? Where do you come from? Where were you born?'

Catalina said nothing for a moment. Then she stammered

something about 'growing up alone' and 'orphan'; 'I haven't got one,' she said, 'no family', 'all alone', she repeated several times, and for a moment she really felt the talons of loneliness clutching at her, but she recovered herself, brushed all that aside, suppressed the feeling and said, 'That's not quite true. No,' she said, 'there *is* still somebody, my brother, the only person I have left. Miguel', she said. 'I want to work so that one day…'—here she faltered and looked at Juan—'I want to earn money, to go to the New World. Miguel went away and never came back, but I know where he is, he's in Potosí. I want to go after my brother,' she said, 'do you understand?'

Catalina suddenly realized that what she had just said was not an invention, and that Juan was the very first person to whom she had confided her hopes. She looked up at him. Juan returned her gaze, and their eyes met for longer than is customary between strangers.

Luck was on their side, and they soon found a man who hired out donkeys. Juan agreed a price with him and told Catalina that with the hired donkey they would be able to reach Vitoria that same day. Then she had to mount. She did everything just as she had seen Juan do it, going close up to the donkey's flank, pushing herself off from the ground as hard as she could and using the momentum to swing her right leg over the donkey's back while pulling herself up with her hands.

It was far into the night when they reached Vitoria. The inns were closed, and Juan invited Catalina to his home for the night. The house that received them was dark and silent, as Juan's mother was already asleep upstairs. Juan led Catalina into a small room crammed with books, cleared some space and brought her blankets, pillows, a basin to wash in and a light. Then he went out, but as he left he turned back towards her and gave the door a gentle push so that it slowly swung to, gradually blocking her view of his face. She heard him say 'good night' before the door closed. They went on standing for a while on either side of the door, unable to see each other.

Catalina lay down with a sense that events were running away with her. She saw all the books in the room, the sheets of paper, handwritten notes, manuscripts. On a shelf above her, which she could only see by tilting her head right back, she discovered transparent containers with strange red, beige, black and brown objects in them. She did not know what they were, but did not get up to find out because she was so full of new impressions that there was no room for any more. She could hear her own rapid breathing, which refused to subside into the gentler rhythm of sleep, and so as she lay there she tried to create some order inside her head. She took one last look back at the girl she had left behind in the cave. She thought—who had that been? A convent child. That girl had done her duty, she had studied Latin and learned how to think, how to calculate, write and do various other useful things. She had fulfilled the purpose for which she had sent herself to the convent, and she was now surplus to requirements. Now, in order to get to the New World, the West Indies, some day—perhaps in two or three years' time—there were things to be learned which a girl could not learn, was not allowed to learn, things which must be learned by someone else—for instance by a man named Francisco. How had she hit upon that name, she wondered. Suddenly a scene from her childhood rose up before her, vivid and crystal-clear, as if by moving aside the debris of her old self in the cave she had made room for this memory. She had been seven years old. Some of the neighbours' children had been teasing her and her second brother Francisco. But their taunts had not been aimed at her and her ugliness, but at her brother, who was rather backward in every way. The children imitated his slow, clumsy, dopey manner; they played the 'Francisco game' with exaggerated contortions of their limbs, nasal moaning sounds, a hobbling gait and dragging arms. Catalina did nothing to stop them. Although she saw the tears in her brother's eyes, she was nasty enough to take a malicious pleasure in his suffering, because this time *he* was the target, not she. For a moment she even felt tempted to join in on the side of the mimics, simply so that *she* should not be bottom of the heap, glad to have someone *she* could look down on. She brushed away the memory with a feeling of distaste for the girl she had once been.

Catalina was awakened—it was still dark—by a loud knocking; habit made her leap up, thinking that it was time for Lauds, and she reached for her things, but there was nothing there. She was still wearing her male clothing. Now it all came back to her. Juan had taken her home with him; when she was alone she had washed her face in a basin; for a long time she had been unable to sleep and had leafed through a book, but at some point she had, after all, stumbled into sleep as if it were a hole in the ground. But she had not slept for long. And now she was standing in the middle of the room, not knowing what to do. She felt dizzy from getting up too quickly. The knocking grew louder. It was not someone knocking at the door of her room: it was further away, probably at the front door.

Catalina put on Juan's shoes, went out into the passage, following the sound, and reached the front door at the same instant as Juan, who was approaching from the other direction. He held the lamp up high and looked at Catalina. For a moment she thought: it's all up now. My face, I shouldn't have washed it. But Juan nodded to her as if they were old friends, saying: 'Already awake?' Catalina answered, 'I can't sleep,' and Juan opened the door. Standing outside were some men in search of a doctor. Anticipating this, Juan had already dressed and even had a bag in his hand. 'If you can't sleep'—Juan lifted a cape down from a hook on the wall and held it out to Catalina—'why don't you come along?'

Catalina took the cape from Juan's hands and slung it round her shoulders. It felt good. Like a shield to protect her from the piercing eyes of the world. Together they followed the men. A few streets away they were directed to a tavern. Inside were swaying figures, drunk from the night's alcohol, and from their midst rose the voice of a man screaming with pain. During a game of cards, Juan was told, someone had drawn a pistol and shot another player. The victim was bleeding like a pig and there seemed no way to stop it. Juan called for some hot oil, but when this request was only met with helpless stares, he sent Catalina off to find some. She headed for the kitchen at once and returned with the oil as fast as she could. In the meantime Juan had examined the wound and established that no vital organs had been affected, but this did not stop the victim from bellowing as if he were at death's door.

'Pull yourself together,' Juan hissed at him, but to no effect, and when Juan dabbed the hot oil onto the wound the patient's screams redoubled, although not for long, as he soon fainted from the pain. At last there was a bit of peace and quiet, and Juan could make a more thorough examination. By now he had staunched the bleeding, and he delved into his bag for some salves. As he bandaged the man, he gave Catalina instructions, and took whatever she passed him as though it were the most natural thing in the world. Finally Juan produced some fresh bandages and a jar containing a decoction of myrrh. He set these down in front of the men, extracted two coins from the victim's pocket and left the inn with Catalina.

'Your first wages,' he said, putting one of the coins into her hand. When she turned a questioning face to him he added, 'I've been looking for an assistant for some time, and now I think I've found one.' Before Catalina could answer he had already placed a hand on her back and pushed her out into the street.

Chapter eight

On good and bad play-acting

Catalina spent the next year working alongside Juan. There was more than enough to keep them busy: nasal polyps, asthma attacks, haemorrhoids, jaundice, gout, diphtheria, fever, erysipelas, visual impairments, syphilitic glandular swellings, and tumours of the spleen. Besides all this, goitre operations and punctures of the pleura had to be performed, using cannulas and drains. In cases of urethral stricture Juan, who favoured the 'bougie treatment', inserted tiny wax candles with rigid wicks into the urethra, by means of which he could administer caustic drops. There were any number of other surgical interventions, from quite minor ones to the amputation of every conceivable body part.

Whatever it was, Catalina soaked it all up. She was not troubled by the patients' screams, nor by the blood or the smells. She seldom felt any revulsion. On the contrary, it was always the most drastic butchery that kept her eyes most firmly riveted on the twitching limbs.

To her it was all new, and anything new was good. She avidly devoured the experiences of each day—the visits to patients, the operations, everything Juan told her, every word she heard, every word she read in Juan's books. She spent hours on end studying the illustrations of the human body or absorbed in the lucid, lightly-tripping style of Bernardino Montaña de Monserrate's *Libro de la anatomía del hombre*. She battled her way through *De recta curandorum vulnerum ratione*, the magnum opus of Francisco Arceo, Juan's former teacher at Alcalá de Henares—not that she understood much of it. Her favourite book was the *Cirugía universal* by Juan Fragoso of Toledo. The volume was still pristine and unread. Juan had only bought it that spring in Alcalá. The very chapter headings sent a frisson through her: 'How it can be shown that someone has died of vexation or grief', 'How to prove virginity', 'Whether a birth should be regarded as legitimate if the mother was pregnant for eleven months' or 'On the question of the ability to beget children in the absence of a penis'.

Once, not long after she had come to Vitoria, Juan was consulted by a man who was doubled up with pain and said he was peeing stones, he was desperate, he couldn't stand it any more, he needed help. Juan led him into a small, separate room, laid out some sharp and terrifying-looking instruments and ordered the man to take his clothes off. Catalina was startled when she saw the man's member before her, so unconcealed and open, so matter-of-fact, cold and naked, so very different from the illustrations she was familiar with from Juan's books. But, showing no sign of inhibition, she studied it closely, memorizing every detail: the two reddish-purple bags of skin, shrivelled, wrinkled like walnuts; the black hair curling right up to the navel, and, lying to one side, the shaft of the penis, lined with veins, with a bald, split, miniature head peeping out like the head of some Tom Thumb. Yes, there was no getting away from it: she might don men's clothing, she might disguise her voice, she had actually heard of a hair restorer produced in Italy which could make even a woman grow a beard; but here she was looking at something that no money in the world could buy her.

It suddenly struck her that sooner or later she would give herself away, and be seized and clapped in jail for what she was doing. She could not possibly hide her body forever from the gaze of others. Could they not already see what she really was? Here, in this room, with a naked man on the table, Catalina too suddenly felt naked and uncovered, exposed and unmasked. She broke out in a sweat, and had the feeling that someone was standing behind her, eyeing her speculatively. Could it be Juan's mother? Catalina looked round, but there was no one there. She closed her eyes and told herself to keep calm. Meanwhile Juan was performing the operation, using the Spanish method. He inserted one finger into the man's anus, which enabled him to reach behind the bladder. Moving his other hand over the naked skin of the abdomen, he slowly pushed the bladder stone from the navel to the pubic area and guided it into the neck of the bladder. Then, picking up the knife, he started making an incision next to the anus and quickly extended it towards the neck of the bladder, parallel to the bundles of muscles, so as to avoid the perineum and the raphe. Catalina had to pass him the *luncino*, a kind of catheter. Juan inserted it, while the man almost bit his tongue off. With a lance-shaped instrument, the *rallón*, Juan made room for the 'cranesbill', a pair of forceps with long, narrow jaws that could be opened and closed by means of a spring. Juan pushed the cranesbill in and activated the spring so that the jaws opened inside. Carefully he took hold of the bladder stone and was starting to pull it out when he realized that it was far too big. He crushed it using a different pair of forceps, and removed the fragments with a small, spoon-shaped instrument. The man survived. Not so Catalina's fear of detection, which faded more and more with each day that passed.

On the contrary, she became increasingly adept at playing the part she wanted to play. Her voice grew firmer and was soon immovably fixed deep down in her abdomen. Even if she had been woken up in the middle of the night, the strangled, high-pitched convent voice would not have been resurrected. Catalina's posture also changed: she stuck out her flat chest (which she hoped would remain flat), often placed her hands defiantly on her hips, and threw back her head. Years spent shuffling along the cloister had left their mark on her gait, but gradually she threw off her nun-like restraint, and in town she watched carefully to see how the young men walked. An advance payment from Juan had helped provide her with clothing: she sported both hat and sword, and possessed a selection of ruffs, as well as stockings, doublets, two capes, and close-fitting breeches; fortunately for her, a small foot was part of the ideal of masculine beauty at that time. She sewed a padded pouch into the front of her breeches, had her hair cut according to the current male fashion, and rubbed her fingers in the dirt of the street every day to make them rougher. She adjusted her behaviour too, quickly acquiring minor skills like swearing, spitting, belching, scratching herself fore and aft, doffing her hat, bowing, and whistling for a coach.

And so her gift for observation matured into a different kind of perception altogether. Seeing was no longer just seeing, but had a specific purpose. Catalina studied men and registered their every action, storing and adapting it within herself before regurgitating it as her own behaviour. The longer she wore male costume, the more deeply she immersed herself in the masculine world, the more at ease she felt. She much preferred fencing to knitting, playing cards to gazing at pictures of saints, riding a horse to passively sitting around. She loved the comfortable breeches and the straightforwardness of men, their taciturnity—their ability, on occasion, simply to keep their mouths shut—but also their direct manner of doing things, their openness, the heedless egotism they showed in their dealings with other people and in the way they ignored rules, hit out, got into fights, and stuck to their own point of view, stubborn as mules. She could do all these things now. On the other hand she accepted that there were some things a man could not do. She knew from the start that she must settle for the one dish or the other: choosing titbits from both was not an option.

For Catalina the main thing, that year, was that she was earning money. She needed it for the voyage. She was quite clear about what was involved, because Miguel had told her all about the journey to the West Indies, and so Catalina knew exactly what was possible and what was not. Or at any rate she thought she did. And even for the man she now was, Francisco Loyola, there was one insurmountable obstacle: the—as Catalina imagined—labyrinthine, dark, sinister corridors of Seville's Casa de Contratación, a gloomy building where thousands of sombre-faced officials carried out their odious business. These officials investigated every traveller to the Far West thoroughly, subjecting him to minute scrutiny and uncovering whatever secrets there were to be uncovered. Never in a million years, thought Catalina, would she be able to conceal her true identity from them. They had long lists and registers; they would easily establish that there was no such person as Francisco Loyola. And even if by some fluke the investigators did fail to notice anything amiss, her access to a ship would still be blocked by the armies of doctors and medical attendants in the Casa who carried out probing examinations of every would-be traveller and would not hesitate to shout, 'Take your clothes off!'

No, for Catalina there was only one way to get onto a ship: secretly and unofficially. And that meant paying money. A large sum. A very large sum. Catalina knew that before starting the ocean crossing the ships of the New Spain fleet made a last stop, for repairs and provisioning, at the Cape Verde Islands. That was where people who had something to hide from the Casa de Contratación would wait, and according to Miguel there were always enough ships' captains keen to earn some extra money who would take them on board. Miguel had told her the price of an illicit passage: 50 *ducados*. A *ducado* was worth 11 *reales* or 47 *cuartillos* or 94 *cuartos* or 188 *ochavos* or 375 *maravedís*. So 50 *ducados* would be 550 *reales* or 2,350 *cuartillos* or 4,700 *cuartos* or 9,400 *ochavos* or 18,750 *maravedís*. To save up such a sum would take her forever.

For the first twelve months, life in Vitoria proceeded more or less smoothly. Catalina improved in everything she did. Especially fencing. This was because the fencing master, a friend of Juan's, spent a long time explaining the theory of fencing to her before she was allowed even to touch a sword, and this method paid dividends, for it meant that when Catalina had her first practice with a sword she already knew exactly how to use it to best effect, and did not fall into the error of rushing blindly into action; on future occasions too she always fought with cool detachment, ruled by her head, not carried away by the heat of the fight. Moreover, by the end of a year she was able to arm-wrestle the theatre doorman Ramón Baroja for a full minute by the clock without conceding. This was a notable achievement, considering that twelve months earlier it would have taken little more than a puff of breath from Baroja to make her unmuscular little arm give way.

At this time Catalina admired Juan without reservation. He was ten years older than she was, and in every aspect of life he was the one with the superior experience and knowledge. Whatever Juan did was right and good, simply because he did it. He displayed the same mastery of his profession as of his life, he had many friends, people stopped to greet him in the street, he was respected; sometimes he stayed out all night with women whom, for whatever reason, he never brought home. But if you are together with someone for long enough, if you share everything with him, house and board, work and conversation, moods and silences, if you live in such close proximity that you see what he is like at times when he thinks he is unobserved, then inevitably there comes a point when the spell is broken. Catalina saw that Juan would sometimes sit alone doing nothing, and not only doing nothing but being oblivious to the world at large. At these times she saw pure, unrelieved sadness lodged in his eye like a splinter. She noticed that Juan often talked about the past, about his time in Alcalá. In his work as a doctor, too, Catalina observed some contradictions as time went on. But it was a whole year before she summoned up the courage to raise the subject with him. First she gathered her ammunition: she read and researched, compared and explored, weighed the evidence and rehearsed in her mind what she wanted to say until at last she felt adequately prepared.

'Tell me,' said Catalina, 'who is right, Geronimo Polo or Bernardo Caxanes?'

Juan was sitting in the sun with a cold drink, fanning himself.

'What do you mean?' he asked.

'One says you should bleed a patient as close as possible to the site of an infection, and the other says as far away as possible.'

'Caxanes is right. As close as possible.'

'How do you know?'

'Experience.'

'And why do those who follow Geronimo Polo say the opposite? Have they no experience?'

Juan shrugged his shoulders.

'If you're right,' Catalina said, 'then the others are wrong and are constantly doing people harm.'

'They are.'

'And you aren't?'

Catalina had to brace herself to ask this short question. Juan, on the other hand, had no idea which way the conversation was heading, and answered without giving it much thought.

'No. I'm not,' he said.

'But there are always two opinions on everything,' said Catalina. 'One book says one thing and another says the opposite. Some authorities say you should apply as much ointment as possible to a wound, and others as little as possible. Some say dressings must be changed every day and others say never.'

'What are you getting at?' asked Juan.

'Do you remember the gunshot wound you treated on my first night in Vitoria, a year ago?'

'Yes. What about it?'

'You put oil on it.'

'That's what you do. Gunshot wounds are poisonous.'

'Do you know Dionisio Daza Chacón?'

'Of course. He was the King's personal physician and a surgeon at the battle of Lepanto.'

'A good doctor, then?'

'One of the best.'

'And what if I tell you that he says gunshot wounds are not

poisonous at all. And that anyone who puts oil on them is a…'—Catalina paused—'…a bungler.'

Now Juan turned to face her.

'Where does it say that?'

'In one of your books.'

Juan said nothing.

'I think,' said Catalina, 'that you doctors just guess.'

'What did you say?'

'You guess. You try things out. You don't actually know the right thing to do, you just work on assumptions. Because if there are two views on everything, how can you tell who is right?'

'Obviously the one who manages to cure more of his patients.'

'And which one is that? In both camps some patients die and some get better. If they get better, the doctor shouts, there you are, I'm right!—and if they die he says, well, it's all in God's hands. Basically you're all just groping about in the dark.' Catalina paused to think, and while she was thinking Juan finished his drink, because he was beginning to find this conversation uncomfortable and wanted to go back indoors. Then Catalina said very slowly, weighing each word, 'But the main thing is that people must never find out. They must never lose their belief in you. They must always think that you're good doctors. That's why you have to defend your opinion so vigorously. As if it were the only correct one. As if it were immutable, carved in stone. In other words you're constantly having to pretend you know exactly what's what, while most of the time you've no idea at all. And that means—'

'What does it mean?'

'It means that you're play-acting, the whole time. And you have to act *well*. Well enough for people to swallow it.'

'I think you've been out too long in the sun,' said Juan. 'We're doctors, not actors.' He stood up, wiping the conversation out of existence as if it were a line in the sand. 'If you want to see actors,' he said, 'go to the theatre.'

❧

In a square in the town, or more often simply in the space between two rows of houses, they would set up wooden structures so as to form a long rectangle. At one end would be the stage, and at the other the *cazuela*, or 'hen-coop', a small balcony reserved for the women. Rooms in the adjoining houses which gave a view of the stage would be rented out as boxes at high prices. Below these there would be wooden balconies for the section of the audience that was not quite so genteel, but still too genteel to sit on the benches at ground level. Only the stage, the *cazuela* and the balconies at the sides were protected by a wooden roof. The remaining area, the pit—comprising a few benches and the space where spectators had to watch the show standing up—was covered by a canvas awning slung between the houses to keep off the sun.

Catalina was standing down there, among the common people. She had got in easily, and without paying, because of her friendship with the doorman Ramón Baroja. In the past year she had been quite a frequent visitor to the theatre and she now had no inhibitions about blowing kisses to the women in the *cazuela*, like all the other young men. She would also cup her hands suggestively in front of her chest, whistle, or stick out her tongue and lick her upper lip. She would raise her hand behind her head and make covert signs with her fingers. She had learned to imitate the lovelorn look in the young men's eyes, and tried to do even better. The result was always the same: the women pelted them with nuts, shells and other objects, ostensibly in annoyance, but really to spur them on to further impudent words and gestures.

After the musical prelude an actor stepped onto the stage and made a speech in praise of his own troupe, who were about to start their performance. The man spoke of the 'genius of the actors', of the 'wealth of content', the 'sublimity of the author' and the unstinting effort that had gone into rehearsing this difficult play. His words were directed towards the benches at ground level. These were the seats taken by the so-called 'musketeers', who were more feared in theatrical circles than anyone else. They were traders and craftsmen—the shoemakers were the worst of all—who closed their shops for the afternoon, turned up for the performance with their cloaks, swords and daggers, and thought themselves great connoisseurs of theatre. The opening eulogy was designed to put them in a gracious mood, for their clapping or their whistles would decide the fate of the play. Indeed, many writers tried to secure the musketeers' favour in advance by offering them money in return for applause—but quite often the musketeers retorted that they would judge for themselves whether the play was good or not.

Catalina had come not for the sake of the play but to observe the actors. She took note of where they placed the stresses in their lines, how they gesticulated, laughed and bellowed, cursed, wept or sang, and how they danced or strode across the stage. All at once she could see herself standing on the stage, or rather she felt as if she were looking out at the audience from the stage: in a flash she had changed places, and instead of looking up at the stage she was looking down from it, she was an actor, an actress, both at once, and suddenly she had no doubts: 'This is what I want!' It had come to her the previous day, following her conversation with Juan: had she not always, all her life, done what an actor does? Pretend, put on a show? She had done it in the convent and had been doing nothing else from the moment she had crawled out of the cave. Being someone she was not was what she did best. If you were as good at something as she was at acting, you had to make it your profession. As Juan's assistant she would have to slave away for a hundred years to save up the money she needed. But as an actor, a born actor, the best of all possible actors, she would earn the money for the voyage in a matter of weeks. Her decision was made: she would stake everything on a single card, exploit her innate talent and become an actor.

Catalina set about it without delay. Coolly, unhesitatingly, certain of what she wanted. She asked Juan for some leave, and spent the next few weeks watching the theatre folk at their rehearsals. And not only watching: she helped them put up or change the sets, was there if anyone needed anything, and would always willingly lend a hand. She talked and ate with them, and the theatre people soon got to know and like her. She also attended every performance, absorbed everything she saw and then, finding a place where she could be alone, tried to copy what she had seen. And then she had a stroke of luck: her friend Juan Bautista de Arteaga was called to attend one of the actors, who was complaining of syphilitic symptoms. Instead of the usual lignum vitae, Juan prescribed mercury ointment and cures using the fumes of particular kinds of incense. He told Catalina that it was unlikely the man would be able to carry on acting for much longer. And Catalina turned this piece of information to her advantage. She learned the sick man's part and memorized all his accompanying gestures. The part made Catalina laugh, being, as one might say, tailor-made for her: it was a part that called for no pretence, since she already carried it within her, underneath her clothes—for in this play the sick actor was playing a woman. Catalina even resuscitated her old voice. It was a bit rusty with disuse, but it still sounded better than the actor's shrill, artificial falsetto. When, a few days later, he did indeed collapse during a rehearsal, Catalina, who was sitting somewhere in the background, could see the other cast members' disconsolate faces: while they were sorry for their colleague and wished him a speedy recovery, they felt even sorrier for themselves, facing a financial loss for which there was no remedy. Catalina, apparently just happening to wander over to them, threw out a line of the part they thought was doomed and done for, and when the actors looked up at her with new hope in their eyes, she switched into her female voice and recited the key speeches.

She was relying on the effect of surprise, and soon she could tell that they had decided to have her. Only a few hours remained before the performance. Catalina had no time for anxiety, agitation or stage-fright. In any case, she was confident of achieving a triumph: she thought she would bowl them all over with her acting, the men and women in the audience would cheer and throw flowers, and in the next few weeks she would earn enough money to take her to the West Indies three times over.

But, as so often in life, the wish and the reality were two different things. For Catalina's acting was unspeakably bad—or so the audience decided, at any rate. They had always been able to make out, under the female costume, the man who was acting the woman's part. The humour of the role lay precisely in the fact that they knew there was a man inside that dress. But now there was no clear separation. 'What's going on?' the audience shouted. This was amateurish, an actor who blurred the distinctions, a hybrid, a mongrel, it was unheard-of! They wanted to see a man imitating a woman, not one who entered completely into the female role. They wanted to laugh at the disparity, not see it obscured. After Catalina's first scene had ended amid whistles from the shoemakers, people began whistling every time she appeared. By the end of the first act, Catalina had to flee from the theatre, so great was the uproar. Before she was even properly outside, she closed that short chapter in her life with a vow never to set foot on the stage again. She knew that she had failed, that she had proved herself unable to do what she was born to do—to play the part of a woman. She was glad no one had seen who she really was, who really lurked beneath that layer of makeup and women's clothes. She was glad no one knew that the person concealed under the costume was Francisco Loyola, assistant to the doctor. And it was to the doctor that she ran. She did not want to be with anyone else. Juan opened the door.

'Yes?' he said.

'It's me,' said Catalina.

'Who are you?' asked Juan.

Catalina was still wearing her female clothes, together with heavy makeup—a base of white lead an inch thick, plus some lurid vermilion and pink—and a wig. She came in, pushed past Juan and took off her dress. Removed the wig, washed her face, wiped away the makeup and with it the woman, and stood there in her men's breeches and shirt, which she had kept on under her costume.

'You?' asked Juan.

'Yes, it's me,' said Catalina.

Then she noticed that Juan had something in his hand.

'What's that?' she asked.

'This,' said Juan, 'is my mother's hair.'

Chapter nine

Fear, relief, horror

It was a duel: on one side stood Juan with every available medical remedy, with knowledge and theory, experience and books—and on the other, marsh fever, creeping, taking its time. At the start the illness was not alarming; it pulled out two clumps of his mother's hair, neither more nor less. But then the marsh invaded her hands: a fever, they called it fever without knowing where it came from, a symbol—the very quintessence—of the unknown, a screech of mocking laughter hurled, in the name of all illness, into the faces of doctors. Not only did Juan's mother's hands grow stiff, she became so weak that she was bedridden throughout the long struggle, which dragged on for six months.

After the tried and tested milk treatments had indeed brought some relief, Juan began to massage his mother's hands every two hours, very firmly, like someone kneading dough, because he thought it was vital to take immediate action and surrender nothing to the illness, least of all the patient's hands. He applied compresses, prescribed sweat cures, baths and diets, and if one treatment proved ineffective he turned to another. He was almost constantly at his mother's bedside, leaving it only to find out from his books what other cures had been tried by the doctors of his day. He sent his friends to the universities of Sahagún, Estella and Oñate to enquire about the latest research. Whenever one of them came back with news of some novel approach, Juan immediately tried it, following the instructions to the letter. He bombarded the fever with every remedy at his disposal, firing from all the barrels of knowledge and experience, keeping the illness on the run and engaging it in bitter battles until at last he forced it into retreat.

His mother's condition improved. The fever subsided. But Juan knew that the campaign was not yet over. He could positively *see* the illness holding a council of war in his mother's body, forging new weapons and gathering its forces. During this pause in hostilities, Juan poured all kinds of tinctures into his mother to arm her for the decisive engagement. Then he waited for two days at her bedside while she slept, breathing peacefully. Her temperature was normal and she lay there, with slightly reddened cheeks, as if she had no idea of the ordeal still to come.

It was on the third day of his vigil that Juan saw the first ulcer. It erupted from his mother's skin like a molehill. At once Juan took measures to force it back; applied salves, herbs, dressings, uncovered his mother so that he could examine her for more ulcers, felt all over her body, regardless of how embarrassing it was for her to feel her son's fingers between her legs. No sooner had he applied a dressing than the ulcer seemed to slip away elsewhere, forcing a way through the subterranean cavities of her body, indeed creating these as it ate its way through, excavating passages and tunnels so that it could keep throwing up its hills at different points on the skin. Meanwhile, the fever and gout returned with redoubled strength. Juan washed his mother, wiped off the new perspiration that instantly appeared on her freshly-washed body, changed the bedclothes and the chamber-pot soiled with diarrhoea, gave her finely mashed food, and had not the heart to refuse her water to quench the raging thirst caused by her dropsy, although most doctors would have said this was bad for her. But what did they know? And he himself—what did he know? Juan could hardly think about a cure, he had his hands full simply applying dressings as fast as new lesions appeared; he could only try to limit the scope of the defeat, he could only hope that it would not be final. And then suddenly he fell asleep, just like that, from sheer exhaustion, with his head resting on his mother's naked breast as she slept: his eyes fell shut, he could not help it.

What awakened him, after some hours of sleep, was a hideous smell. He opened his eyes and did not move, for beside him, inches away, just below his mother's right collarbone he at last saw the enemy, the cause of the illness. The mole had stuck its head out of the rotten flesh and was looking boldly back at him. The first ulcer had burst open, and some thick yellowish-red pus was oozing out of the open wound. For the first time his opponent was showing his true face. And Juan knew that the battle was lost. Though he refused to acknowledge the fact, though he tried everything and left none of the ulcers that burst each day uncovered, though he soon had his mother so tightly swaddled that the skin itself nearly suffocated, though he called upon powers greater than himself—whatever he did, he always saw before him the face of the mole that had ploughed its way through his mother's body and ambushed them both in their sleep.

When Juan finally gave up the fight, he could see that his mother had already made her peace with the enemy. Despite the pain, her eyes were filled with pride in her son, who had done everything he could. She had only a few more hours to live. Juan took off all the dressings, letting the frightful smell engulf him; he washed off the pus and blood, sent out for huge quantities of white lead and began to paint the wounds, one after another, while his mother lay on the bed, nodding because she could no longer speak. Finally he painted over the craters in her face and the holes in her forehead, applied pink and vermilion to her cheeks and mouth, and gave her lips an additional coating of wax to make them shine. He smoothed almond paste and pomade of ambergris into her hair. When he had finished, he put a bottle of rose water to his lips, took a mouthful of the liquid and sprayed his mother's body with it, forcing it out between his teeth. Anna Bianca Arteaga closed her eyes for the last time after looking in the mirror at her white, smoothed face, and the last breath she drew was filled with a red flowery scent which disguised the foul odour of death.

Meanwhile, Catalina's life was undergoing some changes. After her debacle in the theatre, she withdrew to lick her wounds, crouching abjectly in her room like a dog. The woman she had played had been rejected by the audience—on no account must the same thing happen to the man she was playing. To ensure that people continued to accept her as a man, she must be even more of a man than she had been up to now. And so she carefully nurtured Francisco, and did exercises which Ramón Baroja had taught her, to further develop and improve this body of hers. It suited her that Juan was neglecting his work as a doctor and requiring her help less and less often. It gave her more time for herself. However, after a while she realized that Juan was not merely neglecting his work, but had stopped doing it altogether. His patients were having to find another doctor—Juan was not available to anyone. He had no time. He was devoting every spare minute to his mother, or to searching out new ways of effecting a cure. It was obvious where this left Catalina. No doctor—no assistant. No visits to patients—no money for her. She urgently needed a new job.

This state of affairs had been going on for two months when she met her uncle by marriage, Rafael de Cerralta, in the street one Sunday. She recognized him at once. He had lived in San Sebastián for a long time, and as a child she had seen him every so often, even during her time at the convent. It was only three years since this uncle and his wife, a sister of María Pérez's, had moved to Vitoria; now he worked there as a doctor of theology, writing texts of his own, translating others from Latin, publishing commentaries on the Scriptures and earning his living—or so he claimed—by performing various commissions for the Church. Catalina's parents knew better: they said he still lived on the money that had come from his wife, who was now dead.

Catalina gave a violent start when she saw him. But as he drew nearer and showed no sign of recognition, despite looking closely at her, boldness gained the upper hand and she spoke to him.

'Señor de Cerralta,' she said.

'How do you know my name?' asked her uncle.

'Who doesn't know it?'

Her uncle eyed her, mistrustfully for the most part and yet—already somewhat flattered—with a quickly suppressed twitching at the corners of his mouth.

'I heard you were looking for someone who speaks Latin,' said Catalina, and she quoted a few lines from St. Thomas, St. Augustine and other Fathers of the Church that she knew by heart.

'Why should I—'

'For the work that you have to manage all alone,' said Catalina. 'I'm sure you could do with some help. And for me it would be the greatest honour to be permitted to work with you, the author of the famous *Compendium theologiae*.'

Now she had achieved her aim. Her uncle beamed. No one had ever come up to him before to talk about his work. He asked the young man when he had read the book.

'The first time was when I was eighteen,' said Catalina, 'and the second time when I was twenty-one, a year ago.'

In reality she had only skimmed through it once in the convent, and could vaguely remember one or two of the chapter headings, which she now threw out to her uncle as additional pieces of bait. Eventually he said, 'Come round at about midday tomorrow!' In this way Catalina gained an entrée into her uncle's house.

Once there, a curious misunderstanding arose. Catalina had been given—or so she thought—a position, a job, an assistantship similar, she assumed, to the one she had with Juan, but in any event, a post in which she would be paid. She had to sift through texts, read proofs or produce initial rough translations from Latin, but she also had to sit for hours listening to her uncle as he expatiated endlessly on every kind of religious topic. These hours were exceedingly boring, but at least, she reflected, it was easy money. However, it turned out that her uncle saw the situation quite differently: he regarded this young man, Francisco Loyola, as a student, drawn to his house by an interest and a delight in theology. As far as Rafael was concerned, the theological lectures that he delivered to Francisco were the main thing, they were what mattered, what it was all about. Francisco Loyola, Rafael thought, was there to learn. And you did not pay a student—on the contrary, it was eminently fair that Francisco should do something in return for what he, the famous Doctor of Theology, was teaching him, and it was in this light that he viewed all the trifling tasks that the young man performed for him.

When a month had elapsed and Catalina asked, as a matter of course, for her first four weeks' wages, Rafael de Cerralta burst out laughing. Undeterred, Catalina listed all the things that she had done for him during the past weeks. He replied by reminding her of his lectures, through which, he said, his pupil was acquiring knowledge which could one day be turned into hard cash, so that there could be no question of a wage here and now.

Catalina did not give up. She argued with her uncle until finally he rubbed his chin, thought it over and suggested a compromise. 'I won't pay you anything,' he said, 'but you can move in here if you like. You can live here for nothing, the house is big enough, and you can eat here, my cook isn't bad.' Now it was Catalina's turn to think it over, rubbing her own chin. On the one hand she felt affronted by the offer: board and lodging was a very poor wage for all that she did for her uncle; on the other hand there were arguments in favour of it. The smell in Juan's house was growing more and more unbearable, and besides, if she lived with her uncle she would be able—the idea alarmed her, though it also sent a shiver of excitement through her—to discover where Rafael de Cerralta kept his money and, when the time was right, help herself to what was really due to her. 'Very well,' said Catalina, nodding and holding out her hand to her uncle. He shook hands on the deal, not suspecting any ulterior motive.

Now that Catalina was living with her uncle, some streets away from Juan, she no longer saw him automatically every day. He was not there when she got up or when she went to bed. He was not there at mealtimes or in the evening when work was over. She keenly felt his absence from her life. If she wanted to see him she had to go to his house—and she did, every day. For she realized how very much she missed him, how she had grown used to his presence, how she liked listening to him. Besides, things had changed. It was Juan who needed *her* help now. So Catalina helped him. She ran errands, brought him food, and gave him support through the months when his mother was ill and needed nursing, the days when she was dying and after she was buried, and the arid months that followed, when Juan simply did nothing. He allowed very few friends to come and see him. His mind dwelt painfully on the fact that he had lost the decisive battle.

Francisco had been proved right, he told himself. Medicine and all science and experience had failed. What were diets and sweat baths compared to the face of the mole? If a patient recovered, was it really because the doctor had cured him? Or because the mole had chosen not to stick its head out? Had Francisco not said that when it came down to it doctors were simply play-acting? Pretending? How often had he assured his mother that she would make it, even after he knew it was too late?

Catalina's life had fallen into something of a rut. She worked for her uncle, practised her fencing, riding and fighting and spent the rest of her time with Juan. One day in April 1603, Catalina made her monthly calculation: it would be another fifteen months, she told herself, before she would have earned the right to relieve her uncle of the sum she needed for the voyage to the West Indies. She had found out where Rafael de Cerralta kept his money hidden: it was in a small iron box in his study, and he wore the key around his neck day and night.

Utterly lacking in enthusiasm for the task in hand, she had just thrown down her pencil onto the translation she was scribbling when something happened that she had not reckoned with, although in truth it had been inevitable from the moment she had first entered her uncle's house—something that changed the course of her life in an instant. There was a knock at the door. Mechanically she stood up and shuffled along the hall, bored and indifferent. One moment she was thinking of nothing in particular, and the next moment her world came crashing down like a picture falling out of its frame—for the face she saw before her was her father's.

Catalina stood in the hallway, tall and erect. She had had a further growth spurt in the last two years, but mercifully her breasts had remained flat. Powerful sets of muscles now filled out her legs, arms and shoulders. Her back was broad, her stance firm, her gaze piercing, and her posture ramrod-straight. If her face had not been in shadow her father would have seen the beginnings of a moustache on her upper lip. This had been achieved with the help of some hair restorer she had bought from an apothecary. Catalina tended the down like freshly seeded grass. Now, as she suddenly came face to face with her father, seconds passed—and nothing happened. Nothing visible, at any rate; inwardly she collapsed as if she had been blown over, terrified that her father might recognize her, put his arms round her, call her Catalina and with that one word destroy all that she had built up. She was afraid of losing Francisco, that infinitely better substitute for the girl she had been, Francisco, who had given her the place in life that she needed in order to achieve her goal. But all her father said was, 'I've come to see Dr de Cerralta. Is he in?'

It took Catalina some time to register this. She did not react. Her father repeated his question, and she realized that Francisco was safe, that the life she had invented for herself could continue, and her fear changed to relief. 'Of course!' she said. 'Come with me!' Her father followed her. Rafael came and greeted him. And Catalina, on the point of leaving them, paused in the doorway. Her sense of relief evaporated. Who was she? Suddenly she was horror-struck. Her own father did not recognize her. She had a fleeting impulse to go back into the middle of the room and put an end to it all—to pull off her clothes, stand naked before him and say 'Do you recognize me now?' But she did not do it. Leaving her uncle and her father to their own devices, she went to her own room, where she sat by the window and gazed out at the world. There was one person who would recognize her, who was sure to recognize her, she thought. Miguel. She was certain of it. He would see beneath the surface. His eyes would penetrate more deeply, he would look right inside her—he, and no one else. There was no doubt of it. And she *must* find him. Now, more than ever.

Chapter ten

A stone's throw in Seville

That night found Catalina waiting. Her plans were made, her preparations in hand. She had the knife with her under the blanket. She was dressed and even had her shoes on. Five streets away the horse was ready, needing only to be paid for. Catalina looked upwards as though to draw down strength for what had to be done, then she swung herself off the bed. Stepping out of the room, she laid her sword on the floor, turned to the right and moved softly along the corridor. When she reached her uncle's bedroom she pressed an ear to the door. She could hear a puffing sound. In between two breaths, in a single fluid movement, she entered the room. She waited for her eyes to adjust to the darkness, then cautiously approached the bed. Her uncle, in his sleep, had pushed back his thin covers; outside it was quiet, not a breath of wind to stir a hair on anyone's head.

Suddenly, in a vivid mental image, Catalina saw blood flowing from her uncle's chest, the knife that had struck the blow still in her own hand. A tempting voice urged her to do it. Instead she merely shut her eyes for a moment, silently drew a deep breath, took hold of the cord which her uncle wore like a chain around his neck, cut it through, took the key and left the room. She reached the study, which was some way away, pulled the iron box towards her, inserted the key and opened the lid. There was more money there than she had expected. She took the twenty *ducados* which she thought were her due, locked the box and was about to straighten up when she paused. Considered for a moment. Turned the key again. Opened the box a second time, and asked herself why only twenty, why not fifty? Hesitated. Knew that she was doing something she had never done before in her life, and doing it in the presence of her—albeit sleeping—father, whose proximity she could feel through the walls. But Catalina did it: she took thirty more coins, put all the money into a small bag and left the study. Returning to her own room, she trod on her sword-hilt: the blade rose from the floor and fell back, with far too loud a clatter. As she bent down to pick up the sword, she heard the sound of a door opening, and ran through the house and out into the night, to Juan.

'This needs to be quick!' Catalina panted. 'I haven't got much time. I'm going to Seville.'

'When?' asked Juan.

'Right now.'

'So you've come to say goodbye?' asked Juan.

'I've come to ask if you'll come with me. To Seville. And from Seville to the West Indies. The fleet sails in four weeks. What is there to keep you here?'

'Slow down,' said Juan. 'It's the middle of the night.'

'Yes or no, Juan. I have to go now.'

'What's the matter? Is someone after you?'

'Yes or no, Juan?'

'No, Francisco, I'm staying here.'

Catalina threw her arms round her friend, pressed him close, and turned away without looking him in the face again; left Juan, left the life that she had shared with him for almost two years, wiping away—before it could turn to tears—the moisture that running in the cool air had brought to her eyes. She hurried to the inn where the man was to have the horse ready for her, tossed the agreed sum on the table, followed him to the waiting animal, mounted it in the way she had learned, and without a word galloped through the streets of Vitoria, heading southwards.

Two weeks later she reached Seville—and an hour after entering the city walls she was in jail. She had hardly set foot in the city when a pack of youngsters surrounded her, not really menacingly; it was just horseplay, not an attempt to rob her, more a sort of baiting by a bunch of young hooligans—they were throwing stones, just harmless pebbles, nothing that could cause real injury—but the boys had about them the reek of the mob. Catalina was exhausted from the Andalusian sun, the ride had been murderous, the air thick and dust-laden, the ground parched and cracked. And now she was assailed by memories of the Corpus Christi procession, Beatriz de Aliri, the punch in the face, her time in the convent, a life not of humility but of humiliation: it was as though, in Seville, Catalina opened the Pandora's box of all her swallowed revulsion and released the whole accumulation of defiance, rage and fury she had kept inside. This unleashing of her trampled feelings created a cloud of dust which totally obliterated her. She lost her self-control, her self-mastery; the mastery and inner strength that imposed order, restraint and proportion. She no longer knew what she was doing or who she was.

She leaped down from her horse, and it was like a leap into the abyss. In the darkness of her mind she saw nothing. She reached for stones, did not pause to take aim but just threw, anything she could lay hands on, and one stone that was particularly big and easy to grip hit one of the boys on the head. Some local men caught hold of her arm and restrained her. She struggled, but they dragged her off to prison.

Ten days later she was released. She did not know why. As she stepped out of the deep shadow of the prison walls she was blinded by the sun. Then a face detached itself from the light, a tanned face with a pointed black beard: Juan Bautista de Arteaga. Before Catalina could say a word he pulled her into the street. 'This needs to be quick!' he said. 'We haven't got much time!' Juan led her quickly down Calle Sierpes, eastwards, through the narrow streets, past the Giralda—the minaret of the former mosque, now converted into a bell-tower. There, near the cathedral, was the Court of the Elms, the notorious Corral de los Olmos, separated off by thick chains and thus as it were welded for all time to the walls of the cathedral, for the chains indicated that this was an area under the jurisdiction of the Church, which meant no court officials, no officers of the law, no action by the forces of the state against dubious elements. For this reason the Court of the Elms had, over the years, become the main place of sanctuary for all the criminals in Seville.

To the left Catalina saw the Alcázar, one wing of which housed the Casa de Contratación. She was glad that Juan turned off to the right. Crosses abounded everywhere, painted on the low whitewashed houses or set up at street corners purely to discourage the Sevillians from throwing their rubbish onto the street—to no effect, for mounds of filth still towered up on all sides. Now Juan and Catalina could see the Torre del Oro, which had once housed the treasures of the Muslim rulers, and soon they had reached the Arenal beside the Río Guadalquivir, the biggest and busiest trans-shipment port in Europe. The entire city was at work loading up the fleet, thirty-six enormous ships, merchantmen and galleons, lying at anchor in the river with their sails furled. They had all travelled the twenty nautical miles from Sanlúcar, at the mouth of the Guadalquivir, to Seville, with shoal pilots on board to negotiate the difficult entrance, where there had been many cases of ships running aground. Small boats, feluccas and tartans, were used to load the ships with salt fish, dried meat, ship's biscuit, tea, wine and ammunition for the cannons, as well as with the latest merchandise—olive oil and wine soap from Andalusia, coloured ceramic tiles from Triana, mercury from the mines of Almadén, linen from Laval, brocade from Italy and hemp from Lübeck.

Juan raised his arm and waved to someone. 'Aurrea!' he said. 'Come on!'

Following him, Catalina ran towards a man who had returned Juan's wave. The man leaped into a boat, Catalina and Juan jumped in after him, and they cast off and headed towards a small sailing vessel. Juan and the stranger rowed; Catalina sat in the stern. Floating in the river were pieces of wood, bits of orange peel and fish entrails. Catalina hoped she would at last get a chance to ask some questions, but the man would not let her get a word in; he said he was from Genoa, his name was Roberto Maldini, and then, in a score of garbled half-Spanish, half-Italian sentences he told them his life story, or so at least it seemed to Catalina, who could neither understand it all nor give it her full attention, for she was the only one who could see where they were going, and so every now and then she had to guide the two rowers past some obstacle.

They rapidly came alongside the ship and no sooner had they clambered aboard than the anchor was hauled in, as if the crew had only been waiting for their arrival. The ship started to move. The Triana pontoon bridge had just been opened and would certainly not be letting traffic through all day. For a while Catalina forgot all her questions as she saw the battlements of the castle that housed the Inquisition, and on the opposite bank a procession disappearing through the Triana Gate in the direction of the city. 'An execution,' said Roberto, pointing to the condemned man, who was wearing a white tunic and a blue cap. He was riding on a donkey, his hands tied to a cross, the noose already around his neck; two monks were walking beside him, talking to him incessantly and with great urgency, and Catalina could just hear, fading into the distance, the voice of the town crier roaring out, again and again, the crime the man had committed: 'Murder of his own brother!'

It now turned out that Miguel had been mistaken: they were not heading for the Cape Verde Islands, but only for the south-western tip of Spain. There they dropped anchor and waited for the fleet to come by. When it hove in sight, Roberto, Catalina and Juan got into the ship's boat and rowed close alongside the galleon, the *Santa Isabella*, that was slowly gliding past. Juan and Catalina caught the rope that was thrown to them and climbed up it. From down in his boat Roberto Maldini waved to them and started to row back, his face wearing an odd, almost malicious grin.

Once on the *Santa Isabella* there was something that Catalina and Juan found puzzling: the sailors who had helped them climb the rope and pulled them on board did not utter a single word. One of them jerked his head towards the stern. Another led the way. The crew, as though mustered for a silent inspection, formed a double line through which Juan and Catalina walked. They went past the ship's boat. Past the mainmast. Past the cannons on the upper deck, which stood behind closed gunports. Past the mute helmsman, who held the whipstaff tightly in his hands. All the way to the captain's cabin at the end of the deck. The door squeaked as Juan opened it. It seemed to Catalina to be the first sound she had heard on the ship. In the cabin they met the captain, who put a finger to his lips as Juan was about to greet him. He held his other hand out to him, a curved, demanding hollow. Juan got out a purse of money and passed it across the table. Not a word had been spoken.

Part two

Chapter eleven

The aerosol mist

Massed together in the cramped, stifling interior of the pharynx, determined to pounce on whatever they might meet outside, round particles and oval ones, gossamer-thin and spherical ones all jostled together, rather like grains of pollen—about a million of them to each millilitre of pharyngeal secretion. Then a powerful explosion catapulted them out into the air. The smoke produced by the shot could not be seen: it was an insidious, invisible aerosol mist. The viruses tried to keep together, because only by keeping together could they hope to board an enemy body. Attached to their surface were five hundred prickles pointing outwards in every direction and carrying battle-ready proteins of types N and H; in the fresh air of the Caribbean shore they stretched out their feelers for likely docking sites. Some fell to the ground along the way and attached themselves to glistening objects, grains of sand, small pieces of driftwood. These were beyond rescue. The others looked behind them, hoping for reinforcements, but no help was in sight. Then they entered the aura of a living creature. All their prickles perked up. Instinctively they moved to where a breath was being drawn: they must not miss the tide. They could already feel the faint suction; they were breathed in, and used the life-giving air as a Trojan horse that enabled them to gain access, unscathed, to the interior. The concentrated power of all the Ns, which were trembling with eagerness for the fight, instantly perforated the enemy's shields and reduced the bastion of the mucus layer to a viscous fluid, and with each cell that was liquefied a new target was exposed for the Hs to hook onto with all their might. Once they had fastened onto the enemy like so many ticks, the core, the essence, the inner content burst forth: this was the decisive breakout of all the nucleocapsids, invading the host cells, which now lost their capacity to play host to anything or anyone but were carried off by the nuclear storm of the viral strands, which destroyed everything in their path, dividing and multiplying, dividing and multiplying at lightning speed, capturing territory and giving the other side no chance to develop a defence. All this was done with extraordinary swiftness, for experience had shown that it would not be long before the enemy antibodies arrived on the scene. But here, on the seashore, in the unsuspecting body of this indigenous inhabitant, there was a surprise: no enemy came. There was no resistance. This was unusual, but more than welcome, for the further one could drive back one's opponent, the greater the triumph. Even if it was achieved at the cost of one's life: the viruses soon realized that this foreign body, so totally overrun by foreign bodies, had not the slightest chance of survival. But in the few days before the victim gave up his mortal ghost, before he inwardly flickered and died, dragging the viruses proliferating within him to the same death, they fired salvos of coughs and sneezes with unparalleled rapidity at other bodies in the vicinity—a massive and sustained artillery barrage that enveloped the American continent in an invisible, deadly mist. And the influenza viruses received strategic support: smallpox, swine fever and measles overran indigenous bodies in a massive microbial shock attack, musket shot shattered indigenous organs, knife blades stabbed indigenous hearts, empty indigenous stomachs became distended and burst, lashes cut into indigenous skins, and the labour and light-deprivation of mining work drank indigenous blood, so that in barely fifty years seventy million native Americans met their deaths, or as a judge put it at the time, 'If water is lacking to irrigate the land, then use the Indians' blood.'

All counter-measures taken by the natives were doomed to failure. The Aztec Montezuma found himself confronting Hernán Cortés. It was only a meagre troop of nervous soldiers that Cortés was leading into the interior, whereas Montezuma had the whole Aztec empire to draw on, with its hundreds of thousands of warriors. But the Aztecs hesitated, keeping out of sight while they tried to assess the situation, because they were uncertain of the intruders' identity: this might, they thought, be their own god Quetzalcoatl, who had not yet made his long-prophesied return. Fear of the new and unknown was the Aztecs' overriding reaction, and to begin with they tried, by peaceful means, to persuade the intruders to withdraw, sending them first gold and later women. The newcomers were happy to accept these gifts, but showed no intention of retreating. Finally Montezuma tried a ruse. He had noticed that one of his warriors bore a remarkable likeness to the white men's leader. Taking an old helmet and other items of armour that had been found lying about, he kitted him out so convincingly that anyone would have sworn that this was a second Hernán Cortés. Montezuma dispatched the false Cortés, accompanied by a small party of men, to the real Cortés's camp. He had no doubt that when the interlopers saw this powerful demonstration of Aztec magic they would take to their heels in terror and disappear for good. And indeed the conquistadors at first stood transfixed by the sight of this Aztec mummery, only to burst out laughing seconds later. So far from being awed by the Aztecs' magic, they thought the false Cortés was an excellent joke which kept them amused for days. They gave the poor fellow nicknames, teased him, and held him prisoner in their camp, and once again Montezuma could not see where he had gone wrong.

It was this mutual incomprehension that caused the whole problem. It first showed itself when the indigenous people were unable to understand a word of what the newcomers said whenever they left their big ships and came ashore. '*Ci-u-than*!' ('We don't understand you!'), or '*Ma c'ubab than*' ('We don't understand your words'), or '*Uh yu uthan*' ('Listen to the way they talk'), exclaimed the Maya when the conquistadors asked them the name of the peninsula which has been known as Yucatán ever since.

The hairy-chinned newcomers then rammed a stick with some coloured cloth on it into the sand and spoke some sentences into the air, while one of them dipped a bird's feather into a small pot and splashed black liquid onto an object, as flat as a leaf, that they had unrolled. After that they acted as if everything they saw belonged to them. Later on it became more baffling still, when the newcomers once more unrolled the flat leaf-like thing with the black marks on it, stared at it and began to talk to it, though the leaf did not reply. Then it was rolled up again, and the native people had only three options: to fight and be enslaved, not to fight and to be enslaved, or to flee. All this very quickly led them to the conclusion that the misfortune that had befallen them was caused chiefly by the speech-filled mouths of these strangers—by what came out of those mouths whenever and wherever they came ashore.

So it is understandable that in 1600 some dozens of rebellious Indians banded together to perform an act of liberation: they would deprive the newcomers of the attribute that made them what they were. Night had fallen on the Caribbean beach where the crew of the *Santa Isabella* were encamped; they had lit an enormous fire and were drinking themselves into a stupor. A three-man watch had stayed behind on the *Santa Isabella*, together with the captain, Luis de Fajardo, and three officers. The men on the beach had drunk to their successful crossing, devoured nameless birds which they had barbecued on the open fire, bathed naked in the warm water which by day had had a seductive turquoise gleam—joking about the sharks that were supposed to infest these waters and surreptitiously diving down to grab a companion by the foot and give him a fright—and finally they had stretched out exhausted on the beach, sated with their orgies of swimming, eating and drinking. Relaxed and at peace, they were about to doze off when seventy or eighty resolute Indians fell upon them, so quietly, so stealthily, that the sailors did not notice what was happening. They were all tied up by the time they even tried to call for help, but their attackers cut out their tongues and vanished as silently as they had come.

For the sailors this was the most terrible night of their lives. They did not know whether the savages would return, or why their comrades on board ship did not come to their aid; whether those comrades were even still alive, or whether they too, with tongues reduced to throbbing, bleeding stumps, were only capable of inarticulate moans. A few of the sailors died that night, but most of them were rescued the next morning by the men who had remained on the *Santa Isabella*. It was some days later, when pus was oozing from their mouths and the worst of the pain was over, that they succumbed to despair. They tried to speak but could not, opened their mouths to call for something but were unable to wrest any recognizable sounds from their lips, only deathlike, inhuman groans. Sitting on the Caribbean shore, the men began to grasp the full import of what had been done to them and what their fate would be from now on. In silent apathy they stared down at the sand.

Captain Luis de Fajardo knew that he could hardly risk sailing back to Spain with this crew. How was it to be done if an order could not be relayed by a shout from one sailor to the next, right up to the shrouds? At best they might perhaps make it to one of the nearby Caribbean settlements. There, the captain thought, he would have to take on a new crew. But in order to get there he needed the help of the mutilated men, and to obtain it he would first have to rouse them to action, inspire them with new courage, rekindle the fire in them. One evening he leaped to his feet and delivered a stirring speech. His voice rang out into the night. Originally he had meant to say only a few well-chosen words, but when he looked the men in the eyes, when he saw the sailors stand up, one after another, as if to show that they were on his side, he injected more passion into his speech, especially as he noticed that it was only the emotionally charged words that had any effect on the men, words like 'destiny', 'brotherhood', 'comradeship' and 'undying loyalty'. Luis de Fajardo spoke with mounting fervour, heading inexorably towards some sort of climax—perhaps a grand gesture, a great, symbolic deed, or if not an actual deed, at least the prospect of one, a promise, a redeeming vow, and so for his conclusion he declared, without quite knowing *what* he was declaring: 'If I or one of these others who can speak should ever abandon you, then you shall have the right to make the cut that leaves our mouths without tongues and our lips without speech. For we are united forever by what has befallen you and not us!' The tongueless men cheered. That is to say, they cooed like doves, forced stammering sounds from their chests, and growled their approval as they threw their arms up in the air.

Over the next three years it became clear that the men without tongues were taking the captain's words far more seriously than he had intended. That speech had truly given them a new lease of life: they had discovered a new purpose which lay in that very sense of unity that he had invoked, and suddenly they felt themselves to be members of a secret fellowship that could throw all rules overboard and establish new ones, with a captain who had bound himself indissolubly to them by his promise. Moreover, the tongueless men proved, from the very start, to be far better at manoeuvring the ship than anyone had expected. They managed to reach La Habana without any major difficulties. And while they were lying at anchor there, they practised handling the sails and continued to develop the new skill that they had begun to learn on the short passage to La Habana: how to communicate without speech.

With the help of their speaking comrades they worked out a silent system of nautical communication, translating all the commands into hand signals and other movements which could be seen and readily distinguished even from a distance. They bought ship's bells with different tones, ship's lanterns in various sizes, and two dozen animal hide drums. Equipped with these, they devised a combined system of light and sound signals for use when manoeuvring at night, which every sailor had to learn during the wait at La Habana. When the captain saw that there was no getting out of the promise that he had made in the heat of his oratory, when he saw that he had no chance of exchanging his maimed crew for another—if only because the tongueless men never left the ship—he had no alternative but to embark on the return voyage to Spain with the existing crew. And the amazing fact was that during the crossing the men performed the manoeuvres more and more efficiently, and their signals functioned perfectly. On subsequent voyages the tongueless sailors even found time to expand their system of signals, initially designed purely for operating the ship, to include facial and manual signs for daily activities. Sleeping, eating or drinking could easily be mimed. Developing a sign language for abstract concepts was more difficult. During their crossings of the Atlantic they argued about which gesture might best represent which word. Some related the idea of thinking to the head, but others wanted to locate belief there, while a third group felt that belief belonged rather to the region around the heart, and others again claimed that region entirely for feeling. But these debates were never allowed to drift inconclusively: instead, after proposals had been put, a vote was taken and the decision of the majority was adopted by them all.

It was this ship, the *Santa Isabella*, that Catalina and Juan had boarded, without the least inkling of what awaited them. Their silent reception weighed oppressively on their spirits, and when the captain put a hushing finger to his lips, this was accompanied by a melancholy upward turn of the eyes and a jerk of his chin in the direction of the table in the cabin. Juan and Catalina sat down, and so did the captain. Then nothing happened. Twice Juan tried to say something, but each time a gesture from the captain restrained him. Three officers and three sailors entered the cabin, took their seats and joined in the silent waiting. More minutes passed before a gong sounded outside. Only then did the captain stand up and formally announce: 'It is now time to talk.'

The extraordinary scene that Juan and Catalina now witnessed lasted for an hour, from eight o'clock until nine. It was indeed time to talk, in the most literal sense. Grouped together here were the seven members of the ship's company who *could* still talk, and that is what they did: they talked. Loudly, insistently—one might almost have called it shouting—and tremendously fast, all of them talking simultaneously and across each other, interrupting each other, cutting off each other's words, finishing each other's sentences, producing a babel of voices that was quite unintelligible. Juan's pleas that they should take turns to speak were ignored. Only when Juan and Catalina hit upon the idea of listening to just one of the contending voices at a time could they at last begin to make out some of what was being said. And in this way they discovered what had happened, and heard the whole history of the men without tongues.

The more effectively the mute sailors had learned to communicate with each other, the closer the bonds between them had become. Each sought the company of the others maimed like himself. As their silent communication improved, they depended less and less on the tongues of those who had escaped their fate. Indeed, they suddenly began to find speech uncomfortably loud; noticed that the words enunciated by the seven men with tongues hurt their ears. To them the speech of those seven became a distorting mirror: they saw them doing what they themselves could not do, and heard the sounds that they had lost the power to make. But before feelings of pain and envy could grow and fester, they drowned them in a sea of contempt. To the men without tongues, speech, with its movement of tongue, lips, soft palate, teeth, vocal cords and air, came to sound more and more ugly and perverse, while the art of wordless communication grew into a majestic choreography of silence. And were not they, the tongueless men, the ones who mattered? Were not they the heart, the flower of the brotherhood? They were the Elect! The men of destiny! The true, the only ones! The New Men! The others still had their tongues. They were not really part of the group, they were outsiders. They lacked the lack of a tongue: they were poor, primitive creatures, still spitting out words, poking and prodding at language with tongues like elephants' trunks.

Over the last three years the balance of power on board had shifted. On the Atlantic crossings the captain and officers were still responsible for deciding on the destination, for setting a course and navigating, but in all other matters the only ones with a say were those who could not say anything: the wordless men had the last word. They set the rules for life on board—for they were in the majority. They were the dominant ones. They had the power. And since they regarded speech as so much dross, the first rule was silence. Except during that one hour when speaking was allowed.

It is hardly surprising that in the miserly hour allotted to them each day the seven speakers tried to talk as much as possible so as to give the moving parts of their speech mechanism a good oiling. All open or covert attempts to speak at other times had been instantly nipped in the bud by the non-speakers. The penalty for the illicit uttering of sounds of whatever kind was two days' incarceration in the notoriously unsavoury hold. Escape was impossible, for threats hung over the ship, powerful, unexpressed threats: anyone who left the crew in the lurch by jumping ship and trying to run away was breaking the alliance that had been forged on the island, and anyone breaking that alliance would pay for it by having the power of speech cut out of his mouth, just as the captain had promised. Actually by now the tongueless men no longer saw that 'cut' in the light of a punishment at all: on the contrary, they constantly urged the speakers to join their ranks voluntarily, holding out as bait a comforting sense of belonging.

A second gong sounded, and the seven speakers abruptly fell silent. Not another word was spoken that evening. Every time one of the two passengers was about to say something, this was prevented by a finger placed on the lips of one of the 'speakers'. They ate the food, which had turned cold. Finally one of the crew showed Juan and Catalina where they were to sleep: in the fo'c'sle. A comfortable enough place in itself, but on the *Santa Isabella* it was cluttered with barrels, which left little room for them. They had hoped that now, in the darkness of night, they would be able to whisper together, exchanging whatever information they had each managed to hear, but their cramped quarters were already occupied by two of the tongueless men, who were dozing in hammocks. Talking was completely ruled out. Catalina and Juan lay down, as they were, on the floor. Their questions would have to wait.

Chapter twelve

Talking sickness

After my young friend Francisco Loyola, [spurred on?] by exceeding haste, had set off for Seville and—barely interrupted by the wing-beats of his own breath—had attempted to persuade me to share his journey with him,' writes Juan Bautista de Arteaga in one of the few readily legible passages in his memoir, 'I quickly perceived that I had suffered a loss of most grievous magnitude. My thoughts, instead of pursuing their habitual straight course, constantly looped back on themselves. My every train of thought was cut off by the sad image of my departing friend.' In this manneristic style, Juan writes several more pages about the reasons which led him to gather up his money, leave his house and follow Francisco. 'Those matters which required to be ordered' he 'guided into the channels of order', and he persuaded one of his friends to move into the house to keep an eye on it while he was away. Then, finally, he was ready to leave. On his arrival in Seville he at once began his search. The inns, the harbour, the *Arenal*, the ships, the Casa de Contratación: nothing. It was three days before he chanced to hear that a Basque named Loyola had smashed the skull of a local boy with a stone. Juan asked to be directed to the injured boy's home, and gained entry by saying that he was a doctor, had heard about the mishap and wanted to offer his help. The boy was not in too bad a state: the gash in his head was healing and the concussion abating. Juan bought some ointments, which he applied to the wound. Then he went to the authorities, gave them an account of the blameless life of his assistant Loyola, wrote testimonials on his behalf and deployed all his powers of persuasion to convince them that Francisco's act of violence was an inexplicable lapse that would certainly not be repeated. When he added, finally, that the injured boy was now restored to health, the officials agreed to release Francisco Loyola from prison after a few more days.

Now Juan could only wait. On his seventh day in Seville he was sitting in a small tavern when suddenly someone tapped him on the shoulder. He had no idea who this person was. The man laughed, said he was Roberto Maldini from Genoa and enthusiastically recalled their year together in Alcalá. Juan scoured his memory in vain, but in any event, he thought, he must have made a very strong impression on this Genoese, for why else should Roberto be so eager to help him? He actually managed to get him and Francisco onto a ship—a ship which Roberto said did not normally take passengers. Had Juan remembered that they had quarrelled in Alcalá—over some banal affair involving a woman—then the true explanation for Roberto's actions would have been obvious: he was taking his revenge for that defeat. As it was, Juan simply thought that Roberto wanted to do him a favour. And once Francisco had been released from prison there had been no time for reflection.

Juan and Catalina had no chance to talk until they were lying at anchor for a few hours off the southern tip of Spain, waiting for the *Santa Isabella* to come by. Then at last they were able to catch up, at least on the essentials. They stood there in the dusk, looking at the Cadiz coastline. 'I don't quite know how it happened,' Catalina said, as she described the stone-throwing episode in Seville to Juan. To make her actions more understandable, she altered the facts in her favour: suddenly it was twenty hooligans who had surrounded her, they were throwing fist-sized stones rather than mere pebbles, there was no doubt that they were planning to rob her, not just indulging in harmless horseplay, and what she did was therefore clearly an act of self-defence, not an inexplicable outburst of naked violence. She went on talking until Juan gave an understanding nod.

'And then,' Catalina said in conclusion, 'when I was in prison somebody stole the money I had for my passage.'

'I've brought enough for us both,' said Juan.

'But what about you?' she asked. 'Why did you come after me?'

'It was time to make a fresh start.'

Catalina looked at him. Her look seemed to say that this explanation was not enough, that she wanted to hear more, but Juan had fallen silent. They gazed at the Cadiz coast, bidding farewell to their homeland. Then Juan suddenly said a single word, casually, giving it no special emphasis. 'Catalina.'

'Yes?' said Catalina without thinking, turning towards him. And then she nearly jumped out of her skin. It had been almost two years since anyone had called her by her old name, and yet when Juan did so that 'yes' had still slipped out, an automatic response. Juan looked surprised.

'What do you mean, yes?' he asked.

Catalina did not know what to say. There was no way to explain that 'yes'. This was the first time she had given herself away, she thought, and she flushed and looked straight ahead of her.

'I mean that fortress over there', said Juan. 'They've just finished building it. Named after Santa Catalina. Can you see it?'

'Yes,' Catalina said, recovering from her fright.

'There's the fleet!' called Roberto.

The three of them climbed into the ship's boat.

'Which ship is it?' asked Catalina.

'The *Santa Isabella*, over there,' said Roberto, grinning openly for the first time, a grin that did not inspire confidence, but Juan still thought nothing of it; only much later would he remember their quarrel and understand why his former fellow-student had played such a dirty trick on them. Now Roberto added—with gleeful anticipation of what awaited Juan Bautista de Arteaga and Francisco Loyola—'She's a magnificent vessel. A galleon, two-decker, brand new guns. I'm sure when you see her at close quarters, and especially when you're actually on board, you'll be speechless!'

Catalina found the situation on the *Santa Isabella* very difficult. She had so many things to discuss with Juan. She wanted to know more about why he had followed her, wanted to ask him whether he would go with her all the way to Potosí; above all she would have liked simply to lean on the ships' rail and pour out her joy at finding herself, at last, on her way to where she longed to be. But all this was denied her. It was only the morning of the fourth day, and the coast of Africa was still sparkling on the horizon, when Catalina went onto the upper deck, climbed up into the mainmast shrouds, held on with one hand and in one sudden heave spewed out everything that had accumulated inside her during her four days of silence. The 'speakers' exchanged meaningful nods. They knew what was happening: some of them called it talking sickness and others silent sickness. Every one of them had had it, had stood on board raving, vomiting up garbled, meaningless fragments of speech, just for the sake of saying something.

Some of the tongueless men rushed to seize Catalina. They gagged her, bound her hands and dragged her past the guns on the upper deck and down the hatchway to the main gun deck. There was little room there because of the guns and the anchor capstan, but still the gun ports, gratings and hatches always let in sufficient fresh air and light. Catalina was squeezed past one of the capstans and pushed down the stairs to the orlop deck. Here, just below the waterline, it was musty and dark. She was dragged from the cable locker through the galley, the crammed cannonball store and the musty sail locker. They came to a small ladder which took them down one more level, to the hold. Here no light penetrated at all. The men lit a lamp and pushed Catalina ahead of them through the stinking, pitch-dark storage compartments filled with spare sails and ropes, barrels of drinking water and beer, salt meat and other supplies, back towards the bow, past the mainmast and the huge brick-lined oven which reached up into the galley above, and right to the forward end of the ship, the darkest place of all, where they tethered her to the bitts. Now there was nothing beneath her but the bilge, a hollow space that had been filled with stones to keep the ship from heeling over.

The men disappeared, taking the light with them. In a few moments it was so dark that Catalina could hardly make out anything at all. The gag made breathing difficult; the air that entered her nose was nothing but a confection of rank odours, a putrid mix of dirt, damp cloth, moss, salt meat and fish, kitchen smells and mould. Once or twice, when rats came nosing towards her, she had to make quick, jerky movements to scare them off. Down here the fathomless blackness of the ocean was almost palpable and the rolling and heaving of the ship much more immediate. After only a few hours she was so overcome by nausea that she was sick. Her vomit was blocked by the cloth in her mouth. To avoid choking to death she had to swallow the lumps back down.

By the time Catalina was released two days later she had learned her lesson. There was not another peep from her during the voyage, except of course during the allotted hour. However, her ordeal had not dampened her appetite for novelty. She was stuck on this ship, the voyage would take more than two months, there was absolutely nothing to do and she could not even pass the time by talking to Juan, so as an escape from boredom she began to observe the tongueless sailors. She rather liked the movements they made, the signs which every one of them could understand with ease. There were no uncertainties, no ambiguities of the kind she had often met with in spoken conversations: no, each sign had a fixed meaning and could therefore be clearly understood by anyone at any time. There were a mixture of arm and leg movements, simple hand signals, circular motions of the head, gestures made with the fingers, and contortions of the eyes and mouth. The more Catalina watched the mute sailors, the more she began to get the hang of their secret system of signs. She would have loved to go down and join them. At first she did not dare. But then she told herself that there was no rule against it, and one evening, after two interminable weeks utterly devoid of incident, Catalina went down to the gun deck, nonchalantly, as though it were a perfectly normal thing to do.

She found herself in a different world. About half the crew were lounging around down there—all those who were not needed on deck just then. No one took any notice of Catalina. No one stopped her from having a look round. This was a temple dedicated to the pursuit which the men loved more than anything else in the world, and which no one could prohibit now that they had taken over the internal command of the ship; namely, gambling. In one corner Catalina could still see a throwback to the days when the captain had forbidden dice or card games: a group of men were sitting around a barrel and seemed to be cheering the barrel on with gruff growling sounds. As Catalina came closer she saw that a circle had been drawn in chalk on the top of the barrel, and that inside the circle there were some beetles, each of which, she assumed, belonged to one of the sailors cheering them on. The point of the game was obvious enough: the first beetle to crawl out of the circle would be the winner. Catalina moved on to the dice players, but that was a one-dimensional activity, based purely on the chance roll of the dice, and she soon got bored with it. However, when she came to the group who were playing cards, it took only a few minutes before she sat down on a nearby barrel and started to follow the game. It made a welcome distraction from the speechless, grey reality of the ship.

Time passed without her noticing. Here was a challenge for her ambitious nature: she would work out the rules of the game for herself, simply by taking note of the cards that the men took turns slapping down on the table. She made sure to remember which player had played which card and when, and who finally picked up the cards. In addition, she had a clear view of one player's hand and could watch him as he hesitated, selected a card but then put it back, played a different one and was then either annoyed or pleased at the outcome of his choice. Storing up everything in her memory, Catalina used those weeks at sea to become fully initiated into the mysteries of card-playing. The secret of her success against the innumerable ordinary opponents who awaited her in the New World had its origin here, for never, when Catalina sat down to play a game of cards, would she speak—not a single remark, not so much as a word.

It turned out that the *Santa Isabella* was not—as Roberto had falsely claimed—going to be left behind at Cartagena, but was sailing on to Veracruz together with most of the other ships in the fleet. When they had passed the Antilles and were already in the Gulf of Mexico, the *Santa Isabella* was caught in a storm that far exceeded anything the sailors had ever known before. To make matters worse, when the storm began to rage they realized all of a sudden that this was the first one they had encountered since losing their tongues. For three years they had been spared, and they had come to take this good fortune for granted, to believe that Fate had a soft spot for them. They had quite forgotten what such a severe storm was like. When it broke over the ship it brought instant chaos. The bells, lanterns and drums were unusable, or were snatched away by the wind and waves. In the pitch darkness of the storm it was impossible to make out any gestures or signs. However frantically a man might flap and jerk about, there was no chance of his message being seen and understood. Before long the storm had the ship wholly at its mercy and was starting to play a gruesome game with it. Soon there could be no doubt of the outcome: the *Santa Isabella* was going to be lost with all hands, vanishing beneath the waves of the Gulf of Mexico as though she had never existed.

As the ship was going down, the only one to keep his head was Juan Bautista de Arteaga. He could see that the vessel was doomed. When the heavy oak door of the captain's cabin broke free from its hinges and was swept along the deck towards the fo'c'sle where he and Catalina were standing, he acted quickly. Staying cool and calm, but using the full strength of his voice, he shouted to Catalina that they were quite near to the coast and that their only hope of survival was to stay together. He wound a rope around his hips and another round Catalina's, and they tied the ends of the ropes to the cabin door. The vessel was already listing heavily, the ship's boat had been smashed to pieces, and the mainmast was close to snapping, when a wave breaking three feet over the deck washed the cabin door overboard, plunging the two of them beneath the surface and keeping them submerged. Unable to hold out any longer, Catalina was on the point of opening her mouth and taking water into her lungs when the sea suddenly released the door with a violence that robbed them of their senses but did not stop the cry which, freed at last, burst from their throats.

Chapter thirteen

Hail

Catalina regained consciousness. She spat out some water, realized that she could not feel the motion of the sea, and looked about her. A long white beach. She was still tied to the door, and lying next to Juan. She had clamped her arm desperately around his body. Sitting up, she tried to undo the knots in the rope, but her hands were trembling too much. It took her some time to recover herself. With every water-free breath, memories returned. Juan had saved her. He had acted decisively when the ship was going down.

Suddenly she doubted the reality of it all. Tongueless sailors? The hour set aside for talking? The card games? The storm? And now she was lying here. She must do something, must get help, but first of all she must free herself from this door. Gnawing at the rope with her teeth, she managed to unfasten it. Then she stood up, took a few tottering steps with the sun blazing down on her upturned forehead and made out, through narrowed eyes, the green shimmer of some tall trees. Palm trees, she thought. She turned in a complete circle, and began to see things more clearly. The sea stretching away into the distance. The beach sloping upwards at either end. Scattered rocks. Not a soul in sight. The stillness of a sunny day. So this was the New World.

She went back and knelt down beside Juan. She gazed at his arms, his chest, the hair falling across his face, the grains of sand on his cheeks, and she felt an unfamiliar stirring in her stomach. Not queasiness, not hunger, not joy at having been saved, but something else. Something that seemed to come from Juan. But there was no time to think about that now. She untied him, pulled him away from the door, laid him face down and shook him.

Juan took a long time to come to, as though he were waking from a sleep that had lasted for years. Catalina helped him to his feet. They had survived—but what now? Where were they? On an island? Surely not. On the mainland? In New Spain? They sat down on the sand again, and breathed life back into their limbs. It was an effort to talk. 'We must move into the shade,' said Juan. Holding on to one another for support, they managed to cross the beach. Once again Catalina felt a pleasant ache in the pit of her stomach and moved even closer to Juan, but at that very moment the sensation was brutally extinguished, for Juan screamed. It was a single, long-drawn-out scream, and Catalina did not know whether to feel more alarmed by whatever had given rise to the scream or by the fact that he had so utterly lost his nerve.

'Indians!' he screamed, pointing towards the palm trees, from where twenty or thirty armed men were advancing upon them. Now Juan started whispering. Just isolated phrases, as if his mind were distracted, phrases not consciously produced but welling up unbidden, prompted by mortal terror. 'They'll kill us,' he whispered, 'catch us, cook us, eat us, cut our hearts out, we must run…' He turned round. Catalina followed the direction of his gaze and saw that there was no escape. She forced herself to be calm. Reminded herself of Juan's resolute behaviour the day before. That's our only chance, she thought. When they were ten paces away the Indians came to a halt. Catalina walked towards them, raising her hand. Then she began to speak. She did not think about what to say: they would not understand her anyway. All that mattered was to sound as peaceable and friendly as possible. Catalina accompanied her words with gestures she had learned from the tongueless sailors. She folded her hands together and put them to her forehead; curved her left hand into a hollow close to her heart and stretched it out towards the Indians; put the backs of her hands together, fingertips pointing to the centre of her chest, and then spread out her arms.

One of the Indians stepped forward. He was carrying a weapon, a long staff resembling a spear, though without a sharpened head. This he thrust into the sand beside him. Then he cleared his throat and began to speak. To the ears of his European listeners his speech had a cold, raucous sound. Catalina knew she could not understand the other's language, so she thought she would focus her attention on his gestures: would they betoken good or evil? But there were no gestures. The Indian stood there motionless, doing nothing at all other than speaking, if those ugly sounds could be called speech. But still. Catalina concentrated hard. There must be *something* she could understand. She listened more closely, and tried to pick out any word that occurred with particular frequency, for a word that occurred frequently might be the key, the first clue to an understanding. *Et*, she thought, *et*, that might be the word for 'I'. If '*et*' means 'I', Catalina thought, what does…then suddenly it hit her like a blow between the eyes: there was a word that she understood! But that was impossible! There, the same word again. Yes, she understood it! And the next word, she knew that too! It was so incredible that she could not take it in straight away. Only when at last she was sure, when she could almost have laughed with excitement, did she lean towards Juan and whisper: 'It's Latin! He's speaking Latin! I can understand him! Every word!'

For a moment Juan thought that the murderous sun and a murderous enemy had conspired to rob Francisco of his sanity. But then he too started to listen more closely. And when he was no longer expecting to hear barbarous gibberish but the Holy Roman language, his ears too began to identify the familiar words that he had had to learn as a student, and he could suddenly understand what the Indian was saying. This was Latin spoken with a strong Aztec accent, but it was no crude creole; it was pure, classical Latin. Now that Juan and Catalina knew what language it was, it no longer sounded jerky and contorted, harsh and uncouth; on the contrary, the rhythm swayed like grasses in the summer breeze, the vowels became purer, smoothing the angles and edges of the consonants into clearly-defined curves. The Indian was taking great pains to speak distinctly. What was he saying? It was some strange adventure story. At the centre of it was a young Aztec. He had set out to avenge somebody. This was an account of his exploits, especially his fights against the *nonoualca*, as the neighbouring tribe of hostile barbarians were called, a word which Catalina and Juan took to be a name, though in fact it meant 'the mutes', since the Aztecs used that expression for any of their barbarian neighbours who could not talk properly. Learning to speak well and intelligently was a most important component of Aztec education, and their leaders were chosen for their powers of eloquence and accorded the title of *tlatoani*, meaning 'he who possesses the word'.

The longer Juan and Catalina listened, the more obvious it became that the Aztec was reciting a heroic poem; while it bore some traces of classical models, the whole thing was transposed to the world of the Aztecs, and the Latin language had been made to reflect, as well as possible, their own reality, their life in the tropical forest. When the Aztec orator had finished, his companions uttered, one after another, a clearly intelligible 'Salve!'—'Hail!'—and invited the shipwrecked pair to go with them. That same evening saw Juan and Catalina and their hosts sitting together outside their huts, eating food served in pre-warmed pans. The Aztecs wore woven clothes and had their hair tied back. Communication presented no difficulties, and this mystery turned out to have a perfectly clear and simple explanation.

The people assembled here were the descendants of some Aztec nobles who from 1536 to 1540 had attended the college of Santa Cruz de Tlatelolco. This Franciscan college had been founded with the help of the then viceroy, Mendoza. The Aztec elite was to be educated there by European priests and teachers, who would make the Christian religion comprehensible to them. It had been felt that having been made to undergo baptism, the savages must not be allowed just to copy the ways of Christianity without understanding it in all its true greatness, or to hold on to their own gods in secret, merely replacing their names with those of Christian saints. Or indeed to misunderstand completely, and, for instance, take John the Baptist to be Christ's superior, because no one could make them see why the baptizer should be of lesser worth than the baptized. Into such a confusion of religious notions a guiding thread must be woven. The aim had been to bring clarity to these Indian ideas of Christianity and spread among the populace an orthodox form of the faith, purged of primitive superstitions. However, this could not be done without the aid of the Aztec elite. Convince them, so the thinking went, and they would help win over the common people too. Why should not the ancient maxim apply here as well as anywhere: 'What the nobles believe, the peasants will not doubt'?

And so the teaching began. First the catechism, reading, writing, then Latin—the language of the Church—interpretation of the Bible, textual exegesis, history: ever more subjects in ever more detail. And great was the Franciscans' astonishment when they saw how quickly the savages learned. You only had to explain a thing to them once and they got it immediately. They mastered reading and writing in no time at all. It was as if they had a matrix inside them which only needed to be filled: they stored everything they saw or heard and could recall it at a moment's notice. Initially the teachers used crude, didactic exercises involving much repetition and revision, which irritated and offended the Aztecs. So the Franciscans abandoned those methods and instead continually placed mountains of new material before them. Once these members of the Indian elite could read and write, their knowledge expanded like a forest fire. At first the Franciscan Fathers were thrilled with these brilliant students, who made such a refreshing change from the sluggish, apathetic pupils they were used to in Europe, but before long they had reached the point where their reservoir of knowledge was exhausted and they felt they had nothing more to teach the Aztecs—but the Aztecs themselves had no intention of calling a halt to their studies. They had tasted blood. They wanted more—they wanted everything. And as they were being given no new information, they could only satisfy their thirst for knowledge by thinking for themselves.

They subjected everything the Fathers had taught them to the most thorough scrutiny. As long as this did not extend to sensitive areas of knowledge, the teachers continued to be delighted with the amazing results achieved by their students: suddenly the Aztecs were composing Latin verses, they were improving on the plain language used by Caesar, composing texts in emulation of Cicero that came very close to fulfilling his stylistic ideal, constantly thinking of new and simpler explanations of grammar, and translating and interpreting texts at a bewildering rate. But then their craving for new insights shifted its focus to the domain of faith. Every Biblical passage was read afresh, examined to see whether it might not bear a different interpretation from the one their teachers had sought to convey. The Aztecs found endless new issues to raise, and a time of questioning and correcting began.

They pointed out to their teachers various incongruities in their sermons or religious teaching. Here it says this, but there it says that. A contradiction. A false conclusion. An obscurity. A mistake. An impossibility. How can this be so? How did you envisage that? The Franciscan teachers saw Holy Scripture being subjected to a hail of questions which they themselves would never have dared to ask. They were having to defend the Bible against wholly unexpected attacks. Often they could offer no answer but 'That is what is written!' or 'The Word of God is unfathomable!' And this pronouncement became their last refuge, the impregnable bastion—or so they thought—of certainty. But it did not satisfy the Aztecs. They persisted with their questions. Wanted to know why everything was as it was. Why they, Aztecs or Mayas, had to discard their own gods in favour of a Christian God who preached forbearance, yet drove the traders out of the Temple; who pardoned the hypocritical thief but consigned the consistent one to hell. Why they were forbidden to sacrifice the hearts of their dead enemies, while being expected to eat the body of the Christian God. Why the ancient patriarchs were allowed to have several wives, but they were not. In short, there was no end to the Aztecs' questions, and as time went on the conquerors' enthusiasm for this promising venture began to wane. Weary of having to justify themselves, defeated by the questions, overwhelmed by the Aztecs' tireless pursuit of certainty, they finally discontinued the whole project. There was too great a risk that the Indians would turn into heretics. The project had failed. The Indians, they said, had not demonstrated appropriate powers of reasoning.

Juan and Catalina spent several days with the Aztecs, recovering from the hardships of the voyage. It also took them some time to adjust to the climate, which was almost unbearably sultry and humid. Every breath they took was more of an effort, every exertion twice as tiring. Sweat poured off them freely even when they did nothing at all. Then there were the tropical showers, which came from nowhere and ended just as abruptly. And the new, unfamiliar food, which their stomachs had to get used to. Juan and Catalina shared the life of the Aztecs, their cooking, eating and singing, their rituals and ceremonies, and were initiated into the ten commandments of etiquette, which related to insignia, clothes, jewellery and houses. They saw how, when a child was caught telling lies, its lips were pricked with the thorn of an agave; they learned that in *Nahuatl,* the Aztec language, the word for 'liars' was the same as the one for 'Christians'. But when, after some days, Juan and Catalina were present at a birth—it was a girl—and Catalina asked for a translation of the ritual formulae ('You will be in the heart of the house, you will go nowhere, you will never be a wanderer, you will be the hearthstone, the fire contained within the hearth: here our god has planted you and here he will bury you'), and then saw a miniature weaving shuttle and loom being placed in the girl's cradle (for a boy it would have been a little sword and shield), she told Juan that it was time to move on.

Chapter fourteen

New World

Three weeks of steady walking brought them to Veracruz. The city was like a vast building site, expanding greedily into the surrounding land. All around them Juan and Catalina saw Indians or slaves hard at work putting up new buildings, including monasteries and convents to cope with the growing numbers of monks and nuns pouring into the place. Everything was in motion, with never a moment's pause. The city's outer districts were engulfed in the din and the clouds of dust produced by the building operations, while the centre was one enormous market place. Blacks and mestizos offered things for sale from big barrows, Spanish and Creole craftsmen sold their wares in booths that were open to the street, and in many places there were also covered stalls under arcades: everywhere there were people urgently trying to find takers for whatever kind of goods they had to sell. Besides all that, the city was awash with the kinds of activity to be expected in a seaport; the to-ing and fro-ing of ships entering and leaving harbour, the bustle of loading and unloading, of people arriving and departing. Only at night did things quieten down a little, for the districts allocated to the Indians, which were outside the city centre, closed their gates at dusk and their inhabitants were not allowed to come out again until dawn.

For Juan and Catalina this truly was a New World. At every street corner their noses encountered some unfamiliar smell. Wherever they looked they saw something they had never seen before, starting with the people: it would be some months before Juan and Catalina were reasonably proficient at distinguishing nuances of skin colour. They had to learn the West Indian pigmentocracy, a set of designations that ranked people according to an unspoken hierarchy. The Europeans and the Creoles—people of pure European blood who had been born in the new lands—were at the top of the ladder, for the overriding principle was *limpieza de sangre*, purity of blood. The despised, pacified *Indios*, and the *negros,* whom the Europeans could use as they pleased, were right at the bottom. That much was clear. But in between came the various gradations: the mestizos, half Indian, half white; the mulattos, black half-breeds; the *moriscos*, not clandestine Muslims as in Spain, but children of a white man and a mulatto woman; then, continuing down the scale, there were the *albinos*, children of whites and *moriscos*; the *tornatrás* ('turn around'), offspring of a white man and an *albina*; the *tente en el aire* ('stay up in the air') born to a white man and a *tornatrás* woman. In the following centuries this would be elaborated still further in an ever-lengthening chain of forms and colours: an Indian man and a *tornatrás* woman would produce a *lobo* ('wolf'); a *lobo* and an Indian woman a *zambaigo*; a *zambaigo* and an Indian woman a *cambujo*; a *cambujo* and a mulatto woman an *albarazado*. An *albarazado* and a mulatto woman would produce a *barcino* ('bundle of straw'); a *barcino* and a mulatto woman a 'coyote'; a 'coyote' and an Indian woman a *chamiso* ('a dark-coloured piece of wood'); a *chamisa* and a mestizo a mestizo-coyote; and a mestizo-coyote and a mulatto woman an *ahí te estás* ('there you are').

Surrounded by so much that was unfamiliar, trying not to drown in a quicksand of impressions, Juan and Catalina clung to each other for mutual support. If anything more had been needed to confirm their resolve to travel on together, it would have been this onslaught of the new and unknown. After their many days of silence on the *Santa Isabella*, their week with the Aztecs, their long march on foot and the bewildering novelty of Veracruz, the two of them finally found an opportunity to talk. They had so much to say to each other that once they started they could hardly stop. The tongueless sailors, the talking sickness, the two days down in the hold, the card games, the storm, the shipwreck, their survival, the Aztecs—at long last it could all be discussed. Swept along by the very act of speaking, they talked on and on, going further and further back in their memories. Catalina told Juan all about working for her uncle, about her fencing, riding, and fighting, her disastrous failure as an actor, her ride to Seville, the youths, her spell in jail. And Juan? He talked about his mother's death, for the first time. He described his period of mourning and found words which he had never imagined he could find. Those days in Veracruz were spent entirely in revealing themselves to each other. The two of them got closer and closer, but at a certain point this closeness alarmed them and they recoiled as if they had been burnt.

Their aim was clear: they wanted to go to Potosí, the city of a thousand silver mines, perched at an altitude of nearly fourteen thousand feet, a legend and a myth: the place where Miguel de Erauso had charge of one of the mines. Founded only sixty years earlier, Potosí was by this time one of the world's most populous cities, bigger than Paris, Seville, Rome or London. Charles I of Spain had accorded Potosí the status of an Imperial City and presented it with a large shield bearing the inscription, 'I am rich Potosí, treasure of the world, king of mountains, envy of kings'.

Having learned that a carrack was to sail for Panama in a few days' time, Juan and Catalina agreed with the captain that in return for their passage they would help with loading and unloading and also work on board during the journey, and before long the sailors turned the capstan to haul the ship up onto her anchor, the anchor flukes came free, the wind filled the sails, the vessel gathered speed, and during the crossing Juan and Catalina mended yards and yards of canvas, repaired ropes and fed the goats, pigs and chickens; they reached Panama without any major problems, crossed the isthmus, hopping from the Caribbean to the Pacific coast, and waited for a ship bound for Trujillo; and by now it was September and the mosquitoes had had ample time to hatch.

In Panama a female Anopheles mosquito came in to land on Juan's body, plunged her proboscis into his shoulder, and from her salivary glands sent pathogens into his bloodstream that made straight for his liver, where affected cells swelled and burst, so that nothing prevented the pathogen *Plasmodium falciparum* from entering his blood. Juan contracted the worst form of malaria, *Malaria maligna*. It began with seemingly harmless symptoms like headache and pains in the limbs, fatigue, vomiting and a slight fever, but then came the first bouts of high fever, with temperatures of over forty degrees, his spleen became enlarged, and the more serious symptoms appeared: cramps, confusion and comatose states, with the brain increasingly affected.

Once they had arrived in Trujillo, Catalina followed the instructions that Juan gave her in his rare moments of lucidity. She fed and cared for him, took measures to reduce his temperature, treated him with sarsaparilla and earned the money to pay for food and medicines. She quickly found a job with a grocer, Alonso de Urquiza, who owned several shops in Trujillo and the surrounding area. As Urquiza was about to go to Saña for two months to check on his shops there and to arrange for the purchase of new goods, he was pleased to have found a 'true Spaniard', as he put it, to whom he could entrust one of his shops in Trujillo while he was away. Shortly before Urquiza's departure Catalina went to his house, as there were a few final things to settle: he wanted to take her through the lists showing the exact prices of his goods, and give her the black book containing the names of all the customers who were allowed credit. When they had finished Urquiza invited Catalina into the *salón* for a drink. His wife was waiting there, and they were introduced.

Happening to look over the woman's shoulder as she took her hand, Catalina noticed a picture on the wall. An image of Christ, Catalina thought, but already her heart was pounding. A crucified Christ, with a long beard, but there was something wrong about this Christ. The picture certainly showed a crucifixion; the figure on the cross was suffering, and he was bleeding from the wrists. But there was no crown of thorns. And what about that beard? It was much longer than in most representations of the Crucifixion: in fact the beard was the focal point of the whole picture. Nor was that all. Catalina moved closer. Now she was sure of it: the torso was that of a woman. One of her breasts was clearly visible. That was a woman hanging on the cross, a woman with a beard. For the first time ever, Catalina felt that she was not alone.

'Saint Liberata,' said Urquiza.

'I suppose you know her story?' asked Urquiza's wife.

'No,' said Catalina.

Urquiza's wife told her the legend of Saint Liberata, a young girl growing up in Portugal early in the Christian era, in the first few centuries after the death of Our Lord. She was the daughter of the king, a heathen king who naturally wanted to marry his daughter to another heathen ruler, the King of Sicily. However, the daughter was a secretly baptized Christian, and the night before the wedding she prayed to God that He might disfigure her body so that the heathen king would reject her. When the girl awoke next morning there was a beard on her chin. Her ladies fled in terror, and her horrified father could not believe his eyes. He tried to tear the beard from her face, but in vain. When he learned how this had come about he spat upon the daughter who had joined that disreputable sect, and with a single gesture of rejection cast her out of the bosom of the family. He pronounced his verdict: if she chose to pray to that womanish weakling of a God, then let her die as that Jesus had died. And he had his daughter crucified.

'When was she canonized?' asked Catalina.

'She wasn't.'

'But you called her a saint.'

'She's a saint in the eyes of the people. The Church refuses to recognize her.'

'Some people say that she never even existed,' said Urquiza, 'that it's just a story.'

'But then where does the picture come from?' asked Catalina.

'There are pictures of her all over the place, in every country,' said Urquiza's wife.

'She's also known as Wilgefortis,' said Urquiza.

'That comes from *virgo fortis*.'

'The strong virgin.'

'Uncumber in England.'

'Kümmernis in Germany.'

'Livrade in France.'

'Komina!'

'Comera!'

'Cumerana!'

'Hulfe!'

'Ontcommene!'

'Dignefortis!'

'Eutropia!'

'Reginfledis!'

'And whoever calls upon her at the hour of his death,' said Urquiza, 'will die with a quiet mind.'

Those were weary days in Trujillo. Urquiza had let the two travellers move into the small living quarters at the back of the shop. Catalina did all she could for Juan, and spent the rest of her time sitting in the shop—which was slightly off the beaten track—waiting for customers and thinking. Or rather, not so much thinking as digesting what she had seen in Urquiza's house—the picture of Saint Liberata. Her musings put her in a strange mood, and just when she was in this mood a woman called Adeïda de Cárdenas entered the shop. That was the first link in a fateful chain of events.

Adeïda was hardly over the threshold when she espied the new shop assistant. A young man, bored, looking at nothing in particular. A very young man, with the merest hint of down on his upper lip; thin, almost gaunt, his face somehow a little crooked. But there was something in that face, as he looked up at her now, something in those eyes, an expression quite different from that of most men she met; an innocence, a sleepiness. Here was a man who still had no idea of what awaited him when one day he would.... There was only naivety, no lust there, not the suggestive look men usually gave her, which wrapped itself round her like a layer of grease—not the fire that was like a dog's tongue hanging out of men's eyes. Yes, thought Adeïda, it must be far more pleasurable to conjure that fire into a man's eyes for the first time than just to be burnt by it.

She bore down on the young man, greeted him, asked him his name, Francisco Loyola, where he came from, San Sebastián, about his journey to the New World, a shipwreck, a shipwreck? And soon she had him enmeshed in conversation. The shop assistant's natural, uninhibited manner, which showed no sign of crumbling in her presence, only increased Adeïda's eagerness. After she had told him what items she needed and he had noted them down, she leaned towards him, touched his hand, not accidentally, not ambiguously, but with undisguised intent and unequivocal meaning; putting her face close to his she looked into his eyes, and her sensuous lips whispered provocatively, 'Will you bring the things round to me this evening?'

Chapter fifteen

Men or women

When Adeïda held out her hand to her, a bag of air seemed to expand inside Catalina's stomach. It was a feeling she recognized at once. On the beach, just moments after coming safely ashore, she had had the same feeling—a few weeks ago, when Juan had been lying next to her, his arms, his chest, the hair falling across his face. And now here was Adeïda: 'Bring the things round to me this evening!' It was an unequivocal invitation. Catalina knew what Adeïda wanted of her. And she knew how one did the thing that Adeïda wanted of her. She knew it in a precise, anatomical, abstract way, because the 'act' had been described in detail in Juan's books. So what now? Both in the convent and during the years since then it had taken all Catalina's energy to maintain outward appearances, to keep her voice and behaviour under control, and so she had simply ignored the mysterious inner domain of natural urges, thrusting away into obscure recesses of herself any sexual feelings that did begin to stir. But now, here, in Trujillo, now that maintaining her chosen role came easily and naturally to her, those urges, so long suppressed, became more pressing, and Catalina could ignore them no longer.

The evening at Adeïda's house, she could see it now: the room empty and unfurnished, everything unnaturally bright. Under Adeïda's gaze Catalina's chin and nose suddenly possessed a strange beauty. She saw Adeïda take her clothes off, one garment at a time, and finally stand naked before her. But all at once that naked body was duplicated, it stepped out of itself, discarding softness, curves and fragility like a few last, invisible pieces of clothing. Now there were two bodies standing in front of her. Two faces. Juan and Adeïda. They drew closer to her. And not to her alone. They drew closer to her and Francisco. Gently, without haste. The four of them stood there, touched and took possession of each other, and Catalina found herself gazing into absolute whiteness, for several seconds, a whiteness in which she dissolved.

It was some time before she recovered her senses. She was sitting in the shop in Trujillo. With her right hand between her thighs. It was warm and damp there. Her fingers pulled away sharply as if she had burnt herself. She looked around. There was no one in the shop, no one had seen or heard her. Now she was sitting there, breathing hard, with her hand, still damp, on her lap. She brought it up to her nose—an acrid smell, not unpleasant, not pleasant, just new. She licked her fingers, trying to clean off every trace. Felt a deep sense of relief. As though a stone lying in her stomach had been lifted away. But she knew that the relief clamoured to be repeated, and that the fantasy was crying out to become reality.

Summoning to her aid the dispassionate hand of reason, Catalina considered the matter calmly, as though she were setting up an equation. There were two options: men or women. She had to decide. But every thought, instead of clarifying the situation, brought only more and deeper confusion. As Francisco Loyola she needed to find a woman, but at the crucial moment a woman would unmask Francisco, the spurious man; and as Catalina de Erauso she needed to find a man, but how could she do that without first discarding her male costume?

Actually, why not, she asked herself. Why not just drop Francisco? Now. Right away. That would put an end to all the confusion at a stroke. Things would return to normal. Everyone would know where they stood. There would be no more ambiguity. After all, Francisco had achieved his purpose, his mission had been fulfilled, he had brought Catalina to the New World. Now it was only one more step to Potosí, and she could take that step perfectly well as Catalina. But—she would have to tell Juan. Could she do that? Had she not been deceiving him for years? Had she not been putting on an act all the time they had known each other? What if Juan did not understand? What if he simply rejected her? Who could blame him if he did, in his disappointment, confusion, sadness at losing his friend, at losing Francisco Loyola? For Catalina knew how fond Juan was of Francisco. She did not know whether he would be equally fond of Catalina. And she herself had grown accustomed to Francisco. More than that, in fact. Much more. She had grown to love him. To repudiate him just like that would be like murder. No, killing off Francisco was not an option. But then where did she go from here? Her mind was a mass of insoluble contradictions. A woman like Adeïda wants a man, not a woman. A man like Juan wants a woman, not a man. But she, Catalinafrancisco, was both and neither.

All the same, she would go to Adeïda. This evening. She would follow the dictates of desire and take what she wanted—but without giving away her secret. This meant observing just one rule: she must not reveal too much of herself. *She* must be the one to decide what would or would not take place in Adeïda's house. She would use the other's body while denying her her own. That was the best she could do. I've divided my life between myself and Francisco, Catalina thought, and so I'm left with only half the pleasure. She would bring Adeïda to that point of warm, damp relief but then get up and leave her, and at least she would have real, physical images in her mind, images that would go beyond childish fantasy and be filled with the breath of actual experience; she would leave with the smell on her hand that came from touching another's body, and she would put that hand between her own thighs and give herself what she had not been able to get as Francisco. It's the simplest solution, she thought.

She sat in the shop in Trujillo watching the time go by. Muleteers, urging on their weary, shabby-looking beasts would peer in at her as they passed the window and give surly greetings; now and then a donkey brayed. Whenever these dirty-looking men appeared at the left-hand edge of the window and then disappeared off to the right, that was a bit more time used up. Occasionally a customer came. Catalina would name the total to be paid and either take the money or else enter the figure against a name in the black book. This wait for the evening to come was a mixture of pleasant anticipation and uncertainty. But all time eventually comes to an end. Shouldering Adeïda's parcel, Catalina left the shop.

She had no difficulty in finding the address she had been given. The streets were arranged in a regular grid, with the bigger ones named after saints or local guilds, and the rest numbered. Like most of its neighbours, Adeïda's house, a patrician residence, was in the Andalusian style: it was built of stone but with a wooden framework as a precaution against earthquakes, and it had an imposing main entrance, and windows fitted with fly screens through which one could still see what went on in the street. Catalina was shown into the *salón*. There she saw a big chest made of tooled leather, beside it a small writing-desk inlaid with tortoiseshell, and in the middle of the room, two sofas with a low table between them. Corner shelves held all kinds of silverware, big plates and bowls, and alongside them on the walls were tapestries and elaborate embroideries. Catalina did not know whether to sit down or not. She looked at her fingers and tried to avoid thinking of what lay ahead.

When Adeïda de Cárdenas appeared she placed her hand on Catalina's arm, asking, 'Have you got time for a cup of chocolate?' Catalina had anticipated this offensive, and yet now, here, with Adeïda before her in the flesh, she could only nod, completely tongue-tied. She had worked out her plan in the safe haven of the shop, alone with her thoughts. She had never doubted that *she* would be the one dictating the course of events. But now Adeïda's glance, the renewed touch of her hand, her question, softly whispered in a single breath, had scored a palpable hit. Catalina could not match Adeïda in experience. She must take defensive measures. She sat down on the smaller of the two sofas, which hardly had room for two, hoping that Adeïda would take a seat opposite her. She must avoid physical proximity until she felt equal to the situation. But Adeïda promptly sat down so close beside her that their legs touched straight away. For a while nothing happened. Catalina tried to block out all thoughts from her mind. The maid came in with the chocolate. Catalina took the cup and raised it to her lips, held on to it as if for support and sipped her drink, making it last for as long as she could. Then she began to talk. She talked—because Adeïda was not saying a word and the silence had become unbearable—about how beautiful the little town was, about her work for Urquiza, about looking after Juan. She talked away, without Adeïda having asked her anything, clinging for safety to the cup and to what she was saying. As long as she was holding the cup, Catalina thought, her hands could not be touched, as long as she was talking her lips did not present a target.

Adeïda, for her part, simply waited, like a spider that is sure of its prey and watches with a lazy smile as the insect struggles frantically to free itself but only becomes more and more hopelessly caught up in the gluey threads.

As time passed Catalina grew calmer. With every sentence she spoke she felt more at ease. She got used to Adeïda's physical closeness, the touching of their legs, Adeïda's breath, her face. After a quarter of an hour Catalina set the cup down on the table and leaned back. She stopped talking. Looked at Adeïda. Those eyebrows, plucked into a curve, the nose, small and turned-up, the lips, only slightly accentuated with makeup, the skin, delicate, smooth, soft; and finally Catalina stole a glance at Adeïda's breasts, half spilling out of her bodice—much larger than her own, thought Catalina, much more rounded, what would they be like to touch? She pressed her leg against Adeïda's so that the contact was no longer casual but definitely suggestive. It could not be long now, she thought, before Adeïda leaned against her, touched her cheek and parted her lips with her fingers. Now Adeïda was talking. Catalina did not take in what she was saying. Her whole attention was focused on Adeïda's body. But Adeïda suddenly drew back a little. Her leg no longer pressed so hard against Catalina's. Standing up and moving towards the table, Adeïda turned round with an enquiring look, and Catalina realized that she had just been dismissed. She stammered a few words, rushed out of the house and ran back to the shop, where she cowered down in a corner. What was the matter? Why had Adeïda changed her mind? Where had she gone wrong?

She went to see Juan. He was lying in bed, sweating. Catalina asked him how he had slept, whether the pain in his limbs was any better and whether he was hungry. Juan was unable to answer, his mind far away. Catalina fetched a bowl of water. She dipped a sponge into it and wrung it out. Dabbed the sweat from Juan's face. Turned back the blanket and unbuttoned his shirt. Squeezed the sponge out on his chest and could feel his body through it. She washed his sweaty chest, his throat and the back of his neck, and his legs, with meticulous care, her heart pounding. And in the night she lay awake, unable to sleep, and instead hurled herself, as many times as she could, into the abyss of relief. It was already morning when she sank, trembling, into a light sleep.

Chapter sixteen

First killing

All the time Catalina was at Juan's bedside, every second of it, she never stopped talking. She did not know it, but it was her voice that kept Juan alive. As he lay in bed he was crossing a vast, white field, grazed totally bare. Strangely enough it was cool there, almost cold, even though his body was running with sweat. There were no sounds to be heard in the field, no rushing wind, no bird calls. He was not aware of how Catalina was constantly washing him and cooling him down, nor of her sitting at his bedside and holding his hand, starting to stroke his body, resting her cheek on his chest. The one thing that penetrated his consciousness, the one thing that kept him alive was that voice, that muffled voice. Catalina talked because she knew Juan could not hear what she said. She talked about what she hoped to do with Adeïda. How could she conquer Adeïda de Cárdenas? Conquer, thought Catalina, what a strange word to use for what it refers to. She asked Juan how he approached a woman, how he looked at her, how he touched her, undressed her and took her, exactly what he did with her: a man-to-man talk, Catalina said, that was what she needed.

Adeïda, for her part, was satisfied with what she had achieved. She had relished Francisco's uncertainty, the melting away of his nervousness, the awakening of lust in his eyes: she had taken what she wanted to take from their meeting. She intended to drag this phase out for as long as possible. Not until this Francisco was at her mercy, had surrendered to her utterly and lost all will of his own, would she give him what he wanted. Adeïda was in no hurry. She was performing a stately ritual. She let a full five days elapse before showing herself in Urquiza's shop again and asking the young assistant, as before, to deliver the things to her house. Catalina had high hopes of this second evening, and of the three others that followed in the next few weeks—evenings which all turned out very much like the first. Catalina felt each time that she was getting a little closer to her goal, but each time, as the decisive moment approached, Adeïda de Cárdenas stood up, withdrew her body and saw her guest to the door. But Catalina was used to fighting for what she wanted. She was not going to give up just like that. She would not stand by and be made a fool of. Five evenings were enough. More than enough. She was prepared to stake everything on one card. She made up her mind that at their next meeting she would tear Adeïda's clothes off her by force and not let go of her body until her lips had touched every inch of it. But on the sixth evening at Adeïda's she found that this took more courage than she had anticipated. It was only at the very last moment—she was already in the doorway of the *salón*, the moment of departure had come—that she suddenly leaped upon Adeïda as she had resolved to do, seized her by the shoulders and fiercely brought her lips down onto her face. Adeïda reacted with unexpected force. She resisted with all her might, tore herself free and struck Catalina in the face, leaving four long scratches on her cheek. But then a strange thing happened. Placing her hands on Catalina's shoulders, Adeïda pushed her lightly, even gently, out of the house, whispering a few words and smiling. Then the door closed. Catalina was outside. Now at last she understood. She saw that Adeïda was playing games with her and gave a wry smile of her own. It's a game, is it, she thought. Two can play at that.

The next time Adeïda came into the shop, Catalina ignored her oblique remarks and hints. Adeïda asked about the scratches and tried to touch them, but Catalina drew back. When the inevitable invitation came to bring the shopping round in the evening, Catalina said, 'Yes, I'll send someone.' Adeïda smiled at first, but then said, very softly, 'But I want *you* to come, *you*.' Catalina answered, copying her tone, 'But it won't be *me* coming, not *me*.' Then Adeïda leaned forward in such a way that the shop assistant could not avoid looking at her breasts, and said, 'I thought that perhaps this evening we could—'

Catalina put a kerchief over Adeïda's bosom and shoulders, saying, 'You'll catch cold, young lady.'

Controlling herself with difficulty, Adeïda left the shop. Inside she was raging. No man had ever rejected her. She could not understand it. She looked in the mirror. Had she changed? Was something wrong with her? Had she suddenly started to smell? She walked around the town so as to attract male glances and reassure herself that all the men still desired her. But that was no real help. She had to face it: they all did, just not this man Loyola. Her vanity was wounded to the core. She must go to him again, even at the risk of a still worse defeat, she must prove to herself that she could do it, she knew she would never rest easy until she had had her way with this shop assistant and seen his eyes afire with lust, like those of other men. And so Adeïda entered Urquiza's shop once more, feigning self-confidence but no longer mistress of the situation as she had been before. She missed her conversations with him, she said without preamble, she missed *him*, please would he come.

Catalina knew she had won. What an opponent! she thought scornfully. One who collapses as soon as you use her own tactics against her. She looked Adeïda up and down as if she were a horse she was thinking of buying—examined her face, her hair, her body. She's still not completely crushed, thought Catalina, I haven't done with her yet. 'Very well,' she said, making it sound as if she were doing Adeïda a favour, 'I'll be there this evening.' Somewhat relieved, Adeïda turned, lifted the hem of her long skirt and departed with as much dignity as she could muster.

That evening events moved swiftly. The maid left Catalina at the door to the *salón* and disappeared, the door was flung open, Catalina was pulled inside, painted lips were pressed against her mouth and a tongue thrust itself between her teeth. In a single movement Adeïda threw off all her clothes, every stitch she had on. Stood there naked, and Catalina did not know what to feast her eyes on first. Now all the things she had imagined were actually going to happen. Now this body would be hers to possess. She wished she could toss her own clothes aside too, but that was impossible. There was a clear rule that she had to follow. A coldness settled upon her. Now she proceeded cautiously, as though she were descending a steep slope step by step, in constant danger of slipping. Slowly her hands took possession of the other body, appropriated the skin bit by bit, her fingertips like little heads mounted on long necks, taking their time to see and smell and eat whatever there was to see, smell and eat.

Inwardly Catalina was placing every possible restraint on her desire. She would not lose her head, not let herself get carried away. When her hands had conquered the other woman's skin and her mouth had followed where her hands had gone before, when Catalina saw that this body was wholly at her mercy, when she noticed that Adeïda was not *doing* anything, anything at all—her desire suddenly changed its nature and became something very different: a sense of enormous power. An unbounded feeling of dominance. Catalina knew that now she could do what she liked with Adeïda, that the woman was—literally—in her hands. And to make a first sacrificial offering to this new feeling, Catalina curled back her tongue, retracted her lips like a camel, placed her teeth in the vanguard of her attack and bit Adeïda, not playfully but hard. Adeïda screamed. Her areola instantly turned red with blood. Catalina raised her head, curious to see what would happen.

'Now!' cried Adeïda, and Catalina felt herself being pulled down, for Adeïda saw what Catalina had done as a piece of violent foreplay and plunged willingly into submission, touched her breast and put her bloodied finger to her lips, and writhed like a fish under the weight that pressed her down. But Catalina jumped up and stepped aside. 'What's wrong?' asked Adeïda. Catalina raised her eyebrows. 'I have to go now,' she said. With intense satisfaction she looked down at Adeïda one last time, having done exactly what she had wanted to do. And she did not find it hard to leave Adeïda lying there—on the contrary, she drank in the expression of horror in Adeïda's eyes, and every nerve in her body thrilled at her power over the other woman. She sensed that she had destroyed a person, or if not a person, at any rate that person's image of herself. Catalina left the house and never saw Adeïda de Cárdenas again.

Instead, three days later, she met a man named Reyes. This was anything but a chance meeting, for the man was Adeïda's brother-in-law and had been sent by her to exact vengeance. Reyes did not for a moment conceal his intention. He openly threatened Catalina, jostled her, provoked and insulted her and, when she still remained calm, spat in her face. Catalina wiped off the spittle, took a step backwards and for the first time in her life drew her sword in anger. It did not occur to her for a moment that she could be in serious danger.

The fight lasted only two minutes. Then the point of the sword penetrated the epidermis, dermis and subcutaneous tissue, the tiny hair shafts, the *stratum corneum*, pigment cells, capillaries, basement membrane, sebaceous glands and sweat glands, hair muscles and hair roots, and all this happened so effortlessly and with so very little resistance that you would have thought that human skin was specially designed to be penetrated, had there not been an immediate outcry from a whole host of sensory nerve-cells—those nerve fibres which simply stop short in the tissue as if they had been snipped off, and which have always had the job of registering pain. And that Reyes felt pain goes without saying, for in fact his pain only ended when his whole body met its end.

But the sword point was still stuck fast. The limbs still twitched violently as if someone were shaking out the body like a blanket.

Catalina still had the hilt in her hand. She stood bent over Reyes. Saw the blood leaking from his chest. Was reminded for a moment of the blood from Adeïda's breast, which she had tasted. Something seemed to be flowing up through the blade and the hilt into Catalina's hand; she was somehow coupled to that man's death as if she had touched an electric current and lacked the strength to pull herself free. Everything went quiet. Catalina jerked the blade out of the body. For a second or two she thought that the dead man's heart was coming with it, skewered like a fish for grilling over a fire.

From that moment her way of moving changed. Everything she did now was done with more deliberation. She took a single, watchful step backwards, her senses like fine hairs pointed in all directions.

The prison in Trujillo was a single, miserable barred cell. Twelve men were already sitting or lying there, silent, whispering or asleep. There were no blankets, only a floor of trodden earth. Without a word Catalina lay down on the floor, ignoring the men. Moving in her newly acquired, deliberate manner, she crossed her hands behind her head and closed her eyes. She did not know whether what she had done would be regarded as an accident, an illicit duel or murder, all she knew was that she wanted to be out of here, and the sooner the better. She could think of nothing else. She went over all the possibilities and soon had an idea. Her convent days were long past; even so, she would have to steel herself to do what she had in mind. But this was a day when anything was possible; the day when she had killed her first man. She ran over the whole thing in her mind. The idea was as simple as it was foolproof. Catalina stood up and dusted herself down. The men coughed. One of them complained. Catalina took a step towards him, said nothing and simply gave him a look. The man lowered his eyes. Catalina walked over to the bars and called for the guard. He came over, surly and bored.

'I want to speak to a priest,' said Catalina.

'What for?' the guard wanted to know.

'I want to make my confession.'

The man looked at her suspiciously but went off, and half an hour later Father Diego de Ronda turned up, in a threadbare brown habit and with a small black prayer book in his hand. Two guards fetched Catalina from the cell, and she had to kneel down before the priest, who, with an expression of mild distaste, blessed the air around the prisoner and then sat down on a chair and said: 'I'm listening.' Catalina made no mention of the actual reason why she was in prison, the affair involving Reyes. Instead she confessed her meeting with Adeïda de Cárdenas. She described her violent conquest of the woman in such a way that the priest's eyes began to soften. Diego de Ronda spoke a few words of admonition. After he had granted her absolution, Catalina asked whether she could now receive the body of the Lord. Tomorrow, said the priest, tomorrow a mass would be held for the prisoners.

Catalina stood up. With cool calculation she kissed his fingers and then asked whether a man suffering from malaria, Juan Bautista de Arteaga, had been taken to the Franciscan monastery as she had requested. The priest nodded and said that the patient was already there and that his condition was satisfactory. Catalina was taken back to the cell, where she lay down again as if nothing had happened. She did not move again all night, but lay there, not sleeping but staring up at the ceiling, thinking, or pretending to think. Her new discovery—of violence as power and power as violence—had already found its niche in her.

Mass the next morning was held in the small prison chapel. The prisoners had had their shackles removed, and there were guards positioned at the sides and at the exits. Catalina let the mass wash over her as she had so often done as a child, when her mind was on something quite different from what the priest was saying. When it was time for communion, each prisoner knelt down, received the consecrated Host on his outstretched tongue and then made his tongue shoot back into his mouth like a frog's, so that the thin, flat body of the Lord dissolved in the unsavoury morass of saliva and could be swallowed.

Father Diego was anxious not to drop the consecrated Host on the floor. Intense concentration was bringing beads of perspiration to his forehead. Finally it was Catalina's turn. She put out her tongue; out of the corner of her eye she could see the server standing by with a jug of water at the ready. In a minute Father Diego would dip his fingers, wet with the men's slobber, into the clean water and wash them thoroughly. Then he would dab them dry—those same priestly fingers sanctified by the aura of the Host—on the folded white towel. The priest placed the wafer in her mouth. Silently murmuring, 'Forgive me,' Catalina spat the Host out into her hand. The priest's heart missed a beat. Catalina stood up, held the Host high above her head so that everyone could see it, turned a full circle and, ignoring the muttering that was starting up, shouted, 'I claim the protection of the Church.' Then, with the Host clasped in the palm of her hand, she stood perfectly still. The guards were about to rush at the prisoner, but the Franciscan, his voice cracking, placed himself in front of Catalina with his arms outspread and fended off all who came near, shouting, 'No one is to approach him! The man is under the protection of the Church! This is the body of the Lord!'

It seemed as if only his own words fully brought home to Diego de Ronda what had happened, for now he knelt down before Catalina and crossed himself. Catalina knew what she was doing: with her skills honed by years in the convent, she was a schemer of the first (holy) water. Calmly she observed what happened next. After a few moments' thought, the priest rose resolutely to his feet and with vehement bursts of prayer brought the mass to a proper close. Having pronounced the blessing he made a sign to the server, who sidled over to him, his head bowed. They whispered together, and the server nodded and went off. Ronda ordered the guards to remove the other prisoners. They obeyed, if anything rather relieved to get away. Now the priest murmured several prayers, and begged Catalina not to move. She said nothing and waited. A number of monks arrived. Some had brought candles, others censers, one bore the weight of a large cross, another had a black hood at the ready, four of them were carrying a baldachin, and they all followed the instructions issued by their Father Superior, who had accompanied them.

The baldachin-carriers took up position around Catalina, the candle-bearers formed a protective outer circle, the hood was placed on the prisoner's head, the procession, with the cross in front, set off for the Franciscan monastery, and no one could see how, under the hood, Catalina was smiling. The procession was escorted by guards armed with guns, some at the head and others bringing up the rear, and sure enough, in twenty minutes the Franciscans had arrived, unmolested, at the portal of their monastery church. The presence of monks swinging censers had ensured that passers-by fell on their knees before the passage of the Host, which must on no account touch the ground or be defiled in any other way—this was, after all, the consecrated Host, the body of the Lord, which took absolute priority over all worldly concerns. The monks led Catalina to the sacristy. There they extinguished the candles and the burning incense and sang a hymn. After this one of the monks knelt down in front of Catalina, who readily held out her hand to him. The monk scraped the dried wafer from her palm, and while the Host was being locked inside the tabernacle the other monks sat down by Catalina and set about endlessly washing and re-washing the hand that had dared to besmirch the body of the Lord, plunging it into the harshest of soap solutions and brushing away at it so hard in all directions that after a while Catalina began to feel that her skin was dissolving in the noxious liquid. She snatched her hand from the clutches of the scrubbing monks, declaring, 'That's enough!'

Then she said, 'I will avail myself of the asylum of the Church for the next few months—until things have calmed down outside and Juan Bautista de Arteaga is well again. Which cell can I find him in? And another thing: I'm thirsty.'

Chapter seventeen

In the mountain of Potosí

Skeletons. Masses of skeletons. Wherever you looked: by the side of the path, among the sparse mountain vegetation, lying between boulders or actually on the path itself. The closer Juan and Catalina came to the Cerro Rico, the 'rich hill' of Potosí, the more bones they saw, as if the skeletons were multiplying in the night in grotesque orgies of lovemaking. Most were human skeletons. Either already gnawed clean, or still darkened by beetles and crows. Sometimes there were fresh corpses, and then the shadows of larger creatures rose up and scattered at their approach. At first Catalina thought that it was all some weird hallucination produced by fatigue and the unaccustomed thinness of the mountain air. But Juan saw exactly the same thing, so what she had taken for an illusion must be real after all: these were the remains of so-called *mitayos*, Quechua Indians who for decades had been forced to work in the mines. The skeletons were those of men who had not even completed the long trek from their villages to Potosí, which could take as much as three months, or who, after toiling for a year in the 'man-eating mountain', had

had no strength left to combat their mortal exhaustion; men who had set out, often with their wives and children, and who were so unlikely to return that to be on the safe side a requiem mass was said for them before they left.

Catalina heard a rushing, roaring noise, and again it was not an illusion, not just the blood in her own ears: the noise came from outside of her; from the conical mountain which had been visible for some time as a silhouette on the horizon, and which now loomed ever closer. With the streams of water being pumped out of the mountain and gushing down into a single channel, the pounding and turning of the whims and treadmills used to grind the ore, and the mules and men at their unceasing toil, the whole mountain reverberated with a mighty rumbling and humming. And, riddled as it was with shafts, passages and galleries, holes that constantly drew men in and spewed men out, the silver mountain seemed, to the approaching travellers, like a vast beehive.

Juan and Catalina had had to spend a full two months in the monastery at Trujillo before Juan was sufficiently recovered for them to set off, secretly, and on foot, for Lima. There they had stayed for some weeks, had worked and bought two mules which carried them via Arica to Iquique, and from there they had started to climb, extremely slowly and cautiously, treating the ascent with due respect, for they had been told what to expect at high altitudes—thin air and biting cold. Soon the slow pace became habitual, so that they not only moved more slowly but also spoke more slowly, thought and ate more slowly, indeed, it almost seemed to Catalina as if she dreamed more slowly at night, and her dreams were filled with the creatures they encountered on the way; a condor, llamas, wild cats or small animals that would dive head-first into their burrows.

Now, having reached Potosí, Catalina was complaining of nausea, fatigue, headaches and nosebleeds. Despite this she was eager to begin the search for her brother right away, but Juan ordered rest to counteract her altitude sickness, and Catalina curbed her impatience by thinking of the joy to come. Meanwhile Juan was secretly making enquiries, hoping to surprise his young friend. He had decided to try and find Francisco's brother himself. He had naively supposed, only a few days earlier, that he would be able to go from one mine to the next and simply ask. But faced with the 600 mines that gouged their way through the mountain, and 570 different leaseholders, Juan had abandoned that idea and adopted an easier method: he went to the royal treasury to consult the registers that recorded the number of mines, their exact position and the names of the leaseholders. Juan spent a whole morning leafing through the documents. But he found nothing. Francisco's brother was not listed anywhere as a leaseholder. So it was as the bearer of bad tidings that he returned to Catalina.

'He's not here?' asked Catalina.

'No. There's no mine anywhere registered in the name of Loyola.'

'In the name of Loyola,' Catalina repeated tonelessly.

'Yes,' said Juan.

Catalina pulled herself together. Loyola. Of course. The search had not even begun; that was the wrong name. But she did not let her relief show. Juan would expect her to be disappointed by what he had just told her. And by now it was no effort for her to convey the impression of sadness. She assumed a sombre expression, wrinkling her brow and turning her lips down a little at the corners, and then lowered her eyes, while inwardly keeping a tight grip on her true feelings.

Two days later Catalina looked through the registers herself, searching for the right name. The lists were not in alphabetical order, but were arranged according to the date of the entry and the location of the mine. When, on the first run-through, Catalina did not find a Miguel de Erauso she thought little of it, told herself to concentrate harder, and started again. But when the second search also proved fruitless, even though she kept a finger on the page to avoid accidentally skipping a line, she began to feel uneasy. At the third unsuccessful attempt she broke out in a sweat, and after the fourth, when she just rushed through the lists in a breathless panic, she closed the register, her eyes blank. He was not here. If he was not here he could be anywhere. This country was so vast that it made her giddy even to think of it. And perhaps he was not even in this country any more. Then she would never find him. She had to discover some trace of him, some clue, something to set her on the right track.

Over the next few days Catalina looked through the registers for the preceding years and found an entry recording that the mine registered in Miguel de Erauso's name had been closed down three years earlier, with the brief annotation, 'Yield too low to justify further digging, mine to be filled in'. She shut the book, her hopes dashed. Three years. Miguel could be anywhere by now.

She did not give up, however. Her search now entered its most desperate phase. She climbed up to the mine entrances and questioned the overseers. There was the odd one here and there who vaguely recalled a man named Erauso, but no one could tell her where he was now. She questioned the *mitayos*, but many of them knew no Spanish, or could not stop to talk. They were lugging the ore out of the mountain in sacks as heavy as though they were full of earth, sacks which they carried not with their hands but on their backs, held by a thick leather strap that cut into their wet foreheads. Panting and sweating, their cheeks stuffed with coca leaf, they came crawling out of the damp, oxygen-deficient bowels of the mountain into the ice-cold air, tipped the ore into carts and disappeared into the mountain again.

The first time Catalina set eyes on the ore she was disappointed. She had expected to see shiny pieces of silver, but there were only lumps of mineral of an indeterminate, strangely blackish colour. Catalina also questioned the *mitayos*' womenfolk, who, bent double, picked over the ground outside the mouths of the mines for discarded lumps of ore, from which, they hoped, some remaining trace of silver might yet be extracted. To protect them from the cold they seemed to have put on every garment they possessed; skirts, stockings, ponchos, even blankets, one on top of another. Their faces were the colour of brown leather and were framed by multicoloured headscarves, but the dust of the mountain had made their hands as white as those of the overseers.

Catalina went down into the city to ask about Miguel at the grinding mills and at the refineries, where the ore that had been ground was piled up in heaps and mixed with potash and quicksilver from Huancavelica. She questioned the dealers who bought and sold the silver, but from them she heard nothing but words like 'ounce', 'value', 'profit', 'demand', 'costs'; everything revolved around silver, money, making a fortune, every successful deal, however small, was a cause for celebration, while the word 'loss' spelled disaster. Catalina questioned the crippled *mitayos* who were to be found clustered in odd corners of the city, men whose arms or legs had been severed when some gallery had caved in. She questioned workers who were spitting blood, made ill by breathing in mercury vapour or particles of rock. She questioned the many other Quechua who had stayed, whether from choice or necessity, and had found other work in the town. For instance there were dealers in excrement: they had a yard where all Potosí's *mitayos* did their business, so that the dealers could dry it, bundle it up and sell it as fuel, a rare commodity at this altitude. Catalina searched in the thirty-six monasteries, did the rounds of the traders' stalls, went to the brothels and visited all the gambling dens, where the city's eight hundred professional gamblers seemed to be at it day and night. Only the mine owners proved inaccessible. Once she saw a leaseholder and his wife going to church and counted their retinue of servants: there were eighty men and twenty women; Catalina could not even pick out the leaseholder in such a crowd of people. After a month of fruitless searching it was clear that there were no clues to be found here. She could be sure of only one thing: her brother Miguel de Erauso was no longer in Potosí.

It is a measure of her despair that she now grasped at something she had previously dismissed with a smile of contempt. The *mitayos* who were able to speak Spanish had told her about it. Every one of them, without exception. Questioned about a man called Miguel de Erauso, they had thought for a moment, shrugged their shoulders and then said no, never heard of him, but if anyone knew it would be the Nameless One. Catalina had been told horrific tales about this man. She had not believed a word. But now she had nothing to lose. Perhaps, she thought, there might be a grain of truth in those stories. Perhaps there really was still someone who could help her. And that meant venturing, for the first time, into the darkness of the mines.

One of the *mitayos* led her past the main seams—Oñate, Mendieta, Veta del Estaño and Veta Rica—to the northernmost seam, Centeno. Here the galleries had been cut deeper into the rock than anywhere else. When Catalina entered the mine she at once felt her chest tighten. She began to perspire without having exerted herself at all. It was as if a thousand tiny taps had been turned on under her skin. Following the *mitayos'* example, Catalina had roughened her gums with ashes and put a mushy substance into her mouth—coca leaf worked into a paste with plantain and flavoured with aniseed. She noticed that it helped her to breathe more easily and dulled the pain in her lungs. 'If you don't chew,' the *mitayo* had said, 'Pachamama will suck your blood, you'll feel heavy and you won't be able to move.' Catalina walked on, torch in hand. A wave of sweat hit her in the face long before she saw the *mitayos* approaching; the weight of the loads dragging on their foreheads was etched into their faces. The gallery had only a slight downward slope, but the floor was becoming more and more slippery and the small, man-made steps were worn, so that she was afraid of missing her footing.

They were still in the main gallery, which followed the richest part of the seam. But now the *mitayo* turned into a side passage which had been cut into the stone with little regard for such a thing as safety. Here there was almost no air. The workers' sweat and the carbon dioxide combined to form a kind of hot soup which you might possibly drink but could not breathe. Catalina retched. There were more branches leading off now: here a shaft, there a corridor or a deep well. Catalina could hear the sounds of spades, hammers and pickaxes, as well as grunts of effort, groans, commands. They came to a *tío*, and the *mitayo* halted. It was a statue of a devil with two great horns. Coiled around the left horn was a snake, a Quechua symbol of good fortune. The devil was clearly a white man, for he had a pointed beard like the conquistadors. His mouth was open, between the clay lips a lighted cigarette was almost finished, and from down below a huge erect penis reared up. The *mitayo* lit a new cigarette for the *tío*, laid a coca leaf in his lap, swore at him and told Catalina that the *tío* liked to be insulted, and that unless you insulted him you had no chance of surviving inside the mountain. Shrugging, Catalina muttered a few oaths, and the *mitayo* nodded.

They trudged on in the darkness, which was broken only by the light of their torch. The *mitayo* made frequent stops to get his own breath back or to give Catalina a short break. Glistening, viscous smears of purple, or greenish trickles, showed up here and there on the walls. More water was collecting underfoot. There was even less air than before. Catalina put a new wad of coca into her cheek. Eventually they reached a final turning where another *mitayo* was standing, doing nothing: he seemed to be keeping watch. The two forced labourers greeted each other, and the watchman poured a drink into three small bowls. Catalina took one, and the two *mitayos* each poured a drop onto the ground, murmuring 'Pachamama', and then downed the drink at a gulp. Although Catalina did not let it show, she felt as if the brandy were digging a tunnel through her own body. Only now did the watchman address her.

'What do you want?' he asked.

'I want to…to visit the Nameless One,' said Catalina.

'What do you want of him?'

'I've a question to ask.'

'What sort of a question?'

'I'm looking for someone.'

'He'll certainly be able to help.'

'Where can I find him?'

'Just go down this passage.'

Catalina was about to set off at once, but the *mitayo* stopped her. 'What are you doing?' he asked.

'I'm going to him.'

'You have to leave the light here.'

'What do you mean?'

'He lives on darkness. The light would kill him.'

'But how do I find the way?'

'The passage is narrow. You'll get a few bruises, but you can't go astray, because there's only one way you *can* go.'

Then the watchman took the torch from her hand. Catalina set off into the darkness. At first the torch she had left behind still lighted her path, but after the first bend she could no longer see where she was going. She put out her hands and groped her way forward. This immediately brought back memories; there was no way she could shut them out. A feeling of confusion made her stop. Something told her that it would be better to turn back. But still she went on, her hands acting as a substitute for light.

As she continued on she called to mind everything she had been told about the Nameless One. He was one of them, the *mitayos* had all agreed, a Quechua, a man who had long since ceased to be a man. He had been forced into the mine like all the rest, but unlike them he had never come out again. How long ago this was, no one knew. Some said twenty, some thirty years. Since then the Nameless One had spent every day and every night here, in an abandoned gallery, alone, without light, without food, without water; he ate and drank the darkness around him, so they said, and he had vowed not to come out until they stopped forcing the Quechua to work here. And anyone with a question that nobody else could answer would go to the gallery where the Nameless One lived, and would emerge with a definite answer and with knowledge that he had not had before. All in all, thought Catalina, just idle superstition.

She walked on for so long that she began to think she would come out on the other side of the mountain. So far she had remained in control of herself. Cool. Unafraid. But now she stopped. Suppose they're right, she asked herself. This was a sudden, unexpected thought. Suppose it was true? What the devil was she doing here? If what they said was true, then the creature she was on her way to see was no longer human at all. She was about to come face to face with a being from another world. 'Where are you?' she asked, and was startled by her voice: it took on a shape of its own, and its sound floated towards her in the darkness. Then all was silent again, but now the silence, punctured and broken by her question, was an ugly silence, almost unbearable. And to escape that silence, Catalina finally asked her question. Listened intently in the darkness, waiting for an answer. Asked again. And again. In different words each time. The one question she had.

Nothing happened. But before her inner eye something suddenly appeared, and even as she spoke she saw, in her mind, a man stepping out of the shadows. He stood there, close enough for her to touch him. The Nameless One was no more than an outer layer of skin stretched over a skeleton, which was clearly visible beneath. His face was bloodless, lifeless. He said nothing, simply looked at her. This is not really happening, thought Catalina. You've got your eyes shut, she told herself aloud; nothing can penetrate the darkness. There's no possibility of seeing anything here. And suppose she were to reach out her hand? She could grab hold of him and force him to answer, pierce his skin, poke her fingertip into his heart, kill him. Perhaps that was what he wanted. Perhaps that was what she was here for. She raised her hand and made a stabbing movement. The image vanished. Her hand met the cold stone of the mountain, and she opened her eyes, but that made no difference. Her fingers explored what was in front of her: it was the end of the gallery. And there was nobody there. Catalina turned round. As she took her first step back the way she had come she felt—just momentarily—that something terrible had happened. The feeling was the opposite of what we call *déjà vu*: it was informed by what was still in store for Catalina, what would happen many years later, on a day when darkness like this would envelop her again, for a third and last time.

'Did you ask your question?' were the watchman's first words to her. During her absence he and the other *mitayo* had downed several more brandies.

'Yes, said Catalina.

'And did he answer?'.

'No.'

'Then he's dead.'

'Who?' she asked.

'The man you asked about.'

'Or the man I asked.'

The watchman drank another glass.

'What do you mean?'

'I went right to the end of the tunnel,' said Catalina. 'I put out my hands and touched the wall of rock where the tunnel stops. He wasn't there. I don't know if your Nameless One ever existed. But one thing I do know: he doesn't exist now.'

The two forced labourers looked at each other. It took them a few seconds to grasp what Catalina had said. And then they laughed.

Chapter eighteen

The embrace

Three weeks later Catalina did, after all, discover where Miguel was. During the night she ran into a troop of over a hundred men led by the *corregidor*, Rafael Ortiz.

'Who goes there?' called Ortiz.

'Miguel de Erauso,' replied Catalina.

'That's a lie!' said Ortiz. 'I know Miguel!'

Catalina had given up all hope of hearing anyone say that, and was lost for words.

'So who are you?' Ortiz repeated his question.

'I'm his brother,' said Catalina.

'Are you for us or against us?'

'I'm for you.'

'Then come along!'

'Where to?'

'You'll see.'

That was the night the Alonso Ibáñez uprising was put down. Catalina knew nothing about the revolt, she knew only that here was someone who could help her, and she followed Rafael Ortiz and crept through the dark city with his men until the rebels charged them, with cries of 'Liberty!' Catalina killed three of them. More than thirty were captured, and hanged two days later. From Rafael Ortiz Catalina learned that Miguel de Erauso had joined the army and had risen to become captain of a Chilean company, that he was regarded as Governor Ribera's right-hand man and was stationed in Concepción. Juan and Catalina left at once and retraced their steps to Arica. There they had to wait for a ship, for the land route passed through areas that were still unsafe. After three weeks a galleon bound for Concepción entered port. Besides the crew there were two hundred men on board who wanted to join the Chilean army. These mercenaries were eagerly awaited in Chile, where soldiers still faced a real risk of dying and the army suffered from a chronic shortage of troops.

Catalina went on board burning with impatience, and was under unspeakable nervous strain throughout the voyage. She knew that the day she had awaited for so long was now close at hand. Her expectations flew, like agitated wasps, in all directions, ranging from the greatest joy to the most bitter disappointment. She sank into a deep silence. She wanted solitude in which to commune with herself, to pursue her own thoughts. Juan noticed that his friend was strangely withdrawn, even cold in his manner. Despite repeated attempts, it was impossible to get so much as a word out of him. Catalina even lost her temper, speaking to Juan angrily and, for the first time ever, offensively, telling him to stop his tiresome chatter and leave her alone. Juan retreated and stayed out of her way for a while, and Catalina was glad of the peace and quiet. It was some days before she listened to the stirrings of her conscience. She managed to make her peace with Juan, apologizing for what she had said. And then she made an important pronouncement. Facing Juan and looking him in the eye, she put her hands on his shoulders and declared, 'I want us to stay together, Juan. Whatever happens in Concepción. And something will happen there, I know.' But even as she heard her own words, she was conscious of a shadow falling across them. It was as though she needed to make *herself* believe what she was saying. As though her words betrayed a fear that the opposite might happen. The phrase 'stay together' hinted for the first time at the possibility of a separation.

At last they arrived, and Catalina saw the port of Concepción, the city whose byname was 'the Noble' or 'the Just'. Miguel de Erauso, they had told her, would be waiting on the shore to receive the new fighting men. She stood at the ship's prow gazing at the big square facing the harbour and at the soldiers and local people gathered there. As soon as the ship was close enough she began to scan the faces of the waiting men, and it struck her that this was how Miguel must have stood, all those years ago, on board the *San Marco*, scanning the quayside of San Sebastián for one familiar face, for the sister who had not come to see him off.

❧

Miguel de Erauso was inspecting the new troops. He shook hands with each man, exchanging a few words with him, asking him his name and where he was from.

'Let's go,' said Juan.

'What?' asked Catalina.

'He's welcoming the new soldiers. We're not part of that.'

'No. He's welcoming *all* the passengers. Let's stay.'

As Miguel de Erauso drew nearer, Juan saw that a clerk was scribbling down the names of the new arrivals in a book.

'There you are!'

'What?'

'Do you see them noting the names down in that book?'

'So what?'

'It's a register of the new soldiers!'

'Do be quiet, Juan!'

Miguel had a thick beard, and a small nose. His eyes still had the same piercing brightness, but his body was considerably more powerful-looking than Catalina remembered it. A hat covered his hair. His clothes were new, as if he had bought them especially for the purpose of bidding the new men welcome. Catalina's thoughts were in turmoil. Miguel was only a few steps away. Sometimes his eyes strayed from the task in hand and turned towards her, unmistakably, as if guided by some intuition. Now just one more hand separated them—it was a young man from Seville who had made a name for himself back home as a bullfighter. Catalina counted every word he spoke. Then at last Miguel reached her. He held out his hand. Stepped back a pace. Gave her a more searching look.

'Where are you from?' asked Miguel.

With all the others he had asked their name first. To Catalina, it was as if she could actually see time winding back in Miguel's mind. He was searching for something in her eyes. Now he only needed to see through her clothes.

'From San Sebastián,' said Catalina.

Then Miguel stepped towards her and put his arms around her. Catalina could not let go of him. 'It's me,' she longed to whisper, and she held her brother tight until Miguel released himself from the embrace.

'San Sebastián!' he said. 'That's my home town! Have you any news from there? Of my family? My father? My mother? My brothers and sisters?'

Catalina said not a word.

'What's your name?' asked Miguel.

To Catalina it seemed that her heart went into reverse and started to beat backwards.

Chapter nineteen

Wasted

She watched her brother as he slowly moved on, away from her. He was asking all the men the same questions; innocuous, simple, straightforward questions about their origin and identity, questions they could all answer without thinking, because the answers were established facts and as much a part of them as their vital organs. Catalina had given her brother her false name. She had not lowered her mask. And Miguel de Erauso had invited his two 'Basque friends' to spend the evening at his house, saying that he would lay on a supper for them, that he wanted to hear everything, all the news from *Euskal Herria* and from San Sebastián, where his parents lived. Catalina had nodded. She was still nodding as Miguel disappeared from view. Before leaving the harbour she turned back just for a moment, her eyes lowered as though she had dropped something, a handkerchief or a coin.

She spent the whole day in torment. Leaving Juan behind, she went in search of solitude. That's not the end of the matter, she thought. How could it be? How could he have recognized her? Was it not presumptuous to expect him to? Eleven years: she could not blame Miguel. She must give him another chance. She had lived for this moment for too long to let it slip away just like that. This evening, she told herself, tonight, when we've eaten and drunk and talked together, three Basques in distant climes united by the bond of a common homeland, three citizens of Navarra in foreign parts, tonight, when darkness descends on the town, I'll put Miguel, my brother, on the right track, give him signs and clues, for I want Miguel himself to take off my mask. There'll be a high price to pay, I shall have to sacrifice Francisco Loyola, cast him off even though I've grown so fond of him, even though I've become him, but it must be done and I will do it.

Catalina wandered around the town, went to the fortifications, sat down on a tree stump, looked at the water, dried her hands on her breeches, jumped up again and picked some plant stalks which she poked between her teeth, climbed a tree and looked out in all directions, then returned to the harbour, to the spot where the soldiers had been welcomed. Evening came, then night. She went back to their quarters, and found Juan already waiting to leave.

'Where have you been all day?' he asked.

'Let's go,' said Catalina.

❧

'There's everything here that you can think of,' Miguel said as he greeted them. 'You won't have seen food like this in a long while. And all the wine you want. Have a seat, we'll be eating right away. But first—a toast! We shan't run out of drink, I promise you. Boozing, my friends, is the only way to keep sane. So you want to join the army?'

'Yes,' said Catalina.

'No,' said Juan, 'I don't think the life of a soldier is what I want.'

'There's nothing finer,' said Miguel.

'It's quite a step from being a doctor to being a soldier.'

Miguel pricked up his ears. 'You're a doctor?' he asked, and Juan nodded.

While they were talking a slave had brought various pots and dishes of food into the dimly lit room. They piled their plates high and started to eat.

'What's this, Miguel?' asked Catalina.

'Maize risotto. It takes a bit of getting used to.'

'Perhaps you're in need of a secretary?' asked Juan. 'Someone to write everything down—the number of troops, the attacks, the battles, the casualties, descriptions of what happens. For posterity, for all those who come after us. It needs to be recorded.'

'Why?' asked Miguel.

'They'll be interested in what we do. They'll want to know how we acted, what mistakes we made.'

'If you make mistakes out here you end up dead.'

'Well, what do you say?'

'A secretary ? Here? In Concepción?'

'Why not?'

'Well, yes. I could do with a secretary who can bandage wounds and pull arrows out of men's bodies.'

'And what's this?' Catalina asked again.

'The strongest wine you can get. It tastes bitter to start with, but after three glasses it's like honey.'

Catalina drank.

'All the soldiers who turn up here are sent to Paicabí for a few years. To ensure the security of the district, so they say. But I can tell you, it's a nightmare. There's nothing to do there. You just sit around waiting for something to happen, but nothing does. Nothing at all. Not a single Indian tries to attack you. And you can't go hunting for them either. The Indians are too strong and we've got too few troops. The only killing you can do there is killing time.'

Catalina was observing her brother closely. That coarse laugh. Furrows in his brow. The thick, woolly hair. The fleshy hands which at that moment were lifting a chicken leg to his mouth. His teeth, tearing the skin and meat from the bone.

'You've changed,' she suddenly said.

Miguel choked. 'What? Who? Me?' he cried.

'Yes, you,' said Catalina.

'You know him?' cried Juan.

'You know me?' cried Miguel.

'I saw you once. I was young at the time. I was standing on the quayside, watching the *San Marco* sail. I dreamed of being on a ship like that myself one day. Your face stuck in my memory. You were looking back at the shore as though you were searching for someone. Who were you searching for?'

'How on earth have you managed to remember a thing like that?' asked Miguel, wiping his mouth.

'My memory,' said Catalina, stabbing the air with each separate word as if it were a needle, 'my memory has never let me down.'

'I can't believe that! It was more than ten years ago!'

'If you have a dream you remember every detail.'

'I did look back at the shore,' Miguel said, 'because my family were standing there, waving me goodbye. I can hardly remember what their faces looked like.'

'They were all at the harbour?'

'I imagine so.'

'All of them?'

'What's the point of all these questions, Francisco?' asked Juan.

'What are you getting at?' asked Miguel.

'I need some more wine!' shouted Catalina.

'That's the way,' said Miguel, refilling her glass. 'Now tell me everything, Francisco! Do you know my family?'

'What do you want to know?'

'Have you got news of them?'

'I know certain things.'

'About my parents?'

'About your sister.'

'Which one do you mean?'

'Catalina. Do you still remember her, Miguel?'

'Well, vaguely. When I left San Sebastián she was just a child. She must be over twenty now. I haven't thought of her for a long time. And yet I was the one who pulled her out of our mother's belly.'

'How was that?' asked Juan.

'We were on an outing. Mother was heavily pregnant. The baby started coming although it wasn't due. I had to set to and pull it out of my mother's innards. It was dreadful. I had nightmares about it for ages. The blood, all that stuff, even shit, my mother's shit, everything just gives. I had to bite through the umbilical cord with my teeth. I still had the taste of it in my mouth years later. And after that—yes, some memories are dimly coming back now—after that she clung to me like a burr. She really did, she would only let *me* change her, she'd only sleep in *my* bed, only do what *I* told her. I was glad when I could finally get away, to the New World.'

'And that's all?' asked Juan.

'Out here you forget things quickly.'

'How old was she then?' asked Juan.

'I've no idea, six, seven, eight…so tell me, Francisco, what *about* her? What's the news about my sister?'

Catalina took a bite out of a piece of meat.

'Come on, let's have it!'

Catalina chewed the meat and swallowed it.

'Is she dead?' asked Miguel.

Catalina was staring into space.

'She died?'

Catalina nodded.

'When?'

Catalina shrugged.

'When, roughly?'

'About…about three years ago,' she said.

'What of?' asked Miguel.

'You obviously aren't much upset by the news,' said Catalina.

'I've been out here for ages. What do you think can still upset me?'

'It was an illness,' said Catalina.

'Did she suffer much?' asked Juan.

'A quick death.'

'And apart from that?' asked Miguel.

'What do you mean, apart from that?' Catalina threw the question back at him.

'What about my parents? My father? Don't tell me he's still alive. He must be an old man by now.'

'I don't know. He was still alive a few months ago.'

'Then I'll just have to go on waiting.'

'What for?'

'For a piece of news that basically doesn't interest me any more.'

'I don't understand you,' said Juan.

'You'll understand all right when I tell you the whole story.'

As Miguel went on eating, he told them all that had happened to him since he had left his homeland. Catalina ate too, silently, full of her own thoughts but still following every word her brother said, and feeling, with every word, a little further removed from him, and from Juan too.

'After two months at sea and weeks of travelling across country,' Miguel said at last, 'I reached the place I was meant to go to, and became the leaseholder of a mine.'

'In Potosí?' asked Juan.

'Exactly.'

'Do you know a man called Miguel Loyola?' cried Juan. 'He must have had a mine up there at one time.'

'Miguel Loyola? Never heard of him. Why?'

'We're looking for him. He's Francisco's brother.'

'Yes,' said Catalina. 'My brother.'

'No, but up there in Potosí there are as many people as there are stones.'

Miguel continued his story. On his arrival in Potosí he had been met by his grandfather, who had been charged with the running of the mine until then. Miguel soon became aware that something was seething inside his grandfather: anger, hatred, directed against none other than his own son, Miguel's father. For *he* was enjoying a life of leisure in San Sebastián, where it was warm and pleasant, while making his own father, and now his own son, slog their guts out for him in the freezing cold of Potosí. At first Miguel defended his father, quarrelled with his grandfather, called him a liar, a slanderer—no, Miguel shouted, it was just the opposite, his father had sent him here because this country, because the New World was the most wonderful of all imaginable worlds, because this was where life could ripen to its greatest beauty. In those days he still used that kind of flowery language. His grandfather laughed at his naivety and said he would soon see for himself what sort of a life awaited him here.

Miguel threw himself into the work, still seeing everything through the rose-tinted spectacles that his father had placed on his nose. This went on for over a month, until he could no longer avoid facing the truth. 'It really was a terrible time. Eight whole years. It was obvious that the mine was long past its heyday. There wasn't much to be made out of it any more. Our profits were pitiful. A lot of the mine owners were getting richer and richer, but we were getting poorer. As well as handing over a fifth of what we made to the Crown, I had to send the greater part to my father. When the mine was finally shut down—my grandfather was dead by then—I left Potosí. Since then I've always been glad to meet any Basque who comes from San Sebastián, because I hope he'll be bringing news of my father's death. More wine?'

'What about your brothers and sisters, and your mother?' asked Catalina.

'Time has grown like a layer of bark between me and them,' Miguel said, looking for something on the table. Then he murmured, 'The stuff', and was about to turn round to the slave but then stopped. 'Listen!' he said. 'Have you ever owned slaves?'

'What, me?' asked Catalina. 'No.'

'I'll show you what to do. Wait. He's standing back there in the corner. Do nothing yet. Don't look straight at him. He doesn't deserve your attention. Act as though your mind is really on other things. Above all, remember to spare your voice as much as possible. In the art of giving orders, perfection is when no words are needed. Watch this. He'll do whatever you want. I'll show you. Give me your hand.'

'My hand? Why?'

'Don't ask questions. Give it me!'

'Here you are.'

'Right. Now you hold your hand out horizontally, quite far out, that's it, palm upwards. You hold it away from your body. This is only practice, so point it towards me this time. And now quickly flip the four fingers upwards, not the thumb, with a little jerk. If your arm is pointing in his direction he'll come running at once, you'll see. Now wait, we haven't finished yet. Once you've got him here you also have to know how to get rid of him, otherwise he'll be standing beside you the whole time, and we don't want that. You let the lower part of your arm hang down and give your wrist a quick shake, moving it sideways a bit, in a casual, absent-minded way as if you were shooing away a fly, and, I can tell you, he'll be gone at once. Yes. That's right. So here we go. Give it a try. He's over there. That's it, hold your hand out, keep it held out towards him, now, don't catch his eye, that's right. Do you see how he responds in a flash, how he comes running? And now he's trotting off again. Do you want to have another go? It's dead easy. We forgot to ask for the stuff.'

While Catalina summoned the black slave for a second time and Miguel said, 'The stuff' and dismissed the man again, Juan's face gradually darkened.

'This isn't like you,' he told Catalina.

'What are you talking about?' she asked.

'Come on, don't be a wet blanket,' said Miguel.

'What do you mean?' asked Catalina, but she was not even looking at Juan as she spoke.

'I mean that fight in Trujillo,' said Juan, 'and the rebellion in Potosí. All of a sudden you want to be a soldier. And now this?'

'What do you mean?' asked Catalina again.

'Yes, what *do* you mean?' asked Miguel.

'I don't know, but shouldn't we be satisfied if he serves us? Is it necessary to humiliate him?'

'To humiliate a person,' said Miguel, 'he has to know what humiliation is. We can be sure that our slave here doesn't. Take it from me, I've had plenty of experience with these…they're even lower than the Indians.'

'More wine!' said Catalina.

'I've had enough,' said Juan, standing up.

'I'm staying,' said Catalina.

'Are you sure?' asked Juan.

Catalina nodded.

'It's late,' said Juan.

Catalina shrugged.

'You'll find your way back?'

Catalina did not bother to answer.

Miguel gave Juan a parting glance and raised his hand in farewell. Juan waited another moment for a word from his friend. When none was forthcoming, he left the room.

'I can see two of you,' Catalina said to Miguel, after Juan had gone.

'That's the wine, going round and round inside you.'

'I want some more.'

'That's good.'

'The wine…'

'It helps you not to see anything.'

And then came the stuff: a substance ground to a mushy, yellowish-white paste. Miguel smeared some of it under his tongue, allowed it to melt, then chewed it and spat it out onto a plate. Catalina followed his example. Soon both of them were reduced to helpless laughter, they did not know what they were saying, did not know what they were hearing, 'I'm your sister,' brayed Catalina, and Miguel almost choked with laughter. 'My sister,' he roared. 'I disguised myself,' laughed Catalina. 'Disguised,' repeated Miguel, thumping on the table. 'I was looking for you, my brother,' cried Catalina. 'Your brother,' Miguel repeated like a kind of echo. 'I found you in Concepción,' whooped Catalina and in a single movement swept all the dishes off the table. 'It's all on the floor now!' spluttered Miguel, clutching his stomach in a paroxysm of laughter. 'This is good stuff,' yelled Catalina, reaching out her arms across the table. 'Then take me to your bosom, sister of mine,' chortled Miguel, and seizing one another by the shoulders they pulled each other up from their seats. Catalina tried to move her hands up from his shoulders towards his neck, but she had no strength or co-ordination, her hands only twitched feebly, and she fell back onto the seat. 'I need some more of that stuff,' she said, 'You shall have it,' yelled Miguel, and the two of them chewed and ate the mush and spat it across the room, though sometimes Catalina could not even find the strength to spit and so she let the stuff slide down her throat, a lump that pressed heavily against the walls of her stomach, and before long a darkness descended upon her eyes. It was like the closing of a curtain.

Part three

Chapter twenty

Many things come to an end

Francisco Loyola woke up. His head had crashed down onto the table, just like that, without his arms forming a protective cushion. His right cheek was lying in a pool of liquid. There was a powerful stench of wine and vomit. Francisco scoured his brain for any scraps of memory that might remain there. Catalina. A burr. Juan. Miguel. Two faces. Now he was by himself. He stood up. Felt as if his head were still on the table and somebody was sticking a fork into it. Put a hand to his forehead. It was the first time he had let himself go like that. He had never dared before, for fear that if he was not in control of his faculties he might do something that would give him away. Taking slow, careful steps he crossed the room.

On the ground floor he met no one at all. He plunged his head into a basin of water and swept his wet hair back. Then he went upstairs, holding on to the wall and counting the stairs as a distraction from the hammer-blows pounding behind his forehead.

At the top he saw five doors. Without bothering to knock, he opened them, one after another. The first two rooms were empty. In the third Miguel de Erauso was lying in bed with a woman. They were both asleep, although the room was already light. A blanket engulfed the woman's hips and legs. The upper part of her body, which was naked, was uncovered. She was lying on her back, her right arm under her neck, her left hand on her navel. Just then her eyes opened and met Francisco's. Very calmly he put a finger to his lips. The woman did not stir but simply lay there staring at the man standing before her. Francisco turned and left the room. When he was downstairs again he heard the patter of bare feet.

'Wait!' the woman called.

'What is it?' asked Francisco.

'You're Francisco Loyola?'

'If you say so.'

She had only wrapped a thin blanket round herself.

'What's your name?' asked Francisco.

'Ana de Erauso.'

'You're his wife?'

'Have been for five years.'

'There's something I wonder about, Ana.'

'What do you wonder about?'

'I wonder where you were last night.'

'I went to bed early. I wasn't feeling well.'

'Why didn't he say anything about you?'

'Perhaps he did, and you've forgotten.'

'Or perhaps not. Perhaps you just don't matter enough for him to mention you.'

'What makes you say a thing like that?'

'You love your husband, do you?' Francisco did not know where this question came from. There was an unpleasant lump in his stomach. Ana said nothing, but held the blanket closed around her neck. 'And nothing can come between you?' asked Francisco. They exchanged a look which lasted longer than necessary. 'I'll come and visit you both quite often,' he said at last, then nodded and left the house.

He was not thinking that this was really about Miguel, about a devastating disappointment, about having reached his goal only to see it tip over like a bucket of water. He was not thinking that it had all been in vain, his whole life, the long search for what had proved to be nothing. He was not thinking of how fondness can suddenly turn to hatred. No, Francisco did not think at all. He acted. But he took things slowly. He was in no hurry. He proceeded one step at a time.

First he did the opposite of what one might have expected: he set out to curry favour with Miguel. With an unfailing instinct for what would please, he visited Miguel as often as he could, fell in with whatever Miguel proposed, and even anticipated his wishes; he laughed when Miguel laughed, drank and put the stuff into his mouth whenever Miguel did. 'I want,' Francisco told him, 'to be a soldier.' And Miguel arranged matters so that his fellow Basque was not sent to Paicabí like all the rest but was able to stay under his own command in Concepción. Three weeks went by, during which something like friendship began to develop between them—or so Miguel thought, at any rate. Francisco saw it quite differently, for he was merely preparing the ground for what he really intended.

He was ensnaring his patron's wife, exchanging ever more lingering looks with her, and not only looks but also fleeting contacts, hands brushing against each other, a leg resting against the other's leg under the table and not pulling away, a secret caress when they shook hands, words full of hidden meaning when they said goodbye. Francisco was confident of success. He saw the expectancy in Ana's eyes and knew that he only needed to fix a time. But his dealings with Adeïda de Cárdenas had taught him to keep his victim dangling.

Juan, for his part, soon realized that something was happening to Francisco. He was changing, not gradually but rapidly, and in a way that Juan did not like at all. Francisco seemed to have lost all interest in him: he never asked him anything, hardly talked to him any more, and took notice of him only when absolutely necessary; when Juan spoke to him or asked him a question. It was almost as if Juan had died as far as he was concerned. This change dated from the moment they had disembarked at Concepción. After three weeks of this treatment Juan decided to make his friend explain himself. They were up on the ramparts of the fortress.

'Francisco?' asked Juan.

'What do you want?' He sounded irritable.

'I was wondering about your brother.'

'My brother? What about him?' Francisco groaned.

'Aren't you looking for him any more? Ever since we arrived here in Concepción you've not even mentioned him.'

'No, that's all done with.'

'Why?'

'He's dead. I made enquiries. He was in the Chilean army. One of the soldiers knew him well. My brother was killed in battle. Fighting the Indians. There's no doubt about it. The search is over.'

But Francisco's words did not ring true to Juan. He rattled them off glibly, as if he had learnt them by heart. There was something about them—something prepared, contrived—that made Juan suspicious.

'I don't believe a word of it,' said Juan.

'Neither do I,' replied Francisco, with the utmost composure.

With an effort Juan managed not to raise his voice, but all the pent-up anger of the last few weeks burst out of him as he hissed, 'Why are you lying?'

Francisco said nothing.

'We've come all this way together,' said Juan. 'I want to know what's going on. Why you treat me—'

'How do I treat you?'

'As though I simply weren't here any more.'

'You know, Juan, I think a lot about whether we are here at all.'

'What do you mean?'

'The one thing I want now is not to have to talk any more.'

'You're just making it easy for yourself, Francisco. But some things need to be talked about. There are people who care about you.'

'Are there really?'

'On the ship to Concepción you said we should stay together whatever happened.'

Francisco looked out to sea through one of the embrasures. 'I wish the Dutch would come,' he said. 'Right now. Corsairs. I wish I could see them. I would throw myself into the water and swim out to them. Then I would climb aboard and cut down every man who got in my way. Until one of them killed *me*. How many people have you killed in your life?'

Juan made no answer.

'How did it make you feel?' Francisco asked, but he was asking himself, not Juan, for before Juan had a chance to reply he went on. 'I felt that the strength of the dying man was flowing into my body. After killing him I was more than just myself.'

He was still gazing out to sea.

'You've changed,' said Juan.

'Have I really?'

With these words Francisco stepped closer to Juan, as close as he could, as if he wanted to put his face as near to him as possible, and this gave Juan a strangely distorted impression of it, he actually felt that this was a different person, and he was unnerved by the look that Francisco gave him.

'You know nothing, Juan,' whispered Francisco, 'you know nothing at all.'

❧

During his last night in Concepción Juan did not sleep a wink. Some days earlier he had gone to see the Bishop of Huamanga, who had come to Concepción to officiate at a mass baptism. The bishop had appointed Juan as his personal physician, and they were to leave the next day. Francisco knew nothing of all this. Juan wondered whether he should say goodbye to his former friend, as he now thought of him, or simply leave surreptitiously, without telling him. The thought of never seeing the boy again so upset him that he spent the whole of that sleepless night reliving all their shared experiences. He sat down and wrote a letter to Francisco. Just before daybreak he crept into Francisco's room and tucked the letter into one of his boots. As he straightened up and glanced at Francisco's face one last time, he saw something gleaming. Loyola's eyes were open, reflecting the faint moonlight.

'Are you awake?' asked Juan.

'I haven't been able to sleep for a long time.'

'Won't you tell me what's wrong?'

'I'm grown up now.'

'But that makes no difference.'

'I've become a man.'

'What has that to do with us?'

Francisco avoided Juan's eyes.

'I don't understand you,' said Juan.

'Are you leaving?' asked Francisco.

'Yes, I'm going now.'

'Where to?—No. Don't tell me. You won't have fond memories of me. I wasn't what you thought. These things happen. People are deceived in each other. People disappoint each other. Leaving is the best thing you can do, Juan. Then we'll be alone again. On our own, each of us. And besides, by going you're offering me a possibility for the future.'

'What sort of a possibility?'

'The possibility of searching. Perhaps one day I'll decide to search for *you*.'

'But—'

'All my life I've been searching for someone. Ever since I can remember. Now the search is over, and I find that hard to cope with. So go now, Juan.'

Francisco closed his eyes, the gleam disappeared, and he said nothing more, did not get up to embrace Juan, simply lay there and listened as Juan crossed the room, stepping carefully to avoid bumping into anything that might be in the way. Francisco heard Juan open the door and disappear, like an exhaled breath, into the immeasurable vastness of the New World.

❧

As if he had needed that final spur, Francisco took action the very next morning. But first, from a small package, he got out a needle and thread and a scrap of material and sewed Juan's letter into the inside of his doublet, without reading it. This was not the right time. Besides, he could imagine what the letter said, and that was better than actually reading it. Francisco had learned by now that imagination is less painful than reality, that a picture is more beautiful than its model. Now he wanted to do what he had to do and then disappear somewhere where he was unknown.

He took up a position close to the house where Miguel lived with his wife, and waited. The sun moved slowly across the sky. Francisco's eyes never left the door. He thought of Juan, who must have left by now, for some unknown destination. It's a good thing he's not here, Francisco thought. Relief made his throat tighten. At last Ana de Erauso came out of the house. Francisco followed her, like a shark following a trail of blood. When Ana was far enough from the house for no one to be able to see her, Francisco quickened his pace. Now he was walking close behind her. She seemed not to notice him.

He took her by the arm and said: 'Ever since I first saw you, Ana, I've been able to think of nothing else.' And then it all seemed to come pouring out of him—never had he seen anyone more beautiful, her eyes, her mouth, her walk—he reeled off all the compliments he knew a woman wanted to hear. He had thought himself into the condition known as being in love. Without feeling the least trace of it within himself, he knew exactly what it looked like from the outside, the thing they called 'love'—the gestures, the smile, the look, the agitation, the quick, shallow breathing while he spoke, the suffocating fear of being rejected, the churning emotions which made his voice tremble.

'I'll be alone this evening,' Ana suddenly interrupted him. 'Come at nine o'clock.'

That evening she was waiting at her front door and let Francisco in. Ana knew that they had about three hours. They went up the stairs, into the bedroom, and Ana immediately started talking about the image that she could not get out of her head, of herself naked in bed, and of him, the stranger, right there in the room, with wet hair and a finger to his lips; her dreams, her fantasies, her desires. By this time Francisco had pulled her onto the bed, unfastened her dress, his hand had slipped through the layers of underclothes and his fingers were going down to her private parts to do what he had so often done to himself. It was as if he had been practising for months in the rehearsal room of his own body, preparing himself both practically and emotionally for his big scene, and was now at last stepping onto the stage to show what he could do. And Francisco licked up everything, every drop of perspiration, every bodily fluid, the traces left behind by his own saliva; his tongue poked its head into every orifice as though looking for a place to make its home. Francisco gave Ana no chance to do anything, no intervals in which to recover, just one arousal after another.

Ana's eyes filled with tears. Not only her vision but her sense of reality became blurred. She forgot about time and danger, about her husband or any other disturbing possibilities, she was nothing but a body and its responses—until a sound brought her back to herself. Downstairs the door slammed, and she knew that her husband was home and that time had deceived them, had fled by far too quickly. She began to whisper to Francisco. Only now did it strike her that he was still fully dressed; she had no time to be surprised, but told him to slip into the adjoining dressing room; there was a chest there that he could hide in. She wrapped a blanket around herself, tidied her hair as best she could, opened the door to the other room and with a nod of her head urged Francisco to be quick and do as she said. Already she could hear her husband's tread on the stairs. She could gauge exactly how drunk he was from the sound of his movements.

Today, she thought, he was quite sober; his footsteps were strangely quiet, not as heavy and resonant as usual. Once more she whispered sharply to Francisco to get a move on, but he had no intention of obeying. He did not go into the dressing room. He got up from the bed with an almost exaggerated display of calm, buckled on his sword, and went and stood in front of the bed in the middle of the room, facing towards the doorway which any moment now would frame the figure of Miguel de Erauso. There he waited, his arms folded on his chest, his face wearing an expression of supreme satisfaction, as though what he had worked towards for so long was finally about to happen, as though at last he was being given a chance to get his own back.

Ana was reduced to silence. There she stood, with her hair still somewhat dishevelled, with patches of flushed skin on her face and all over her body, which was only inadequately concealed by her nightdress, and with no chance at all of coming up with a plausible explanation for her husband. And now it was already too late, for Miguel de Erauso was entering the room. He saw Francisco by the bed and his wife at the door to the adjoining room, he saw her desperate expression, he saw Francisco's sneering, spiteful smile mocking him, and in his overpowering rage he reached Francisco in a single bound, so that Francisco barely had time to draw his sword.

The force of the attack took him by surprise, for the very first blow sent his sword flying across the room. He retreated, stumbled, landed on his back and felt the point of the other's sword touching his chest. He looked at Miguel, who was standing over him, only needing to plunge the sword home to kill him.

Miguel was breathing more slowly now. You couldn't call that a fight, he thought. It would be nothing short of murder. This boy here is no opponent for me. And with a quick flourish as if he were signing a document, Miguel made a deep horizontal cut in Francisco's chin. Francisco screamed. 'Get yourself ready!' said Miguel. 'Tomorrow you're off to Paicabí. Don't ever show yourself here again! Call yourselves Basques! One hangs on to the bishop's skirts and goes off to Huamanga, and the other…take yourself off before I change my mind!'

With a hand to his bleeding chin, Francisco hurried down the stairs, but once he was outside the door he stopped, turned round and whispered to himself, 'I'll be back someday.'

The next morning he left Concepción and rode to Paicabí. From then on he seemed not to know what to do, and so he did the one thing he had learned to do: he imitated whatever he saw around him.

Chapter twenty-one

The lieutenant nun

Any attempt to chronicle the next twelve years of Francisco Loyola's life would become mired in repetition. His experiences and activities roll like waves through his life, endlessly the same, and from this point on they seem wholly to define what he is. Unconnected with anything so intangible as an inner life, characterized by the flavour of violence and the outwardness of action, they consist solely of card-playing and his military career.

Francisco spent three years in Paicabí, where, as his memoirs record, he 'ate, drank and slept in armour'; he played cards, practised and improved his fencing and fighting skills, complied with the prevailing rules and conventions, and blended into the army community and hierarchy. He kept his eyes peeled and copied what he saw. Each soldier lived like all the other soldiers, simply *because* that was the way all soldiers lived, and man is like a ruminant, endlessly re-chewing the same thing. Watching the others, Francisco Loyola saw what he was expected to do and did it. That had been his way in the convent, and that was his way now. The need to conceal his secret forced him to be not just more manly than a man but also more soldierly than a soldier. The copy turned out sharper than any original: the soldier-by-imitation became the best soldier imaginable, one who himself became a model for others and thereby reinforced the ideology of violence. It is a curious thing: Francisco Loyola rebelled outrageously against his own sex, and yet he adopted the other sex without reservation, obeying the seemingly fixed rules that a man and a soldier had to obey. In this way the supreme rebel was also a supreme conformist.

After three years the long-awaited battles began, and at last everything he had learned could be put into practice. The simulated killing was filled out with flesh: now there were living targets that reacted to being penetrated by pistol and musket bullets not with a muted, meaningless plop but with sounds genuinely produced by a human throat. There was no need to spare a thought for the targets of these attacks, for the world was divided into two distinct parts, a fact that was endlessly drummed into the soldiers. Everything that was out there, that was alien, that fought against you and made things difficult for you was evil that must be eradicated; the vast, filthy South American stable that you had to clean out, Hercules fashion, until one day at last the fighting would stop—or so they thought, for they did not know then that this would never happen. On the other side was all that was good and right, namely civilization and Christianity, which must be helped to triumph and take root here, and therefore one might risk one's life with a good conscience in this cause, since the reward, if one died, bore all the traits of Paradise. It was like a surgical transplant: the dead, useless old tissue must be excised from the continent-body once and for all, and replaced by what was new and valid. These Indians absolutely refused to be converted to the truth, to the one and only truth, to what was good for them. They could not get it into their thick skulls that they were being offered peace, prosperity, work and salvation, no, they were stubborn children who would not eat, who spat out anything they did not like the taste of, because in their natural benightedness they had not yet grasped that without food there was no survival.

The countless battles always followed the same pattern. Out on the open plains the Europeans set up their camps and made their preparations for killing. They cleaned and oiled their muskets thoroughly, stripping them down and re-assembling them, so as to avoid dangerous barrel bursts. Even at night they always kept one hand on their muskets and the other on the hilts of their swords. They spent every free moment sharpening the blades of their weapons, simply to fill the void of waiting; they trained, switched positions, discussed techniques of close combat, exchanged ideas on how best to evade the enemy's battleaxes, and in the meantime their bodies decayed both inwardly and outwardly, they gave up washing, their skin was reduced to a layer of dirt, their clothes disintegrated—each man wore whatever he chose, uniforms were unknown in those days—and they simply waited for the moment of battle.

Francisco Loyola was always at the forefront of the fighting. As an embodiment of what the Europeans were trying to achieve he was without equal. When he went into battle against the Indians he threw himself into it heart and soul. He rode straight at them, oblivious of himself. He gave no thought to dying, and this admittedly made him a good fighter. He raged. He cut down everything in his path. It was as if, when he fought, two green scales slid down between his eyes and the world outside; lenses that bathed everything in a poisonous green light. He revelled in every slaughtered enemy, counting aloud as he performed his butchery, and judging each day of battle good or bad according to the number of victims he had dispatched; he acquired an ever harsher manner and more economical, clear-cut movements, and his voice became rougher, more guttural, through his constant roaring on the battlefield. He quickly rose up through the ranks. In his eyes, his actions glowed with a certain beauty: the stabs and blows seemed to him like benedictions and the clashing of metal like the peal of bells, the shots left trails of incense fumes, the teeming masses of Indians recalled the great processions, and whenever one of the enemy sank to his knees he looked as if he were about to receive the Body of Christ. For Francisco, weapons were instruments from which he coaxed musical notes, a symphony of cries. And in the thick of the fighting, when he looked closely, he thought he could see the presence of death like boiling water flowing around the corpses of the Indians, or like an invisible hand gathering forfeited lives like mushrooms.

Then came the five great battles on the plain of Valdivia. The Governor of Chile was now Alonso de Sarabia, and the remnants of his army had shrunk to a bare five thousand men. These were difficult days for the heirs of the conquistadors. They just about managed to win the first four battles, but the Indian side was continually reinforced by waves of new arrivals, so that the Europeans lost the fifth and last Valdivian battle and the defeated army was forced to withdraw.

When Francisco saw his company's flag being captured by two Indians he charged at the enemy. The flag was by now a mere caricature of itself, torn, dirty and covered in blood, but it had to be saved for the sake of the symbolic power that it possessed. Though Francisco did his best to avoid the arrows, he could not prevent one of them from embedding itself in his leg. Betraying no sign of pain, he caught up with the flag-stealers, swooped down on them like a bird of prey and thrust them from their horses, clawed the flag from the hand of the falling warrior and heard the distant cheer that went up from his own troops.

This episode won Loyola the rank of lieutenant, the first half of what would eventually become his legendary sobriquet, 'the lieutenant nun'. Now he killed as a member of Alonso Moreno's company, which soon afterwards was placed under the command of Captain Gonzalo Rodríguez. For more than five years he killed as a lieutenant, all the while hoping to be made a captain himself. He killed in Potosí and Cochabamba, Tucumán and Las Charcas, Mizque and Chuncos. 'As we rode inland,' he says at one point in his memoirs, 'we came upon lush plains with countless almond trees, just like the Spanish plains with their olives and other fruit trees. The governor had taken it into his head that we should grow cereal crops to make up for what we had lost, but the infantry refused. We said that we had not come all this way to be farmers but to conquer and take gold for ourselves, and we would get hold of food along the way.

'We made all the speed we could, and on the third day we came to an Indian village whose inhabitants immediately took up their weapons, but as we approached they fled in the face of our musket fire, leaving several men behind, dead. Without an Indian guide who knew the region we rode on and took the town, and as we were leaving it again, Bartolomé de Alba, who was weary after the assault, took off his helmet to mop his brow, and a devil of an Indian boy, not more than twelve years old, who was perched up in a tree close to the road, shot an arrow at him. The arrow went straight into de Alba's eye, and he fell to the ground at once, so badly wounded that he died three days later. We tore the boy into ten thousand pieces. In the meantime more than ten thousand Indians had returned to their village. Eager for battle, we fell upon them again, and butchered so many of them that blood ran like a river across the square, and we chased them to the Dorado and beyond, slaughtering furiously all the way.'

Just as, in the convent, the watching eyes of the nuns had encouraged Catalina to live like a saint, so now the admiring looks of his fellow-mercenaries spurred Loyola on to do what he had been trained for and what he had an overwhelming urge to do, for his blood-lust grew from day to day, and so, consequently, did the other soldiers' respect for him. Never flagging, he continually led audacious new raids, heedless of possible losses. Sometimes he seemed to be fighting not *against* the Indians but *for* his own soldiers, as if the battle were no more than a performance, a game, for the entertainment of his own men. Nor was he satisfied merely to set an outstanding example. He wanted to enthuse the others, to inspire and lead them. When fresh young recruits, uncertain of what to expect, were sitting, ashen-faced, on their horses, he talked them out of their fears. The novices blossomed under the leadership of Loyola, who knew no fear and hurled himself recklessly into the fray. And when the battle was over the young men forgot that they had ever been afraid. Blotting out the past, they celebrated their victory over the heathens; the dead were left where they lay, and the survivors baptized.

At the battle of Puren, the commanding officer was killed during an early stage of the fighting, and when the leaderless troops looked for a man to replace him, Loyola was the only possible choice. For the next few months he commanded the company and led the men to great triumphs of killing, culminating in the battle against the Indian chieftain Quispiguaucha, who, despite having gone through the motions of being baptized, was at that time one of the greatest enemies of the realm. Loyola succeeded in taking Quispiguaucha prisoner. Before his heart had stopped pounding from the exertion of the battle he had strung the enemy chieftain up on the nearest tree. This was a mistake, for Loyola had not realized that the governor had really meant it when he gave orders for the chief to be taken captive and on no account killed. He swallowed the governor's reprimand with bad grace, and when, to cap it all, the governor informed him that he could not depend on people who disobeyed his orders, and that in future it would not be he, Loyola, who would command the company as its captain but instead a man by the name of Casadevante, Loyola exploded. He shouted abuse at the governor, calling him a weakling who had no idea of how things really were out there. This would have been enough to get Loyola arrested, but when he also drew his sword on the governor, and was only restrained from attacking him by the intervention of armed guards, he was instantly thrown into prison, where this time he had to serve a lengthy sentence before being discharged, not just from prison but from the army as well.

In every free moment of his ten years as a soldier, whenever there was a brief pause that required some diversion to fill it, Francisco Loyola had taken his pay, sat down at a card table and played. And so, when his military career came to such an abrupt halt after the battle of Puren, he was admirably prepared for civilian life: he found it easy to earn his living as a professional gambler. Like the battles in his soldiering days, the card games also followed a set pattern. Francisco watched the cards being dealt, but without touching his own cards and above all without losing the imperturbable calm with which he dominated the whole game. While the other players immediately pounced on their cards, Francisco observed his opponents. He paid close attention to each card that was picked up and whether it was added to the player's hand with a smile or with a look of annoyance or disgust. Only when all the cards had been dealt did Francisco pick up his own hand. Determined not to let anyone look at his cards, he devised a technique to prevent it, and worked every day on improving his speed: he took only one quick look at his cards, five seconds at the most, and in that time he memorized the suits and values. After that, instead of holding the cards in his hands as the others did, he laid them face down on the table. Then he would place his elbows to left and right of the cards and form his fists into a protective canopy on which he would rest his chin, a position from which he could once more observe the other players at his leisure. Not a single word passed his lips during the game. He soon noticed how often this taciturnity led to victory, for the other players found it extremely disconcerting. At the end of a game it would often happen that Francisco's opponents, in a combination of disappointment at losing and rage against the arrogantly silent Basque, would reach for their weapons. This led to numerous fights, which Francisco was not averse to. If, in the autobiography of the Lieutenant Nun, you count up the number of opponents killed during or after a game of cards, you arrive at a significant total. The statement, 'I drew my dagger [or sword] and he fell to the ground', comes to be a stock formula.

Why Francisco won all these fights is something of a mystery. Many of his opponents could fight at least as well as he could, and were physically stronger than he was, and Francisco's particular style of fencing could not always outweigh that disadvantage. However, in those years of fighting, both as a soldier and as a card-player, Francisco seems to have given free rein to his temper. He was the opposite of what Catalina had been. Whereas the girl in the convent had meekly swallowed whatever was done to her, Francisco would not stand for anything at all. He would mete out punishment for the most insignificant trifles, almost, it seemed, inflicting punishment for its own sake. He would never try to avoid danger: on the contrary, he was drawn to any situation that seemed likely to escalate. Even so, a violent temper alone would have made him a less effective fighter. Franciso's achievement was to combine the energy of his anger with something that might be called serenity. He united mindless, barbarous savagery with the clear-sightedness of supreme detachment. He might draw his sword with fiery cheeks, but he fought with a cool head. Here he did manage to achieve a reconciliation of opposites, and this was the reason for his extraordinary success as a fighter.

At the end of this period Francisco met a man known as 'El Cid', a giant of a fellow whose mere presence could shatter the self-confidence of an opponent at the card table. He always had a group of cronies with him who had proved useful allies in many a card-table brawl. The Cid was not used to losing. When he realized that his card-playing skills were no match for Francisco's, he plastered a shark-like grin on his face, reached across the table and drew a handful of Francisco's coins towards him. Acting as if nothing had happened, Francisco played on and won the stolen money back again. This did not disturb the Cid's composure, and after he had lost the pile of money a second time he made as if to draw it over to his side again, but as the Cid incautiously stretched out his hand, Francisco, with a single movement, skewered it to the table with his dagger, and then leaped up and, pressing down on the dagger with his whole weight, sliced off his opponent's hand. He then fled from the gaming den before the Cid's companions could move to stop him.

While Francisco soon dismissed the incident from his mind, the Cid, that very day, swore the exact opposite—that he would never forget what had happened—and from that moment on Francisco Loyola, though he did not know it, had an extremely dangerous enemy at his back.

Chapter twenty-two

In the dark

In 1616, Francisco Loyola was thirty-one and, thanks to his way of life, already had a furrowed brow and pendulous jowls. He was in some town or other—they were all the same to him—when he ran into an old acquaintance from his army days, Carlos de Silva, a lieutenant like himself. Silva was cursing the state of calm that had descended upon the country, bemoaning the leaden tedium of such periods of peace. Battles were few and far between, there were not so many Indians fighting now, and it was a matter of luck whether you happened to be in the right place when a chance of fighting did present itself. 'A gutless breed,' was Silva's verdict on the Indians, who in his view had given in far too easily. The soldiers, robbed of their raison d'être, were condemned to idleness.

That night, Silva told Francisco, he had what he called an 'assignation with a sword'. His adversary's name was Acosta. The grounds for the duel were trivial, a mere pretext. The truth was that the men missed the thrill of battle. They wanted to smell danger again, wanted that sense of being alive which they only had when their lives were in jeopardy. They wanted to be fighting for their lives again, not having to wonder if they actually had lives worth fighting for. Silva asked Francisco to be his second, to support him, for the second was expected to come to the aid of the principal if the need arose. Francisco agreed at once.

There were eight hours to go before the appointed time. The duel was to take place in secret, in a small wood, at eleven o'clock at night. The two men had something to eat, then lay down and slept for two hours. When they woke, they had a drink and did some arm and leg bending exercises to warm up before practising duelling moves.

'Always remember that you mustn't just watch your opponent's sword!' said Francisco. 'Your eyes have to be everywhere—on his sword, his feet, his free arm and especially on his face. Concentration is everything. You've nothing to lose.'

'How can you say that? I have my life to lose!'

'If you're keen to stay alive, that makes you a good fighter. But if you don't care you'll be unbeatable.'

'What about you? Aren't you keen to stay alive?'

'I've often imagined how it would be if I were the one being run through. I've seen a lot of faces as men fell to the ground. What's so terrible about it? In the end, when all the screaming is over, there's just silence, without even the mechanics of breathing to disturb it any more. It's simply quiet. Do you see what I mean? What could be better than that? And when I'm fighting I see only that silence before me, and not the darkness that comes with it.'

'Tonight it will be dark,' said Silva, moving over to the window. 'A cloudy night. The moon won't stand a chance.'

'What news is there? Tell me all that's been happening,' said Francisco, to distract him, and Silva talked about the townspeople and the newly arrived white prostitutes, especially a woman from Córdoba whom he was going to visit tomorrow—it did him good, he said, to talk of tomorrow, it gave him courage. Talking about the future made him feel stronger, and tomorrow, incidentally, the Bishop of Huamanga, who had been in town for two days, would be holding a high mass, and he would go along to it and give thanks for the successful outcome of the duel. Francisco looked up. The Bishop of Huamanga. And Juan Bautista de Arteaga. Francisco thought of times long past, and of the person he himself had once been. All of that lay buried under the detritus of years: Miguel, Ana, the weeks spent in Concepción, their parting, the words that Juan…Francisco ran his hands over his doublet. Juan's letter. He had sewn it in there. But this wasn't his old doublet—because of heavy wear and tear he had had to replace his clothing several times over. He had never thought of Juan's letter, which would now be mouldering away on some battlefield or in the soil of Paicabí.

'The bishop,' said Francisco. 'Has he still got the same physician? Juan Bautista de Arteaga?'

'I don't know.'

'Then we'll make enquiries tomorrow.'

'Tomorrow!' said Silva. 'I like the sound of that.'

Francisco and Silva went on talking, we are told, 'about this and that, until ten o'clock, when we heard the bells striking the hour, and we took our swords and cloaks and set off. The darkness was so impenetrable that you could not see your hand in front of your face, and when I noticed that, I suggested we should tie handkerchiefs around our arms so that whatever happened in the next couple of hours we would still be able to recognize each other.'

They went into the wood. The last few steps to the appointed spot were difficult, they could hardly see where they were placing their feet, and now and then a small animal darted across their path. They arrived early and had to wait. Francisco had an odd sensation. It felt as if he had been here before, in this very place. But it was only the darkness that he was remembering, the darkness and the feeling he had had when he destroyed the image of the Nameless One in Potosí. He drove the memories from his mind. At last their opponents appeared; they too had come without a light. Now that their eyes had overcome their vain craving for light, Francisco and Silva were at least able to see the ghostly figures approaching. Not their faces, only shadows emerging from shadows. Dark shapes that were only a fraction lighter than the surrounding darkness.

Acosta and Silva each took a step forward, while Francisco and the other second drew back so as to give the duellists enough space. Without a word the fighting began. The seconds heard the clatter of blades, the combatants' panting breath and the scraping of their shoes on the woodland floor. When Silva took a definite hit, though not a dangerous one, Francisco moved forward to his side. Without hesitation the other second followed his example. For a moment the two principals paused. Silva took advantage of this lull to lunge at Acosta and deliver a fatal thrust right into his adversary's chest. A yell of triumph spurted from Silva's lips, polluted with blood, for his cry of triumph was also a cry of pain and of death: his lunge had brought him victory, but also defeat. It had only succeeded because he had not side-stepped Acosta's weapon. The two swords entered the men's chests simultaneously, and plunged in deeper and deeper. Each seized the other's shoulders and pulled him nearer, until their faces were close together. They saw themselves in the gleam of each other's eyes, mistily, for the last time, and then they tipped over sideways, dead. For a split second all was still.

Francisco and Acosta's second took up the fight. Francisco dealt the first blow. After they had spent some minutes cautiously testing each other out, it was clear to Francisco that the other was not his equal. He could tell that he must have been a good swordsman once, but he was hampered now by the sluggishness of one no longer young. His reactions were slow, and so he was repeatedly forced into a desperate defence. His mental slowness became more apparent the longer the fight went on, and his lack of fitness was betrayed by his laboured breathing. And there was a fear in him that Francisco could positively smell—for Francisco's opponent had recognized that he was outmatched.

Francisco now deliberately began to make Acosta's second look foolish. He had already had several chances to land a fatal thrust, but instead he inflicted only light scratches, as if he were making notches in the other's skin to record the points he scored. He was like an orca on the Patagonian shore playing with a seal it has caught, killing it only after having some fun with it first. But Francisco was to pay dear for this self-indulgence, for his adversary now saw an unexpected chance: he would stake everything on one throw, summon up all his remaining strength for a final, decisive thrust at a moment when the other did not expect it. So he risked everything and suddenly, in apparent surrender and weakness, offered his broad chest as a target for Francisco's sword. Once more Francisco spurned the offer, but he could not resist inflicting another scratch and then twirling round on the spot, confident of victory, enamoured of his own prowess and delighting more in this sport the longer it lasted; but as he completed his pirouette he saw his adversary's eyes, alert again, panther's eyes in which the will to survive was not yet extinct, and the panther suddenly sprang at him, in two long bounds, with all the unforeseen strength of a body that has already been written off. The blade pointed straight at Francisco's unprotected chest and would have reached and penetrated it, had not the thrust been diverted at the last moment, for the man tripped over Silva's hand where he was lying prostrate on the ground, the blade found only Francisco's arm instead of his chest, and it was the white handkerchief that turned blood-red.

Angrily Francisco Loyola plunged his sword into his adversary's body and then pushed him away. 'As you see,' he said mockingly, 'I had already bandaged the wound even before receiving it.'

The man was lying on his back, about to breathe his last. Francisco bent down. Now he looked into the dying man's face. He could not believe what he saw. Taking his handkerchief and grabbing up a stick from the ground, he cobbled together a makeshift torch, lit it and rammed it into the ground next to the dying man. He looked at him again. He did not know what to feel.

'What's your name?' he asked.

'Miguel de Erauso,' said the dying man.

'I didn't recognize you,' said Francisco.

He opened Miguel's shirt and took a look at the wound. Then he started to remove his own clothes. One by one he laid the garments down beside the man who had once been his brother, matter-of-factly, as if he were performing a duty. He took off his doublet, his shirt, his undershirt. Finally he unwound the bandage that he fastened round his breasts every day to flatten them. He knew that his brother was past saving, but acting under a strangely mechanical compulsion, as if he could not do otherwise, he wrapped the bandage round his brother's wound.

Miguel de Erauso looked at the female torso before him and said not a word. By the light of the torch he saw the deep scar on his adversary's chin and said not a word. He looked into the eyes of the other, who was kneeling over him, and said not a word. He put together all these things that he saw, and remembered all that had happened many years before. At the moment when insight began to dawn in him, when he suddenly saw with the clear vision of one who is close to death, and opened his mouth for a final word, a name that he wanted to utter, as a surmise, as a question craving an answer—at that moment his heart ceased to beat. There would still have been enough breath in him, the name could still have issued from his lips like a last look, but Francisco Loyola, instead of closing the dying man's eyes, placed a hand over his mouth.

Chapter twenty-three

Wanting a different death

This was by no means all that happened that night. When Francisco drew back his hand it was wet with the blood from his brother's mouth. He wiped it off on his breeches. The torch, which had almost burnt itself out, cast a meagre light over the scene. Francisco turned and walked a few steps without knowing where he was going, or why. He simply kept walking until he saw the lights of the town. By this time the clouds had cleared from in front of the moon, and Francisco could see that a man holding a torch was approaching from the direction of the town. The man deliberately barred his way. Not only that, but he laughed and suddenly grabbed him by the shoulders. Francisco made to draw his sword, but it was not hanging at his side, and now it came to him that he was still half naked. The man pushed him with such force that Francisco fell over backwards, and his assailant threw himself on top of him. At once Francisco felt the prickly beard in his face and an evil-smelling tongue trying to push its way between his lips. The man's bulk was so massive that Francisco could not shake him off. He rubbed Francisco's breasts with his hands, squeezed them together and gave a loud belch. Then he tore open his own breeches, Francisco heard grunting sounds, and the man's hard member, stiff as a pole, pressed against his abdomen.

Francisco struggled but had no chance at all against that hairy colossus. Finding himself powerless to get the fellow off him, he stopped struggling and lay still beneath him, took a quick breath, then ran his tongue over his lips, closed his eyes and whispered some lascivious, obscene words. Snorting, the man put his mouth inside the open lips of his victim. Francisco licked up the foul little lake presented to him before slowly extricating himself from the kiss, then he steered his lips past the man's cheeks, opened his mouth as wide as he could, and buried his teeth in the man's neck, trying with all his might to make his teeth meet. Immediately his mouth filled with hot blood. The man screamed and started using his hands to hit out at Francisco and try to throttle him, but Francisco hung on to his neck and would not let go. His jaw was an iron clamp; he did not move, breathed through his nose, felt the blood trickling down his chin, felt the man's movements grow weaker and stop. Still Francisco did not release his grip, but dug his teeth even harder into the man's neck. Then it was all over.

He rolled out from underneath him. Spat out everything that was in his mouth, blood and scraps of skin and flesh, turned on his back and looked up at the sky, exhausted, still tasting blood on his tongue. He stood up, still moving in an oddly mechanical way, as if he were being controlled by some other agency, went back the way he had come, into the wood, to the site of the duel, picked up his clothes and got dressed, covering up the breasts that had betrayed him. He buckled on his sword, returned to Silva's house and gained entry to it, went to the washbasin, washed his face, rinsed his mouth out, gargled and spat until there was no more water left, took his things, loaded them onto the mule, mounted his horse, and left the town in which all this had taken place. He did not give Juan Bautista de Arteaga another thought.

Now he rode. First along the coast, until he came upon one last freshwater stream, where he paused for food and drink before taking the path leading to the mountains. Francisco wanted to reach the high ground: some impulse drew him towards a place where he could gain an overview. He made few stops on the way, sometimes eating, drinking and even falling into a doze while riding along. He hardly noticed when two men approached him. They rode up to him and asked him the way. They themselves were completely lost. Francisco shrugged and said that he had no idea where he was either. The men decided to travel with him. That way, they said, they all had a better chance of survival. They had underestimated the terrain: no matter where they came to, behind every hill, behind every mountain peak lay the vastness of the Andes.

Francisco did not care. He felt a deep indifference, an almost cynical resignation. Let destiny take its course: what was going to happen would happen anyway. There was nothing *he* could do. He did not know the way. He was lost in the labyrinth. From above their heads came the hoarse cries of the vultures, patiently biding their time. Not only did the landscape become desolate and bare of vegetation, but the air also grew noticeably colder. Altitude sickness often made the three of them stop and throw up whatever they had put into their stomachs. And there was not much to be had now—a few herbs growing beside the path, roots. If they were lucky, a dead animal that had only just expired and had not yet started to rot—though eating it made them feel twice as nauseous as before. Eventually one of the exhausted horses collapsed, trembling. Francisco's companions finished it off with a bullet and threw themselves upon the meat, though they found only a few scraps; the horse had become almost entirely skin and bone. The other two horses and Francisco's pack-mule did not last much longer.

Lack of water was not the main problem, for every so often it would rain, or they would come upon a stream with drinkable water. Far harder to contend with was the cold. There was scarcely any wood to make a fire, and the icy chill of the nights slashed at their bodies. Francisco lay by himself, but the other two huddled as close together as they could, rubbing each other's hands and dirty faces to warm them, and using the horses' hides as blankets. These kept out the worst of the cold, but because the shreds of flesh had been imperfectly scraped off there was a penetrating stench of decay about them.

While his companions constantly bewailed their lot, Francisco barely said a word. He was totally wrapped up in himself and had only a superficial awareness of pain and privation. He was waiting for something, though he did not know what. One day, towards dawn, he heard shouts of joy coming from his companions, who were walking ahead of him. He looked up and saw what they saw: two figures leaning against a rock, people who might be able to help them, who would know where they were. Francisco's companions ran towards the strangers but stopped a few paces away from them. Francisco caught up with them. What he saw made him too stop and stare: the figures were no more than caricatures of human beings, dead, frozen, their mouths hanging crookedly open as if they were laughing. Only just dead: no beak-marks yet. The three lost wanderers now had to pass close by the starved corpses.

While Francisco paid no attention to the dead men, the others could not take their eyes off them. They felt they were looking into a mirror that showed them the future, and that what they saw was themselves in a mere matter of days. And so it proved: one collapsed after another week, and the other soon afterwards. While Francisco registered the death of the first man with his usual equanimity, he closely observed the second man's dying. It's the other who's dying, he thought as he watched, his eyes riveted on the spectacle. The man was leaning his head against the rock, with his eyes half closed. His breathing made his ribcage heave as if he were vomiting, and the breaths were irregular and came less and less frequently. Finally there was a pause as if something in the dying man were gearing itself up, and then a last breath burst from his lips. He stayed in the same sitting position, and an invisible hand stroked his body smooth. The incessant beating in his chest had stopped.

Now there was only the clattering of the vultures' beaks. Showing due decorum, they sat some distance away, waiting, their throats ringed with red and white as if they had tied serviettes round their necks. Francisco had to go on. He left the birds to their meal. That night he could not sleep—something made him start up. It was really only a noise; an odd, flapping noise, as if someone had tossed a long black cloak back over his shoulder. But there was nothing there. He was alone. And he suddenly knew that what awaited him out here was meant for him alone. No one would take it from him.

Francisco left that place while it was still night, and went on his way, just so as not to have to sleep any more, just to get on. He was on a dangerous path which took him past fissures, past precipitous slopes and deep chasms. He saw the end of the path, rising up before him more and more clearly. And now at last his indifference gave way to a deep fear, a fear which, once present, refused to be banished. Not like this, he kept thinking, not like this. Again and again he sank to the ground, again and again he struggled to his feet. He felt hands gripping his shoulder. He shook them off. Not yet, he thought, not yet. There was nothing left in him but instinct driving him on, a last powder-charge of life. His one desire was not to hear the flapping of that cloak again. And he walked on, even when all his strength was gone, even when the blood was barely flowing in his veins. The only muscle that kept him moving was his willpower, propelling him round this bend and the next and the one after that. He put everything into this last march, his eyes gazing fixedly ahead towards the one hope that still remained, for he knew he was so deep in the Andes that he could never find his way out again by himself, and so over there, around this bend, behind this hill, here, now, up ahead, some people must appear and reach out a hand to him. Only that image sustained him, the image of rescuing human hands offering food and warmth—an image that he tried with all his might to superimpose on reality. And Francisco Loyola must have looked like a walking skeleton, emaciated to his very bones, pallid and bloodless, when he rounded a rocky corner and saw two Indians. Francisco did not know whether to feel joy or terror; with a last flash of awareness he wondered, 'Are these cannibals or Christians?' He would have loaded his musket, but he had thrown it away long ago, and so he could only resign himself to whatever was to come. 'And I wept,' we read, 'for what I think was the first time in my life.'

Chapter twenty-four

A feather

Now, surely, we may expect to see a change in Francisco, a profound transformation, a new life-altering understanding. For he returned to the religious life for a full half-year. He never left his monastic cell, but confined his life to the ten square yards that they had given him, ate what they brought him, sat on his stool, lay on the bed or sometimes beneath it so as to have the underside of it before his eyes, stood with his back to the wall or rested his forehead against the door, and when he did move about, it was only an endless circling, six months of pacing round his cell and round his life. His rescue had come like a bolt from the blue. Ironically, after all that he had done, it was two Indians who had saved him from death, had covered him with blankets and made him drink hot water with herbs, men who knew exactly what and how much they should give him to eat, knowledgeable men who had experience of desperate situations like this and who saw no reason to let someone die or actually kill him in order to tear the last few clothes off his body. 'They're Christians!' it says in Francisco's text. His rescuers not only gave him what he needed in order to regain his strength, but also guided him out of that labyrinth of bitter cold, to the nearest place of human habitation. They left him when the town was within easy reach, and just as they had appeared from nowhere, so they vanished again.

On reaching the town Francisco Loyola immediately went to a monastery and agreed a price with the monks for a secluded cell. There he gave himself over to introspection. Looking back in time, he drew the events of his life like beads from a necklace and laid them out in front of him. The contorted faces of the men he had killed fused into a single face. Their screams merged into a single scream. Then, going back still further, he saw the great quest, his life's mission, on which he had embarked so long ago. And lastly, he considered Juan Bautista de Arteaga: the feeling he had once had, that had twined itself around Juan like a vine, had been hacked to pieces. For six months he plumbed his own depths. Surely he would find something there. Something pointing towards the future, towards the life ahead of him. He was looking for something inside himself that was not modelled on what others did; not the piety of the convent, not the soldier's obedience—something of his own. Like a burrowing animal, Francisco dug down through the layers of himself, shovelling aside the dirt and debris of his life so far, yearning to make some discovery, to come upon a treasure, an answer, a direction. He was indefatigable in his search. But instead of light, illumination, alleviation, or any pointer for the future, he saw only desolation. He was gripped by the fear of finding nothing but what he was creating: a hole.

Eventually he called a halt. He had dug so deep that nothing at all could be seen now. Only an emptiness quite unlike the emptiness of Ekain. An emptiness that crushed him. No sign of a new possibility, of a fresh start. Just a deep pit that showed him where his life had been heading from the outset: he knew now that it would end in darkness. He wished he had not seen what he had seen in the Andes and now in the monastery. But the flapping of the cloak and the blackness of the hole formed a pair that were to haunt him from that point on.

After he left the monastery nothing changed. Francisco Loyola lived exactly as before. He still often had to draw his sword, defend himself and sometimes cause an adversary to 'fall to the ground', for by now he was widely known—he was the card-player, the intrepid lieutenant, who was easily provoked and given to violence. A man who gave way to his gut reactions and did not stop to think before making his thrust. An impulsive man who acted instead of waiting, who was quicker to kill than to show compassion, who gave vent to his rage, and yet did so calmly and smoothly, with movements that belonged to a different world. Frequently shadows from the past caught up with him. Everywhere there were people with a score to settle, people thirsting for revenge.

By now, Francisco Loyola was Francisco Loyola through and through. His creation—the man he had incorporated into himself—had been developed to the point of perfection. All his gestures and movements seemed utterly natural. His voice was where he wanted it and had rusted solid in that position. Sometimes he himself actually forgot about his real body, remembering it only when he touched himself at night or when he found blood in his underclothes, when his breasts hurt or when he fancied having a full beard. In any case, there seemed to be no way back. Francisco no longer knew who the person called Catalina really was. She was a distant figure whom he had once known, but had lost sight of over the years—just like Miguel and what he had called the burr. No, he really wanted to be the person he was, because he wholeheartedly believed in himself, because he enjoyed being held in high esteem, because he loved his freedom to do and say what he pleased, because he had become someone who could set his own stamp on things.

Even so, there were times when he was uncomfortably aware that something was not right, that he was concealing something; that he was a deceiver and an impostor, pretending to be someone he was not. And on those rare occasions, he had a sense of being not genuinely alive, of being a puppet version of himself, an unconvincing substitute, a dubious creature controlled from outside, a traitor to his own self and to reality. And he would sometimes feel an urge to throw off everything he was wearing in a once-and-for-all act of liberation, to show the world who he really was. But he did not do it, for he could easily foresee the devastating consequences. The news would get around. Everyone would know who he really was. His secret would be out, and with it his advantage over others would be lost. People's respect for him would crumble away. They would start to whisper and point, to laugh at him behind his back and make malicious comments. No, he must keep the secret to himself. He had no need of anyone else. Being in control was what mattered to him most of all. It suited him to go on being his own master.

❧

From this point on Francisco Loyola drifted 'like a feather in the wind', as it says in his memoirs. He took on all kinds of work and, letting fortune's donkey carry him where it would, blundered at random from place to place, never staying anywhere for more than a few months, working as a shepherd, shop assistant, hired hand to load and unload goods, porter and mule-driver, and once even for the forces of law and order. Francisco writes: 'I was sent to Piscobamba and the plains of Mizque, to investigate and punish certain crimes that had been reported in that region. When I reached Piscobamba I arrested a certain Lieutenant Francisco de Escobar, who lived there with his wife. I accused him of having robbed two Indians and of having treacherously murdered them and buried them under his house, which was in a quarry. We dug down and found the bodies. I followed up every clue, however slight, and when I had finished I summoned the parties before me and condemned the defendant to death. He appealed, I allowed the appeal, and the case was transferred to the court at La Plata, together with the defendant. But at La Plata the verdict was upheld and Escobar was hanged.' In his very next breath Francisco turns his back on this occupation too. 'I went on to La Paz,' we read, 'where I stayed for a time, during which nothing of note occurred.'

Over the next two years, since he found no goal or aspiration within himself, Francisco resumed his habit of observing the people he came across in the course of his various employments. He looked at the humdrum everyday pattern of civilian life, the men and women who had their lives neatly laid out like flower beds, tidy, clean, raked smooth: there was the wedding and the vows they exchanged, the house and home they shared, there was the work they did, there were the children who might be produced, and all of this under the benign, warming sun of ordinariness. People were born, ate, worked, had babies, suckled them and died. However much Francisco tried to view all this with contempt, however much he looked down on this ordered futility, it seemed nonetheless to radiate a magical calm, and secretly he felt a growing desire for what he saw. Once he went to stay with a friend called Pedro de Chavarría and his wife María. The couple were still childless after ten years of marriage. This did not seem to cloud their idyll. Francisco was much moved by what he saw during his visit. It was something of which he had no experience—namely, happiness, sparkling like a multi-faceted jewel; a life shared by two people, their intimacy a kind of mutual absorption. Was this what was called love? Each was there for the other. The brightness that enfolded the two of them, their gentleness towards each other, the passion conveyed by their looks, their permanent state of happy contentment: to all of this Francisco found himself sentimentally attracted. He wished he could be like these people, he yearned to find someone who might be his to share his life with.

Francisco stayed with the Chavarrías for a week. And then came the catastrophe. After taking his leave of them he went to buy a few things, and when he had got everything he wanted and was heading out of the town, deep in his own thoughts, he saw three people hurrying towards him. Two of them were monks, and they were escorting a woman between them. It was María de Chavarría. Francisco came to a halt; María was frantically pointing at him. He had no idea what was going on. It was some time before he could make head or tail of what they were saying, as they were all shouting at once. All three were hysterical. There had been a murder, Pedro had killed someone, the bishop's nephew, Pedro had caught him, the nephew, *in flagrante* with María, his wife, and now he was after her too, after María, he was going to kill her as well, she must get away, disappear fast, someone must take her to Huamanga, to the convent, to her mother, that was the only safe place for her, and before Francisco could object the monks had lifted María up and sat her behind him on the mule, and from either side their flat hands, more often joined in prayer, gave it a slap on the rump, so that it set off with somewhat more alacrity than usual.

Chapter twenty-five

The ride to Huamanga

Francisco did as the monks told him, but he could not believe what he had heard. It was beyond anything he could imagine, and it utterly demolished his previous assumptions. He demanded to know exactly what had happened, and as they rode along he forced María de Chavarría to tell him every detail. He needed certainty. He wanted to wash his illusion right out of his head. Completely. And that required words.

His agitation mounted. Not only as a result of María's vivid descriptions, but also because of his own increasingly disturbing thoughts. Everything, thought Francisco, absolutely everything that he had seen there, the whole sugary idyll of the Chavarrías, that togetherness, the depth of that so-called love, that intimacy, even the happiness in María's eyes, was merely an appearance which was utterly different from the reality. All of it untrue, thought Francisco. All of it a sham. And a new idea formed in his mind, and hardened to a certainty that was as simple as it was terrible: people were all like that. It was the same everywhere. They pretended to one another. They deceived one another. Just as he put on an act in front of people, so they put on an act for each other. They deceived and were deceived in return. The whole time. And that meant that they were no different from him. Not a whit. But did they know what they were doing? Did they know what they wanted? Did *he* know what he was doing? Did *he* know what he wanted? He had spent six months confined in the monastery, searching, and had found nothing worth pursuing, nothing that was worthy of him and of his strength of will. So what made him still live as he did? What made other people live as *they* did? The whole thing was unbearable! How could anyone find their way in this morass? How could anyone tell what was real and what was not? Surely it was high time for him to come out and show himself at long last, to let people see him, if only for a moment, as his true self?

In parallel with the agitation aroused by these thoughts, he was also being aroused in another way: the constant up-and-down motion, his widely splayed legs, the contact with the animal's scratchy back, the way they were sitting close together and their sweat was mingling…María was holding on to Francisco, clasping him round the middle, her breasts pressing into his back; Francisco could feel the woman's softness from behind and María could feel his breath from in front. Each had the feeling that the mule's pace was growing quicker and the contact with the other's body closer, the boundaries seemed to dissolve, in their minds their clothes fell away and their skin touched, Francisco heard María moaning and did not know if it was real or if he was only imagining it, but now María laid her hand on his thigh, and Francisco unhesitatingly seized it, opened the cord of his breeches and guided the woman's hand inside, and delved with it beneath the pouch of padding—now at last there would be no more doubt, now at last someone would know him for what he was. Francisco sat more upright, held María's hand firmly clamped between his fingers and drew it down through the bush of hair to what should not have been there; he felt María suddenly go rigid behind him, but he had no intention of giving up now, and far from releasing her hand he kept on putting her fingers just where he wanted them, until at last, in a shower of relief, he closed his eyes.

Francisco brought the mule to a halt and they both dismounted. Just ahead of them was a river. Francisco walked right up to the bank and looked across. María, who was trembling, stayed close to the mule. Francisco pointed to the water. 'No sign of a ford,' he said. 'We'll have to go along the river for a bit.'

María had her hand clamped tightly under her armpit.

'Do you know this area?' Francisco asked.

María shook her head.

'Let's hope your husband isn't following us,' said Francisco. 'I only know roughly which direction Huamanga is in. He'll know the best routes for getting there. Are you ready?'

María said nothing.

'Let's ride on then,' said Francisco.

María did not stir.

'Come on, nothing is going to happen. Or would you rather stay here and wait for your husband?'

María shook her head and sat on the mule behind Francisco, but tried to avoid touching him. They soon reached a point where the river could be crossed, and although they got into deep water half way across and the screaming, overburdened mule drifted downstream a little, they made it to the other side and rode on. Before the fading daylight could blur the outlines the fugitives saw the first houses of Huamanga in the distance.

It was already dark when they reached the convent. Francisco handed María in at the gate like a parcel. He gave the nun on gate-duty precise instructions: no one must be let into the convent. The girl must be safely locked away. Preferably with her mother. Her husband was after her. And when Francisco had said all this he suddenly had a feeling of revulsion for the woman he was setting down here. For what she had done. And what he himself had done on the way. He felt he had been seen through. Something disgusted him. Francisco beckoned María to him again and bent close to her. The nun was all ears. Francisco motioned to her to go away. 'Listen,' he said to María, when the thwarted eavesdropper had moved away into the shadow. Francisco lifted María's chin and made her look into his eyes. 'Not a word to anyone about what happened on the way, do you hear? That's the only price I ask for helping you.' María nodded, then turned and disappeared into the convent.

Francisco rode pensively into the town, where he stopped at an inn, took something approximating to a room, changed into some dry clothes, settled down in the tap-room and let time go by. He was drinking something or other out of a cup. He had no idea what time it was when the cup suddenly fell to pieces in his hand. Or why it had done so. It took him a while to realize that it had not shattered of its own accord, but had been smashed by a pistol bullet. So someone had fired a pistol. He raised his eyes towards the source of the shot and saw Pedro de Chavarría standing in the doorway. The smoke still hung in the air.

Francisco had not the least desire to fight Pedro, he would much rather have discussed matters, to clear up what was evidently an unfortunate misunderstanding. But Pedro rushed at him and Francisco had no choice but to take to his heels. They ran through the streets of Huamanga. Pedro had his sword in his hand and had thrown away the pistol. Francisco took refuge in a church. This, he thought, might be the right place to make a maddened pursuer see reason. Certainly the place for a conciliatory talk. By this time darkness had fallen. In the church a number of lamps and candles were burning. Moments later Pedro's shadow appeared at the main door. Francisco had miscalculated: being in a hallowed place had no restraining effect on Pedro at all. Like an animal unleashed he charged at Francisco, storming down the central nave in mighty bounds, and looking into his eyes Francisco could see that this was not the Pedro de Chavarría that he knew but someone quite different, who no longer knew what he was doing, who would dispatch him into the next world without a moment's hesitation.

Francisco was only carrying a dagger. He managed to parry his adversary's first blow using that small blade, but the dagger was sent skidding several yards along the floor. Francisco took a few steps sideways, a few back again, and went on dodging about nimbly, constantly watching out for the other's blows, which whistled past his head. And that head had better come up with an idea in double-quick time if he did not want to be with Him in paradise that very day. Then he saw the crucifix. It was a cross carried in processions and was propped against one of the columns. Diving beneath his adversary's weapon, Francisco ran over to it. The cross was not too heavy, and was about the height of a man, with a Christ figure made of clay. Francisco lifted it off the floor and held it up towards Pedro like a protective shield, as if he were a devil or some sinister apparition that could be put to flight by its symbolic power. Now, surely, Francisco thought, here, with the cross right in front of him, he must stop, he can't possibly strike out at the cross. But nothing and nobody seemed capable of bringing Pedro de Chavarría to his senses. He was obsessed with a single goal: the annihilation of his enemy.

By now a number of people had entered the church, drawn by the noise of shouting and running. A blow by Pedro struck the cross. The people gasped, drawing in their breath in unison. Now Francisco had no choice. He had to fight, and so he turned the cross round in his hands so that the Lord's head pointed downwards and the feet heavenwards. As he took a firm grip on the shorter end of the cross Francisco saw that it made a perfect sword, and that the headstand that the Lord had performed had given him an ideal weapon for keeping his assailant at bay. True, he could hardly make any sort of meaningful attack with it, but at least he had an adequate defensive weapon with which to parry Pedro's blows. He only needed to hold out until someone finally came to his aid and took Chavarría's sword away from him. There were so many people in the church! What were they waiting for? Could they not see what was going on? Would no one protect the crumbling body of the Lord? His hands and feet were already falling off, and now his legs; with each blow of metal on clay another limb clattered to the floor. Soon only the chest and head remained, modelled in an austere style, grey and gaunt, and wreathed with thorns. Pedro made another lunge with his sword, but this time he only hit the gap between Jesus' back and the wood it was stuck to. Leaping backwards, Francisco suddenly performed a ninety-degree turn; Pedro's blade, jammed between the clay and the wood, was jerked out of his hand, while the naked torso of the Lord broke off at the neck and crashed to the floor. Then Francisco raised the cross and slammed it down on Pedro's head, so that, with a bemused expression on his face, Pedro fell flat on his back, unconscious. Francisco turned the cross the right way up again and held it to his adversary's throat. Gasping for breath, he could not form the words he wanted to say. He could only stand and stare at the head of the Lord which hovered, disembodied, directly in front of his own. It seemed to Francisco that the crown of thorns was slightly askew and that, like him, the crucified Christ was panting with the effort of the fight. Then he looked past the Lord's head at the bystanders who were at last showing signs of movement, making way for someone who wore bishop's robes and who was beginning to speak in a loud voice. But the meaning of what he said did not penetrate Francisco's brain, for behind and slightly to one side of the bishop he saw a man who was of far more interest to him than any episcopal words.

Chapter twenty-six

Death by the rope

'I recognized you at once,' said Francisco, when he could bear the silence no longer.

Juan Bautista de Arteaga looked at him.

'Why shouldn't you have recognized me?' he asked.

They were sitting in the bishop's house, that same night. Pedro de Chavarría had been arrested.

'You're right,' said Francisco. 'Why shouldn't I have recognized you?'

'Were you looking for me?' asked Juan.

'No.'

'But you knew I was living in Huamanga?'

'I knew that you went to Huamanga. I didn't know if you were still living here. It's been a long time since then.'

'The old bishop died. I stayed on with his successor.'

'As his doctor?'

'He's never ill, this new bishop. I go about with him, I write down everything that happens, I collect events. We travel a lot. I suppose you could say I'm a kind of secretary.'

There was a pause. Every question that Francisco tried out in his mind sounded somehow ridiculous.

'And then there are my own memories,' said Juan.

'What do you mean?'

'I'm making a collection of my own memories too. Everything that has happened in my life.'

'Including me?'

'Including you.'

'And Vitoria?'

'Home?'

'Call it what you like.'

'Of course.'

Francisco said nothing.

'You must tell me everything,' said Juan.

'It's late,' said Francisco.

'Tomorrow, then.'

'Yes, tomorrow.'

But the next morning, the door of Francisco's room was flung open by two men who stood there, their faces grave and impassive, and one of them said, 'You're under arrest!' Francisco thought this must relate to last night, to the destruction of the cross and the fight in the church; he had nothing to reproach himself with and readily followed the two men. But the questions he was required to answer were nooses being knotted for him. Yes, before the quarrel with Pedro he had gone into that inn, next to the gaming house. Yes, this was his dagger, he had lost it, who had found it?

'With this dagger,' his interrogator told him, 'a man was murdered last night. Near the inn. Before your fight with Chavarría. And there are two men who saw you commit the murder.'

Everything happened at such breathtaking speed that Francisco felt giddy. During his brief hearing he recognized one of the two supposed witnesses who were testifying against him. The man had no right hand, only a black cloth covering a stump: it was the Cid. Now Francisco understood the plot that had been hatched against him, but could do nothing about it. Obviously the Cid must have been somewhere in the crowd watching the fight in the church. He must have fallen to his knees, not out of piety but so that he could surreptitiously pick up Francisco's dagger from the floor. And he must have used the dagger to commit the murder.

Francisco Loyola's case was quickly dispatched. The concrete evidence would have been insufficient in itself, but the witness statements carried considerable weight. Juan Bautista de Arteaga's hands were tied. He was not even allowed to visit the condemned man in prison. The sentence was death by hanging. 'Now I was a bit worried,' reads Francisco's text. But the position was truly serious: Francisco's appeal for mercy was rejected. The sentence was ordered to be carried out in three days' time.

The preparations for a death were in full swing; an execution was a major social event. Two days were devoted to the work of construction. With the aid of a tree-trunk the hangman tested the strength of the rope and of his structure. Among the citizens of Huamanga the atmosphere was electric, as if a thunderstorm were approaching. People were looking forward to watching someone die. The short struggle with Death after he had laid his stringy hands around the victim's neck, the faint death rattle just before the end, the water running out of the legs of the breeches following the moment of death when all control is lost—for the spectators all this had the character of a play, and because it was genuine, it was more convincing than any other show that was on offer. But what gave them more comfort and pleasure than anything was that *they* were not hanging there. The death of the man who *was* hanging there confirmed the plain fact that they were still alive. His life was being snuffed out, while they were still breathing. As long as it was someone else dying, their own lives were inviolable.

On the eve of the day appointed for his death Francisco was sitting in his cell, thinking. So the following morning was to be his last? It was strangely unimaginable. But what if it were so? What if he really had reached the end of the road this time? Just then a priest entered the cell and said he had come to hear his confession.

'Confession?' asked Francisco.

The priest nodded.

'Confession!' repeated Francisco, laughing now.

The priest began to mutter some words in Latin.

'Stop!' shouted Francisco.

'What do you mean?'

'I refuse.'

'That's not possible. If you don't confess you can't be executed.'

'That's right.'

'I mean, if you don't confess, you can't be admitted to the communion of saints.'

'You said it.'

'Well then. Shall we begin—'

'Go away and leave me alone.'

Francisco stood up and advanced upon the priest, who leaped up in alarm and left the cell. Shortly afterwards the judge appeared, a man called Vega.

'No confession?' he asked.

'No confession,' said Francisco.

'What's the idea of that?'

'Putting me to death when I have not made my confession—I doubt if you can square that with your conscience.'

Vega rubbed his chin.

'You may find you're wrong about that, Loyola.'

And then, we are told, it 'rained priests'—clerics who hammered away at Francisco Loyola from all sides, imploring him to change his mind. They painted in lurid colours the everlasting torments of hell which awaited 'that poor wretch, Loyola' if he refused to be confessed. But

Francisco would not be moved. By morning the priests had become even more agitated and would not leave the cell at all, even when Francisco demanded to be left in peace. They began to raise their voices, but their pleading and scolding achieved nothing.

The light of day tolled the knell for a human life, and the priests had to put the habit of taffeta on the condemned man and sit him on a horse. They accompanied him on his way to the gallows. They begged Vega to delay the execution: it was far too soon. This man, they said, needed to be prepared for his last journey, he must not be left without spiritual succour. But Vega replied, with perfect composure, 'He is to hang, right now. The decision has been taken. Death is already at his side. If he insists on going to hell that is his affair. I have not forbidden him to confess.'

Francisco had not reckoned with this. He had hoped to obtain a postponement, a breathing-space—a couple more days of thinking time. But now here he was, perched on the horse, wearing the black taffeta habit, a caricature of himself, with these tiresome priests, like a swarm of mosquitoes, alongside him. He saw the gallows looming ever closer, and beside it the man who was going to operate it. The whole town was gathered there. Francisco was pushed up the four roughly carpentered steps. Now at last the priests stood back. Only one of them accompanied him all the way to the noose that trembled in the morning breeze. He was still insistently whispering to Francisco that he must change his mind, there was still time, a single word would do, just 'I repent', he was ready to grant him absolution, he just required that one word, no more and no less, or even, when he was beyond speaking, a nod or a sign using his eyes.

Francisco was not listening. He refused to believe that the event that was already casting its oval shadow right before his feet was actually going to happen. He gazed into the assembled throng of people and at once picked out the Cid, who was standing in the front row, grinding his teeth in anticipation, hatred bringing beads of sweat to his forehead. He was gesturing triumphantly with the stump of his arm. Juan Bautista de Arteaga was standing behind the bishop, who was sitting on a raised platform. As for the other people: unknown faces, a chaotic mass of strangers who were there to claim Francisco's death as their due. They had come to see a man die, and they would be satisfied with nothing less.

Then Francisco suddenly recognized María de Chavarría. He realized that she must have been looking at him all this time, for when she saw that she had at last caught his eye, she acted instantly. She made a sign to him by squeezing her breasts together and pushing them up, ignoring the men standing near her, who nudged each other, jerking their chins in her direction and making lewd remarks. Francisco considered for a moment. That was certainly a thought. He stood there, soberly reflecting, on the platform which was all that stood between him and the abyss, death and damnation. Then he heard a question being addressed to him.

He knew they were asking the usual last question. Francisco nodded and said yes; of course he had a wish. His features became more animated. A last wish that could be granted very easily, he said, but one that mattered to him more than anything else at all. For a moment he closed his eyes as he put together the right words. He wanted to have them all ready on his tongue before he opened his mouth. And then he said, 'I would like to die just as I was born.'

Those around him said nothing. They looked at each other. Vega suspected another ruse, but Francisco's expression convinced him that he was serious. Nobody would be joking, with death so close at hand. Even so, Vega was mystified.

'What do you mean?' he asked.

'I would like to die just as I was born,' Francisco repeated.

'He wants you to take his clothes off!' shouted María de Chavarría.

'Do it!' cried the priests. 'It's his last wish, you can't refuse him!'

'Yes, why not?' the spectators shouted.

'Naked!' shouted some others. 'Let him die naked, if that's what he wants!'

Vega looked around: on all sides people were nodding. Last of all he looked at the bishop, who was still undecided. Then Juan

Bautista de Arteaga bent down and whispered briefly into his ear. The bishop nodded. Two of the hangman's assistants approached and pulled the taffeta habit over Francisco's head. Underneath it he was wearing his normal clothes. When they were about to undress him further, he said, 'No, please. I would like to do it myself.' They cut through his bonds. He rubbed his wrists to restore his circulation. Then he looked into the crowd.

What he now did, he did slowly. He turned his hand against himself, beginning by removing his shirt. Garment by garment he stripped his body, yet he felt as though he were doing the opposite, as though with every piece of clothing he took off he were putting a new one on—as though for him nakedness was a disguise. Then he spread his arms wide.

There was total silence. The onlookers could not take it in all at once. What they were seeing was an impossibility! María de Chavarría was nursing a smile. Juan Bautista de Arteaga was leaning for support on the arm of the bishop's throne. The judge, the hangman and the priests all stepped back a pace. In the crowd, no one moved.

'Hang Francisco Loyola!' said the condemned man. 'But not me. I am Catalina de Erauso.' But his voice sounded full of regret at what he had just done. In a slightly lower voice he added, 'Don't be misled by what you see.'

At last the crowd erupted into a hubbub of yelling, shouting and roaring. They pointed at the spectacle before them, demanded answers, explanations, demanded to be told what was going on. 'Cheating swine!' someone shouted. 'All the more reason to kill him!' And others: 'Him? You mean *her!* Jezebel! Cheating whore!' Uncertainty prompted some nervous laughter. There were cries of 'Satan!', and people began frenziedly crossing themselves. The priests, too, held aloft their holy water sprinklers as if to fend off higher powers; their mouths moved continuously, mumbling, chewing their Latin prayers that no one could hear.

The Cid was standing close to the edge of the scaffold, his eyes staring. Never had the word 'dumbfounded' had a fitter application. Close by him someone cried out: 'That's right! It was Francisco

Loyola who was condemned to death! This can't be him! He mustn't be hanged!' At this the Cid drew his pistol. The people around him backed away. Some of them screamed. The Cid raised an unsteady left arm. He levelled the gun and took aim. There was a moment's silence, and then the shot rang out. Francisco fell to the ground, naked and wounded. A number of men pounced on the Cid, took the gun from him and held him fast. Juan pushed aside the people who were in the way and leapt up onto the scaffold. He knelt down beside Francisco, whose eyes were open. He was lying, naked, in a pool of his own blood. Juan raised the upper part of Francisco's body and examined his chest and shoulder. The bullet had passed right through him, and the wound was not dangerous.

All this time Francisco was trying to read Juan's expression, anxious to know how badly hurt he was. Juan gave a nod. 'It's nothing,' he murmured into Francisco's ear. 'There's no danger. But all the same,' he added softly, raising his eyes briefly to the noose, 'it would be no bad thing if you fainted at this point.'

Francisco raised himself in Juan's arms and, bringing his mouth close to Juan's ear, whispered, 'A gunshot wound, Juan? Then do me a favour and don't use hot oil.'

Chapter twenty-seven

Dictation

The death sentence was quashed. The man who had attempted to kill the prisoner was one of the witnesses who had testified against him at the trial. This fact was more than enough to discredit him. He was tortured until he made a full confession. The townsfolk of Huamanga got their execution after all and were content.

But now everyone wanted to know what was to become of Francisco Loyola, who had saved his life by stripping off his clothes. The bishop had his eye on him. After three days he sent several nuns to Loyola to examine that mysterious body of his. The nuns approached the figure lying in the bed and turned back the cover. They felt his breasts, and Francisco could not help laughing because it tickled. He made a suggestive remark, causing one of the nuns to start saying her rosary at the top of her voice. Then they pulled his legs apart and fingered his sexual parts; one of them reached her hand into the orifice, looking for something, and then nodded, withdrew her hand and whispered two words which were soon making the rounds: *virgo intacta*. This inspection aside, Francisco was sealed off from all visitors in order to prevent him from telling his story. The bishop wanted to be the first to know the truth about this person. After a week had passed he entered Loyola's room.

'It is time for you to speak,' the bishop said, sitting down on a chair.

'Where is your…your secretary?' asked Francisco. 'Arteaga?'

'He will not be present.'

'Why not?'

'I must first judge whether what you have to tell is suitable for other ears than mine and those of the Lord, if you understand what I mean.'

'What do you wish to know?'

'Tell me everything!'

For the past few days Francisco's one wish had been to tell his story, from the beginning—to Juan Bautista de Arteaga. But now it was the bishop sitting here, and he too was waiting for words from him. Francisco could only toss him a few bones, no more, no less: the barest skeleton of his life.

'Very well,' said Francisco, and this is how it appears in his memoirs. 'The truth is that I am a woman. That I was born in such and such a place. That I am the daughter of this man and that woman. That at a certain age I entered a convent. That I was brought up there. That shortly before taking my vows I left the convent for this and that reason. Went to such and such a place, undressed and dressed myself again, cut off my hair, travelled to one place and another, took ship, landed and went rushing around the country, killing, injuring, wounding, leaving a trail of havoc and roaming around until I finished up here, now, at the feet of Your Eminence.'

'Is that all?' asked the bishop.

'That's all I can say.'

The bishop looked at the person before him, whose body was concealed under a blanket.

'But why?' asked the bishop.

Francisco remained silent, turning his head away slightly.

'And…and how?' Confusion overcame the bishop as the profile

of this person was presented to him, he could see it now, clearly, the cheek really was that of a woman, but what was that on the upper lip? And those arms, muscular as a cowman's, and that look, hard as a rock from Arica. And yet, that body, yesterday? It was all beyond his comprehension. 'Have you nothing more to say?'

'No.'

'There will have to be an enquiry into this.'

'Into what?'

'Everything. Your life. Your conduct. Your deception.'

'I'd like to get up,' said Francisco. 'Tomorrow. I'm free. My sentence has been rescinded. I ask to be given some clothes. That's my last word.'

'Clothes?' asked the bishop. 'I don't know what clothes I should give you, Loyola. I really don't know. What you have done is outrageous. Such a thing is unprecedented. The case must therefore be referred to His Holiness. Only His Holiness can decide what is to happen. You will be taken to Rome. Two of my servants will accompany you there. And Arteaga. You already know him, of course. He insists on taking personal charge of this important matter. May His Holiness show leniency in deciding your fate.' With that the bishop rose and walked to the door. He turned round once more, quickly blessed the room, with a brief glance at Loyola, and said, 'The *Santa Barbara* will sail in three weeks' time, for Seville. You will be on board. From Seville you will take a ship to Genoa. From there you will travel straight to Rome, making no detours on the way. That is *my* last word.'

Juan had one leg crossed over the other. His hands lay flat on his thighs. He was waiting. Francisco was pacing up and down. The boards creaked under his boots. He was wearing his habitual clothing. They were in the small cabin which had been allocated to the bishop's secretary for the voyage. The *Santa Barbara* was setting sail. Footsteps and shouted orders could be heard from outside. The waves breaking against the ship made a continual sucking and snorting sound. A wind had come up and was taking the vessel out to sea. Their 'big talk' could now begin.

'They told me that on the day when Miguel pulled me out of my mother's womb it rained even though there wasn't a cloud in the sky. Can you believe that?' Before Juan could answer, Francisco went on: 'Once, in a cave, I threw a stone up as high as I could, and it was caught by a god called Mari. Can you believe that?' Juan realized that these questions did not require an answer but were complete in themselves. And now Francisco formed the words that were needed. As if he were obeying an impulse that had been frozen for a long time and was now, at last, thawing. He did not stand still but strode rapidly to and fro in the cabin. He made no attempt to gloss over anything, nor, however, did he inject any remorse into his words. They were simply a true reflection of what had happened. No more, no less.

The 'big talk' lasted for four days; Francisco told his story until evening brought exhaustion, until darkness fell, until he ran out of words. The time that was not filled with speech he spent alone on deck, sitting in an odd corner and letting the shavings from his narration waft away on the wind. On the fourth day he was within sight of the end.

'Then seven nuns came, they pawed me all over and one of them stuck her wormy little fingers into my private parts and poked about as if she were trying to free a drawer that was sticking. Can you believe that?'

This time Juan nodded. He listened to the remaining bits of the story, the last few crumbs—the interview with the bishop, and the order to leave for Rome—and with that Francisco's narrative had caught up with the two travellers, as if it had actually joined them in the cabin. Everything had been said.

'We must note it all down!' said Juan.

'What?'

'Your life!'

'What for?'

'So that it doesn't get lost.' And Juan took a sheaf of paper and writing materials out of the drawer of the cabin table and set everything out in readiness. 'Now for the writing,' he said. 'I'm going to write it down.' Juan stared at the paper. He was about to start. But then he looked up.

'What's the matter?' asked Francisco.

'I don't know,' said Juan. 'I think I can only understand you if I write as if I were you. That's the only way for me to see the things that you've seen.'

'Meaning?'

'You start again from the beginning, and I write as you go along.'

Francisco told his life-story all over again. What he had already said lay before him like a road; he could simply follow it without having to think about what direction to take, and so the sentences came bubbling out so fast and so fluently that Juan Bautista de Arteaga struggled to keep up. Juan wrote down what he could, but many words and sentences were lost. He was like a bucket standing out in the pouring rain: most of the water always falls outside it. The sound of his breathing was mingled with Francisco's words, the scratching of the pen with his footsteps. Drops of sweat splattered simultaneously onto the paper and the floor. In the act of writing Juan bundled together what was said and what he managed to hear, and from this combination a text took shape. By the time they had spent something like two days and nights on end in the cabin, neither eating nor sleeping but only speaking and writing, and were approaching the last stage of the narration for the second time, they were impatient to get to the end. They had not changed their clothes for days, they were trapped in their own sweat, out of breath and suffering as much pain, one in his wrist and the other in his jaw, as if the hand were sprained and the tongue dislocated.

Before they could return to normality, surfacing like divers after a long underwater swim; before Juan could gather up the pages of writing from the table to put them in order, and then read them through again at his leisure, days later, on his own, attempting to decipher and correct passages that were unclear; before Juan realized that the text was but a stunted version of Francisco's life and that he had only recorded the bare facts; before he had to admit to himself that in the dictation process an immense amount had been lost—feelings, thoughts, anything that might have afforded an insight into the inner self of this human being; before Juan finally asked his companion, 'What shall we do with this text?' and Francisco replied, 'You keep it. You wrote it!'; before Juan died many years later, leaving the carefully preserved manuscript to the Sevillian branch of the Urquiza family; before the autobiography of the Lieutenant Nun took its tortuous path to its first publication in 1829 under the title *Historia de la monja alférez, doña Catalina de Erauso, escrita por ella misma*—before any of this could happen, the last sentence had to be spoken, for the last sentence always has to be spoken sometime. And when the last sentence had fallen from Francisco's lips and Juan had caught it, Juan laid his pen down on the paper. Francisco was leaning against the wall. Juan stood up, and Francisco moved towards him. They stopped just a small distance apart. They gazed at one another as though seeing each other for the first time. They did not take their eyes off each other. At last they each stepped forward and closed the remaining space between them. But their embrace lasted only for a moment. Then they drew apart.

Chapter twenty-eight

A decision in Rome

Even faster than the *Santa Barbara*, rumours flew across the sea, rumours spun around a truly incredible individual: rumours about all the things done and experienced (as well as about many things *not* done or experienced) by this remarkable personage. Like a gathering storm, Francisco's reputation gradually brewed up and then broke in the form of a single name—a name that had attached itself to him even before he landed on Spanish soil again after almost twenty years in the New World: the lieutenant nun, the nun lieutenant, *la monja alférez*. Francisco could do nothing about any of this. Nor did he wish to. People pounced on his story and continually told and retold it. They exaggerated it, distorted it, elaborated it, with no regard for what was true and what was not, but even so the core remained the same. Furthermore, in the story as it was handed down, people of every century have found inspiration for writings of their own, recasting the material in new forms. This process will never cease, because far more is involved than the fate of a single human being.

In her book *The Lieutenant Nun*, Sherry Velasco discusses a large number of texts revolving around Catalina's life: not only the official and authentic documents, such as a letter written by the Bishop of Huamanga, another by Pedro de la Valle (a member of the circle surrounding Pope Urban VIII), the *relaciones* of 1625 and 1653, or an account by Fray Diego de Rosales, but also a multitude of fictional works. These include a play by Juan Pérez de Montalbán written while the lieutenant nun was still alive; Thomas de Quincey's Romantic version of the story, entitled *The Nautico-Military Nun of Spain*; Carlos Coello's *Zarzuela, La Monja Alférez*, published together with a critical prologue by José Gómez de Arteche; Juan A. Mateo's play *La Monja Alférez*; an anonymous manuscript from 19th-century Mexico; the two-volume historical novel by Eduardo Blasco, *Del claustro al campamento o la Monja Alférez*; a host of 'warrior nun' comic strips; Emilio Gómez Muriel's 1944 film with the improbably pretty María Félix as Catalina; works by Ochoa, Morales-Alvarez, Rodríguez, Keller, and Miras; Aguirre's film made in 1986, and others far too numerous to mention. But many of these fictional versions unjustifiably romanticize the return voyage to Seville and give us a sentimentalized relationship between two people, a purely postulated act of love, a Catalina who slips back into her 'innate' role and reverts to an incongruous femininity.

The reality was quite different: that one fleeting embrace on the *Santa Barbara* did not lead to anything more. For even if Juan saw the act of writing as a kind of union on a higher plane, which might indeed have led to their finding each other in a more tangible way, Francisco had arrived at a different point. His dictation was also a diktat. He was the one setting the terms. It was his own life he was relating. What he said concerned him alone. Or so he thought, at any rate, and he not only dictated his life-story to Juan but determined everything else too: the pace and the rhythm. He did not realize that Juan could only get down on paper a tiny fraction of what he said. But he was not concerned about that. Francisco was dictating his life to himself, cementing it with every word he spoke. Francisco Loyola was ramming Francisco Loyola, like a peg, more and more firmly into the ground. He could not be anything now but the man he had become. And after he had said it all, he had said all there was to say.

After a two-week stay in Seville, another ship carried the two travellers to Genoa, where the Papal coach was waiting to convey them to Rome. People there already knew who was coming, and gossip was rife. Passers-by turned their heads and tried to peer into the coach, but the curtains were drawn. The Pope received Francisco in audience and listened to his story—and a strange thing happened. One assumes that the Pope will see what Francisco did as a blasphemy against God, an outrage against the fundamental values of the Church. Each individual must occupy his allotted place in the world, the Pope will surely say. The ordinances of Nature must be obeyed. From now on, Loyola, you must cease to live as a man, you must renounce this clothing, which disfigures you and robs you of the identity that was bestowed on you once and for all. Look into your heart, and go back to leading the life that you were elected and chosen and destined and intended to lead—the life of a woman. But Urban VIII said none of these things. He listened to what Francisco Loyola told him, kept putting questions to him, and enquiring into details, was astonished at all the things this person had experienced. No doubt he had difficulty seeing a woman beneath the mannish garb, but could see the man who had taken up the cross and the sword and helped to 'pacify the heathen'. One of the many 'valiant men who had opened up a New World to Christianity'.

The Pope granted Francisco Loyola permission to continue living as a man. He could go on wearing those clothes. Certainly, for a verified *virgo intacta* there was the option of entering a convent again. But the decision was entirely his, Francisco Loyola's. And Francisco's response? How one wishes he would rise from his kneeling posture and say: 'Why not both? Why not a life without this rigid separation? Instead of two poles that exclude each other, why not two points on the same scale? Not merging into one, and not set apart as opposites, but steadily moving closer. Always seeing otherness as part of oneself.' But that is not what he said. For Francisco Loyola had made up his mind, and he announced his decision in forceful terms.

The Pope nodded benevolently and dismissed him. 'Most graciously,' Francisco adds to the account recorded by Juan, 'His Holiness gave me his permission to go on living as a man, while impressing on me that it was my duty to lead an honest life from this day forward; that I must refrain from harming my fellow-men and that His commandment, Thou shalt not kill, carried with it the vengeance of God for those who disobeyed it.' Francisco kissed the ring and left the Vatican, and as he came into the city he 'heard the giggling of two "ladies" who were leaning against a wall and had just accosted two young men. They looked at me and I looked at them, and one of them said, "Senõra Catalina, where are you going, all by yourself?"—"My dear whores," I replied, "I have come to give each of you a hundred strokes on your pretty little necks, and a hundred slashes with this blade to the fool who would defend your honour!" The women fell silent and then hurried off.'

While Juan Bautista de Arteaga set off for his home town of Vitoria, Francisco was enjoying the high life. 'My fame had spread, and it was remarkable to see the crowds that followed me everywhere—famous people, princes, bishops, cardinals. I found doors open to me wherever I went, and in the six weeks that I spent in Rome hardly a day went by when I did not dine with princes. One Friday a gentleman invited me to dinner and I was given all manner of presents, and then, by special order of the Roman Senate, my name was entered in a book as an honorary citizen of Rome.' *Which* name, he does not say.

People wanted to know all about him. What intrigued them more than anything was how Francisco Loyola had managed to keep his body hidden all those years. Francisco answered their questions patiently, describing his meticulous precautions and extreme vigilance. He had often simply not washed, and had smelt abominably. He had made a little tube to urinate through and learned to pee standing up. The wounds he had received had generally not been in places that posed any danger of discovery, and he had treated minor wounds in the chest and posterior himself. Above all, however, he emphasised how blind people were: they were influenced by what they saw, what they wanted to see and above all what they were accustomed to seeing. Eventually his listeners began to lose interest. The public's curiosity ebbed away, and people went back to their everyday concerns. This was something of a relief to Francisco. Once he had soaked up all that respectful admiration and been introduced everywhere as a novelty, it became increasingly burdensome to be constantly recognized in the street. Suddenly Europe seemed to him like an ink-blot in comparison to the huge land masses of the American continent. He yearned to go back to the New World, where he had become the person he was, back to the vastness and immensity that would give him one thing: anonymity.

First he made one last visit to the Basque country, starting with his home town, San Sebastián. His parents had died. The Whale was now occupied by his sister Mariana and her husband. Francisco signed—as Catalina de Erauso—a document in which he renounced his share of the family inheritance in return for one thousand *reales* and several letters of credit to be redeemed in Seville. Then he went to a gambling den in San Sebastián, where he embraced his brother and namesake Francisco de Erauso, the masturbation attendant. After that he set off for Vitoria. This was the last of the farewell visits he made before returning to the New World.

He met Juan Bautista de Arteaga in his old family home. Both of them recalled words they had spoken long ago.

'I'm going to Seville,' said Francisco, smiling.

'When?' asked Juan.

'Right now.'

'So you've come to say goodbye?' asked Juan.

'I've come to ask if you'll come with me. To Seville. And from Seville to the West Indies. The fleet sails in four weeks. What is there to keep you here?'

'No, Francisco, I'm staying here.'

They looked at each other.

'Then we shan't see each other again?'

'It's unlikely.'

They were sitting in Juan's room.

'When are you leaving?' asked Juan.

'Very soon. When it gets a bit cooler.'

Juan sipped his chocolate.

'You don't want to go back to Huamanga?' asked Francisco.

'No. What I want now is peace. Look at this house of mine. As soon as I came back I felt sure that nothing could ever persuade me to go away again.'

'Nothing?'

Now Juan turned his head towards Francisco. The slowness of the movement made Francisco uneasy.

'You always knew more than I did,' said Juan.

Francisco nodded. Then he said, 'I'm sorry.'

Juan drew a deep breath. It sounded like a groan. 'Before you go,' he said.

'Yes?'

'There's one more thing I need to know.'

'Ask away!' said Francisco, sitting up straighter in his chair.

'That time, on the beach, when we were both lying there in the sun, and I was unconscious. You came to before I did.' Juan made a long pause, then continued. 'You said, you know, when you were telling me everything, your life story, on the *Santa Barbara*, you said you saw me then, you saw me lying there, you looked down at me, you said something about a feeling. Tell me what sort of a feeling it was.'

'It was lust,' said Francisco.

'Nothing else?'

'Nothing else. It was no different from feelings I had later—towards women.'

'It wasn't…stronger?'

'Do you mean love?' asked Francisco scornfully. 'That only exists in people's imagination.'

'Tell me something else.'

'Well?'

'What would you have done if I—'

'The Indians have no way of saying "would have", do you remember? With them everything is clear-cut: either a thing happens or it doesn't.'

Francisco set out alone and rode to Seville, as he had done all those years before. Now and again he looked round to see if Juan Bautista de Arteaga was following him, but he knew that this time he was not. Francisco Loyola reached Seville. His last sight of his homeland was of the fortress of Santa Catalina.

What kind of a death can a person like Catalina de Erauso, the Lieutenant Nun, expect, after a life like hers? A violent one, no doubt. One of her many enemies, we may be sure, will finally track her down and corner her. At some point in the past Catalina will have taken from him someone he loved. Probably she herself has no memory of who it was or when it happened. But, like the Cid before him, this enemy is hot on her trail, hell-bent on retribution: she has done him an injury and he is going to take his revenge. The insatiable cycle of killing that never ends. Like a desert wasp, the enemy never stops searching for the tarantula's burrow in which Catalina hides, desiring only to be left in peace. He runs her to earth and her last battle begins.

Even before they start Catalina knows that she will lose. And yet she fights for her life with all the strength she can muster. But this time she is the one into whose body the notches are cut. Her adversary is younger, stronger, more agile, more implacable. He can play with her as he likes. He is certain of victory. Eventually Catalina hears the flapping of the cloak that she recognizes all too well. Her last cry is to Santa Liberata, who will help her to die with a quiet mind. There it comes now, the wasp's deadly sting. As the sword is plunged into her she sees, in a single image, all the bodies she has pierced with her own sword, and knows that she has brought this death upon herself.

But none of this is certain. We are not able to relate how death overtakes her. How her body jerks convulsively. How the blade is forced into her. There is no evidence whatever of that last—and first—penetration, that orgasm of death, that cruelly symbolic confirmation of what *seems* to be her true identity. For the fact is that we know nothing of how she died. Her trail simply peters out, somewhere in Mexico. Like a trickle of water, the life of the Lieutenant Nun seeps away into the ground. Our last glimpse of her comes from a man by the name of Nicolás de la Rentería, who dictates an account of his meeting with her to a fellow Capuchin friar. He last saw Catalina de Erauso, he says, in 1645, in Veracruz. The Lieutenant Nun was calling herself Antonio de Erauso, and was a person of courage and skill. She worked as a mule-driver. She wore male clothing and had a sword and a dagger ornamented with silver. She was then about fifty years old; strong build, dark complexion, a few hairs on her chin. The work suited her: she compared herself to a weary mule which only the blows from her stick could induce to set one hoof in front of another.

Epilogue

And yet—we do know the date of her death. The evidence is not of a kind to convince scholars, but that does not matter. The person we have to thank for the precise time of her death is none other than Juan Bautista de Arteaga. Who else would it be? Essentially it is Juan we have to thank for everything. It is there in just one sentence that he wrote. A tiny sentence. Easy to overlook. Not even the concluding sentence of his memoirs. It is tucked away, surrounded by a mass of tedious description, and is neither striking in itself nor accompanied by any comment. Perhaps Juan himself did not realize the significance of that sentence.

Juan had grown old. He was living in Vitoria, having settled in his parents' house. Still writing. Since nothing much happened these days, since everything seemed steeped in monotony, he would often pursue his own thoughts—and Catalina figured prominently in them. Again and again Juan recalled those years of his life that had meant the most to him. Chances that had passed him by. Losses that no earthly search would ever restore. You have to hand it to him, he could write the same thing in endless different ways.

Juan now worked only sporadically. He still had a few patients left, just enough for him to scrape a living. He seemed content with that. Age had taken away his appetite, and life had robbed him of his hunger. He spent most of his time at home. Friends were thinner on the ground now. He had few visitors. Contemporaries died. A new generation was launching itself into the world. Only one colleague from earlier days occasionally looked in on him.

'How old am I?' Juan would ask him every year. Every year his friend told him the figure. And every year Juan muttered, 'As old as that?'

Pleasure of any kind was a thing of the past. None of life's diversions held any appeal for him. Every evening's bedtime was burdensome, for the dreary days ahead cast the gloom of endless sameness before them.

One night Juan woke suddenly. As if something had startled him. He peered into the darkness. Nothing there. Not a sound. Nothing stirring. He went over to the window and leaned out. He could see two stars. They seemed to him like eyes gazing at him from infinitely far away. At that moment it started to rain. It was 30 August 1649.

'And I had the feeling that something was wrong.'

Bibliography

This novel was inspired by the autobiography of Catalina de Erauso, who by her own account was born in 1585, though the San Sebastián baptismal register suggests that it was more probably 1592. Her autobiography may be found in the following editions, amongst others:

Historia de la monja alférez, doña Catalina de Erauso, escrita por ella misma. É ilustrada con notas y documentos, por D. Joaquin Maria de Ferrer. Paris, 1829.

Vida y sucesos de la monja alférez. Autobiografía atribuida a Doña Catalina de Erauso. Ed. Rima de Vallbona. Arizona State University, 1992.

Lieutenant Nun. Memoir of a Basque Transvestite in the New World. Translated by Michele Stepto and Gabriel Stepto. Foreword by Marjorie Garber. Boston, 1996.

I wish to thank the authors listed below, whose writings have contributed greatly to this book. I would particularly like to thank Cornelia Lotthammer, who first drew my attention to this subject.

Jesús Altuna and Pedro Diaz de González: *Ekain und Altxerri bei San Sebastián. Zwei altsteinzeitliche Bilderhöhlen im spanischen Baskenland.* Übertragen, herausgegeben und mit einem Vorwort von Gerhard Bosinski. Sigmaringen, 1996.

Georges Baudot: *La vie quotidienne dans l'Amérique espagnole de Philippe II. XVIe siècle*. Paris, 1981.

Marcelin Defourneaux: *La vie quotidenne en Espagne au siècle d'or.* Paris, 1964. (English translation: Marcelin Defourneaux: *Daily Life in Spain in the Golden Age.* Translated by Newton Branch. London, 1970.)

Stephen Ferry: *I Am Rich Potosí, The Mountain That Eats Men*. New York, 1999.

Olwen Hufton: *The Prospect Before Her: A History of Women in Western Europe. Vol. 1: 1500-1800*. London, 1997. (German translation: Olwen Hufton: *Frauenleben. Eine europäische Geschichte: 1500-1800*. Aus dem Englischen von Holger Fliessbach und Rena Passenthien. Frankfurt am Main, 1998.)

Mark Kurlansky: *The Basque History of the World.* London, 1999. (German translation: Mark Kurlansky: *Die Basken. Eine kleine Weltgeschichte.* Aus dem Englischen von Holger Fliessbach. Munich, 2000.)

Cornelia Lotthammer: *La Monja Alférez. Die Autobiographie der*

Catalina de Erauso in ihrem literarischen und gesellschaftlichen Kontext. Frankfurt am Main, 1998.

Dr W. Krenger, 'Medizinisches aus dem Goldenen Zeitalter Spaniens', *Ciba Zeitschrift*, No. 69. Basle, May 1939.

Ludwig Pfandl: *Spanische Kultur und Sitte des 16. und 17. Jahrhunderts. Eine Einführung in die Blütezeit der spanischen Literatur und Kunst*. Kempten, 1924.

Wolfgang Reinhard: *Missionare, Humanisten, Indianer im 16. Jahrhundert. Ein gescheiterter Dialog zwischen Kulturen?* Regensburg, 1993.

Jonathan Rutland: *See Inside a Galleon*. London, 1977. (German translation: Jonathan Rutland: *Eine Galeone. Ein Einblick-Buch.* Hrsg.: R. J. Unstead. Deutsche Bearbeitung: Friedrich Johannsen. Esslingen, 1977.)

Eberhard Schmitt: *Atlantische Expansion und maritime Indienfahrt im 16. Jahrhundert*. Bamberg, 1992.

Sherry Velasco: *The Lieutenant Nun. Transgenderism, Lesbian Desire and Catalina de Erauso*. Austin, 2000.

Tzvetan Todorov: *La conquête de l'Amérique. La question de l'autre.* Paris, 1982. (English translation: Tzvetan Todorov: *The Conquest of America. The Question of the Other.* Translated from the French by Richard Howard. New York, 1984.)

About the Author

Markus Orths

Markus Orths was born in 1969. He studied philosophy and French and English literature, and now lives and writes in Karlsruhe. He has received various awards for his novels and short stories, including the Limburg Award (2003), the North Rhine-Westphalia Award (2003), the Marburg Literature Award (2002), the Moerser Literature Award (2000), and the Floriana Award. In 2000 he won the Berlin open mike, which is one of the most prestigious and important literary contests for young writers in Germany.

The fonts used in this book are from the Garamond family